TWILIGHT PASSION

"Down this way is the last of the bedrooms," Travis said, leading Laine down the hallway.

He pushed the door wide open to reveal a spacious, open room with wood ceiling beams and a gleaming wood planked floor. A massive bed with a high dark wood headboard dominated the white-walled room, and two high windows framed the stand of cottonwoods just beyond them outside. A low white stone fireplace occupied the wall opposite the bed, and in several wall niches sconces held thick candles.

"Ah, the master bedroom," she declared, not stepping inside.

"Yes, sometimes it seems too luxurious for a man like me. I should probably have a bunkhouse with a cot or something," he laughed.

"On the contrary," Laine said thoughtfully, "it suits you, I think."

"I think it would," he responded quietly, "with the right woman in it."

Travis stepped into the room and drew her in with him. Her heart thumped wildly against her chest, and his hand over hers generated a heat she'd never known before.

She withdrew her hand slowly. "I think we should start back now. The sun is already setting, and it gets dark so quickly out here."

"That's the wonderful thing about this room."

"What is?"

"Watch," he said as he raised the window shades to expose an expanse of sky above the trees, then lit all the candles. The flames bathed the room in a soft glow.

"It's beautiful," Laine whispered. In fact, it's magical, she thought, the kind of room that casts a spell over a person and makes her feel ethereal, awake inside a fantasy. She walked to the windows to gaze out at the mauve-shadowed twilight.

"And you are beautiful," he whispered from behind her.

HEARTFIRE ROMANCES

SWEET TEXAS NIGHTS   (2610, $3.75)
by Vivian Vaughan

Meg Britton grew up on the railroads, working proudly at her father's side. Nothing was going to stop them from setting the rails clear to Silver Creek, Texas—certainly not some crazy prospector. As Meg set out to confront the old coot, she planned her strategy with cool precision. But soon she was speechless with shock. For instead of a harmless geezer, she found a boldly handsome stranger whose determination matched her own.

CAPTIVE DESIRE   (2612, $3.75)
by Jane Archer

Victoria Malone fancied herself a great adventuress, but being kidnapped was too much excitement for even Victoria! Especially when her arrogant kidnapper thought she was part of Red Duke's outlaw gang. Trying to convince the overbearing, handsome stranger that she had been an innocent bystander when the stagecoach was robbed, proved futile. But when he thought he could maker her confess by crushing her to his warm, broad chest, by caressing her with his strong, capable hands, Victoria was willing to admit to anything. . . .

LAWLESS ECSTASY   (2613, $3.75)
by Susan Sackett

Abra Beaumont could spot a thief a mile away. After all, her father was once one of the best. But he'd been on the right side of the law for years now, and she wasn't about to let a man like Dash Thorne lead him astray with some wild plan for stealing the Tear of Allah, the world's most fabulous ruby. Dash was just the sort of man she most distrusted—sophisticated, handsome, and altogether too sure of his considerable charm. Abra shivered at the devilish gleam in his blue eyes and swore he would need more than smooth kisses and skilled caresses to rob her of her virtue . . . and much more than sweet promises to steal her heart!

Available wherever paperbacks are sold, or order direct from the Publisher. Send cover price plus 50¢ per copy for mailing and handling to Zebra Books, Dept. 3763, 475 Park Avenue South, New York, N.Y. 10016. Residents of New York and Tennessee must include sales tax. DO NOT SEND CASH. For a free Zebra/ Pinnacle catalog please write to the above address.

GARDA PARKER
ARIZONA TEMPTATION

ZEBRA BOOKS
KENSINGTON PUBLISHING CORP.

ZEBRA BOOKS

are published by

Kensington Publishing Corp.
475 Park Avenue South
New York, NY 10016

First printing: May, 1992

Printed in the United States of America

Prologue

Silver Grande, Arizona Territory
November, 1870

Laine Coleridge squeezed her eyes shut, and huddled on the bed wrapped in a blanket, attempting to keep her thin twelve-year-old body warm.

Her mother's shrill laugh rose over the shouts and laughter in the saloon, a room Laine knew was full of smoke and foul-smelling men. She could hear chairs scraping across the gritty wood floor, glasses slamming down on tables, and tinny music from the out of tune upright piano. Clamping both hands over her ears, she meant to block it all from penetrating the thin walls of the room they shared in the back of a crumbling wood frame hotel.

Laine hated this place, couldn't remember when she hadn't hated it. She hated that saloon the most, especially the men there who followed her mother, raking their eyes over her like hungry buzzards. Laine had seen that too many times when, against her mother's admonition, she'd peeked out of their room.

7

She wanted to grab her mother's hand and run as fast and as far away as they could, leaving the dust and people of Silver Grande behind them. But every time Laine approached her about it, Elizabeth Coleridge would say, "Don't you worry, honey, Mama's going to get you out of here, get us both out of here, soon as she can, soon as she makes enough money. Back east to Sarah's. She'll take us in, and I'll get real work, and you'll go to a nice school. Soon."

Laine wouldn't miss Silver Grande, nor any of the people in it. She'd had no real friends here, except one.

Travis Mitcham.

Travis, two years older than Laine, the hero of her dreams. His mother named him after a distant relative, the famous Colonel Travis who died at the siege of the Alamo in Texas. The romantic name of that dashing hero fit perfectly into Laine's fantasy world.

Travis was the only one who would listen attentively to her stories. She had regaled him with tales about how someday she would be a great lady and live on a hill in Boston in a magnificent mansion with servants.

"And I'll bet you will, too," he had smiled. "I know you will do anything you set your mind to. You're already a pretty girl, Laine. Everybody knows that. Someday you'll be a beautiful queen of society in San Francisco, or Denver, or some other wonderful place you've been dreaming about."

Laine's spirits would lift, and she would gaze adoringly up at him.

Then he had cupped the tip of her face in the palm of his warm hand, and Laine remembered thinking he might kiss her. Her insides had knotted in a combination of hope and fear at the prospect. Instead he had hugged her the way an older brother might a little sister.

"Ah, little Laine, you've got to stop living in a fantasy world. You've got to live in the present and work toward the future."

"I hate living in this present, this here, this now," Laine had countered vehemently. "And I don't know if there is a future for me that's any different. And . . . and maybe if I keep dreaming, my dreams will come true."

She had never told him out loud that he was living in her dream mansion in Boston as well. Nor had she told him how very handsome she thought he was with his chestnut hair curling over his collar, and his brown eyes that darkened to green or sparkled with gold when he talked. Sometimes the words pushed out of her heart with such strength she had to force her jaws shut, lest they tumble off her lips and surely mortify her with their sound and meaning.

Laine believed that Travis was the only person in the world, other than Elizabeth, who understood her. He declared that Laine was his best friend, and never appeared bothered when his other friends teased him about it. She loved him for that. He was her own special hero, but she never put that into words either.

Travis had left Silver Grande two years before to attend a private school. The moment he left, Laine was plunged into a deeper loneliness than ever before, missing the times they'd spent together and aching for his return.

Laine remembered her mother telling her she was just about three years old when they moved into the hotel. Elizabeth could find no work in Silver Grande, and Jackson Smithers, the aging, kind owner, offered her a meager sum for serving drinks in the saloon. The free room was a benefit. It was more than he could afford, but he was sympathetic to the young woman and her little girl.

Elizabeth's beauty was a great draw to the saloon for local men and cattle drovers. With her porcelain-fine skin, eyes so blue they appeared violet, and lustrous honeygold hair, she stood out from the other women, the upstairs girls, with their heavily painted thick skin and unnaturally brash red or yellow hair. Business got better for Smithers and the hotel, but Elizabeth's friends dropped to none. She became a social outcast by the respectable ladies of the town, and they included her young daughter in their whispered opinions.

Smithers grew to care for Laine as the daughter he'd never had and, without her own father, Laine gave her child's love to him, and called him Uncle Jack. Saying he hated the slights and insults Elizabeth suffered, eventually Jackson offered marriage, or money, or both, if she would stop working in the saloon. Elizabeth refused both offers, saying she had to earn the money with work. Laine had often heard them arguing over this.

She thought about the special relationship she

shared with Elizabeth. None of the other girls in Silver Grande could say they had that with their mothers. But, then, they had their fathers. She didn't. When she was little, Laine vaguely remembered Elizabeth saying David Coleridge, her father, was coming back for them anytime. Gradually Laine came to know that was only her mother's dream. Her father was faceless to her, nothing. She couldn't remember him, didn't want to remember him.

Laine's heart and spirit hardened as she grew up in the saloon, and she could not conceal her dislike toward some of the people who lived in Silver Grande. Elvira Hadley, the self-appointed leader of the town's social class, and her daughter LaBelle stood out as the most contemptible of all. They were cruel in their open remarks toward Laine and Elizabeth, and they gossiped about David Coleridge.

Elizabeth had sobbed into her pillow one night after she'd heard Elvira say he'd made and lost a fortune several times over during their short marriage, and couldn't face the last humiliation of losing everything through gambling and bad business deals. Then he'd run out on them. Laine loathed the very sight of Elvira Hadley after that.

Reed Hadley had tolerated the rude behavior of his wife and daughter, but then Laine remembered that he had suddenly changed, urging them to treat Elizabeth and Laine more charitably. Laine thought it must be awful for him to be married to such a mean woman and have such a spiteful daughter. Mr. Hadley had a son named Jamison, but she'd seen him only once that she could recall. It wasn't a pleas-

11

ant memory. Something about his eyes made her feel uncomfortable in her own skin.

"Why do they have to be so mean to us, Mama?" Laine had asked one day when in the mercantile she had overheard Elvira Hadley utter a particularly biting remark about Elizabeth's failure as a mother.

Elizabeth had swallowed so hard Laine thought for a moment her mother had swallowed her voice. Finally Elizabeth said, "It's because I don't have a husband. You don't have a father. They think we're worthless trash."

"Why don't we, Mama? Why don't we have a husband and a father? Why doesn't he ever come back? Doesn't he like us?"

"Of course he does, darling. He . . . just can't come back yet. But he will . . . someday."

"Why not, Mama?"

"I wish I could tell you, honey, but I can't."

Laine knew later that the reason Elizabeth couldn't tell her when her father would come back was because she didn't know. She didn't know where he was either. Or even if he was alive.

Even though Elizabeth had spoken nothing about David in many years, Laine always knew when she was thinking about him. Elizabeth would grow despondent and withdrawn, and Laine would hear her crying in the night. During those times the roles of mother and daughter interchanged. Laine would become the strong one, reassuring her weary mother that their dream of getting out of Silver Grande was just a short time away from coming true. She would reach into their special hiding place in the wall and take out the painted tea tin, and together they counted the small savings it contained. It was always just a little short of being enough, according to Elizabeth.

Sometimes Laine wondered if Elizabeth's claiming a lack of money was just an excuse to keep them there. She probably still believed David Coleridge was coming back for her. Laine knew in her heart he never would come back, and without knowing him or knowing anything about him, she hated him for doing this to her mother and to her.

Laine decided in her young heart that the only way she could live with her feelings about this man she couldn't remember was to bury him. In her conscious mind she did just that.

Now the laughter and shouting from the saloon grew louder, and the language more hurtful to Laine's ears. Suddenly Elizabeth's forced laughter turned to screams. Furniture crashing and breaking, mingled with the scuffling of feet, the crack of an open hand against tender flesh, cloth ripping.

Laine's gaze darted around her cramped quarters. There was no place to hide, no place to feel secure. She scrunched herself into the far corner of the bed, drew her knees up under her chin and hugged them with her thin arms, rocking and trying to make herself as small as possible.

The pounding of her heart fairly burst in her ears when the door flew open. Elizabeth rushed in, slamming and bolting it quickly. She slumped against it, breathing heavily, and Laine saw with rising apprehension that her dress was torn.

13

"Lainie, honey . . ." Elizabeth gulped air hungrily.

Even in the room's dim light Laine could see her mother's face was hot and flushed, and she stared in horror at the mean red streaks across her throat and above the neckline of her dress. Elizabeth's long hair, always neatly coiled and pinned, fell around her shoulders, and her hand shook visibly as she hooked one lock behind her ear.

"Listen, honey," Elizabeth began again, "we're getting out of here. Tonight." She breathed a nervous laugh. "Get some things together . . . not much. We'll be leaving shortly."

While Elizabeth talked she moved quickly around the room, grabbing things and stuffing them into her travelling bag. Then she stopped abruptly, turning pleading eyes on Laine.

"Lainie! Please, honey, get moving! We have to be ready!"

Laine was paralyzed with fright. The downy hairs on the back of her neck stood up, and her hands tingled. A feeling that something terrible was about to happen hung over her like a dense fog.

"Honey," Elizabeth placed both hands on her daughter's trembling shoulders in an effort to steady them both. "Mama has one more thing to do. Something she doesn't want to do, but she just has to do it so she can get us out of here. For good."

"What, Mama?" Laine could barely hear her own small voice above the raucous sounds coming through the patched walls.

"Now don't you worry about that."

Elizabeth hugged Laine so tightly their mutual

trembling made their bodies shake wildly. She leaned back and her blue-violet eyes glistened with fright and withheld tears.

"Lainie, remember that I love you, have always loved you and want a better life for you. Will you remember that . . . always?"

"Yes, Mama. We can talk about this later, can't we, after we're away from here?"

They stared at one another as if it might be the last time, tears streaming down their faces.

Elizabeth put both hands on Laine's shoulders. "Now listen very carefully, Lainie, I'm counting on you. Put your things in this bag and take it to the back door. Wait for me there. And don't forget the tea tin."

A loud pounding and a hard voice yelling through the door made them both jump. Looking over her shoulder, Elizabeth whispered huskily, "You understand, honey?" Her fingers dug into Laine's small shoulders. Then she stood up.

Laine reached out and clung to her mother. "Mama, no! Don't go! I'm scared!"

"I know, baby, I know." Elizabeth picked Laine up off the bed and put a thin coat over her nightgown. "I am, too. Now remember, get to the back door as fast as you can. And don't look into the saloon. You hear me? Don't!"

Laine stood in silent numbness, tears still falling in a steady stream down her swollen face. Elizabeth blew out the light, and kissing her daughter's tear-damp cheek, clasped her tightly.

"It'll be over soon," she whispered. "Remember I

love you." Then she quickly left the room.

Laine stood motionless for a moment, then ran to the bed to get her beloved doll with the china face. She rolled it up in her Sunday dress, and stuffed it into the bag, then drew their precious tea tin out of its hiding place.

Outside, dragging the bag behind her, she crept carefully, feeling her way in the murky darkness along the wall toward the back door. Reaching it, she propped herself up against it and waited in the dark, shivering in the damp night air. Not even the moon will come out to light this place tonight, she thought. In back of the building, the sounds coming from the saloon were muffled. A welcome relief.

Laine grew more fearful as she waited in the shadows for her mother. Desperately she wanted to believe they were actually getting out of Silver Grande. She shifted to lean her other hip against the door. Already she felt as if she'd been standing there for hours, and her mind raced in a thousand different directions.

Shivering in the damp air, she peered around the corner of the building, hoping she would see Elizabeth coming, her heart sinking when she didn't. How she wished her mother would hurry. She was so scared.

As she always did at night when she was afraid or unhappy, she fantasized about what it would be like when they lived safely in Aunt Sarah's house in Boston. She thought of Travis again.

Her fantasies had once taken her to a beautiful white house in a green valley where she lived with him as his wife. Once she asked her mother what it was like to be married, but Elizabeth avoided answering her.

Where was Travis now? She needed him. Why didn't he ride in on a big white horse right now and whisk her and Elizabeth out of Silver Grande and far away into the night? He couldn't, because heroes on white horses only lived in little girl fantasies.

Laine wasn't a little girl anymore, and she knew what she'd felt for Travis all these years was real love. In a way, she believed she was very much like her mother. Both of them loved too long, too deeply, men who left them behind and forgot them. Never again, Laine vowed. I won't let myself feel like that for any man, and I'll help Mama do the same. We'll start all over again in Boston, and love will never hurt us again.

Suddenly, from inside the saloon, two shots boomed in rapid succession into the heavy night air, their thundering echoes bouncing off nearby rocky hills. Laine jumped back against the door, her shoulder blades grinding into the wood strips, her heart pounding deafeningly in her ears.

She waited for what felt like hours before the commotion in the saloon died down. Then running footsteps plodding into the hard earth came close to her hiding place. She backed deeper into the protective darkness of the doorway. The footsteps stopped and all became silent, except for the heavy pounding in her ears. She was afraid to move, even to breathe.

Thick low-hanging clouds thinned like the spreading of fingers, letting a little of the hidden moonlight filter through. Eerie shadows undulated over the ground. Out of those shadows Laine saw the figure of a tall man take shape not more than ten feet from her. She gasped. The clouds moved more rapidly, uncovering the moon, and a silver shaft of light flashed like a beacon into the doorway.

"Laine," the man whispered huskily, "hurry, we must go!"

Laine backed farther, plastering herself against the door. "No," she said weakly, but she didn't cry. She'd learned long ago not to cry. "Mama told me to wait right here for her. I've got to wait here. Mama's coming for me."

The man walked closer to her, holding out his hand. His voice was gentle, and seemed oddly familiar to her.

"Lainie . . . your mother won't be coming for you tonight. She . . . she sent me to take you to the train in Flagstaff. You'll be going to Boston alone."

Laine's small body went rigid with fright. "No! Mama told me to wait for her. We're going to Aunt Sarah's together! I . . . I don't know you." She gripped the travelling bag tightly, hugging it to her.

"Lainie, listen to me," the man pleaded, "we've got to hurry now. Your mama said for you to go ahead. She'll see you at Sarah's as soon as she can." He started toward her again.

From inside the saloon, sounds of shouting and scuffling grew louder and closer, as if they were right in the room she'd been living in.

And then, the jolt of a mind-splitting explosion and its impact against the back door propelled her forward into the man's arms. He caught her and ran to a waiting buckboard, whipping the horse into a tear away from the building.

Laine stared in horror over her shoulder as fire burst through the back of the hotel. A shooting pain in her head thrust her face into the soft fabric of the man's coat, and she slipped into black nothingness.

Chapter One

Black Canyon Road, Arizona Territory
Spring, 1883

The steady beat-clop of horses' hooves plodding into thick brown-red dust, and the rocking of the Black Canyon Stagecoach made Laine's stomach churn. Long past its prime, the coach groaned and creaked over the winding stretch of brush-bordered road out of Flagstaff. She wasn't used to riding in such a contraption. It didn't surprise her to remember that she had never ridden in one when she was a child in Arizona. There had never been money enough to step even one foot out of Silver Grande then. And in Boston she always rode in a private buggy.

The stage driver, a leathery-skinned man of about fifty named Buck Harmon, had apologized several times to her about the condition of the coach because of its age, but Laine could tell by how clean it was that he was proud of it. She'd found that endearing about him and wouldn't complain, even if she did feel as if the bones in her bottom were jarring her teeth.

Moistness crept over her throat and temples, and with a limp hand she brushed a stray curl from her cheek and secured it behind one of the tortoise side-combs which held her long hair up off her neck.

How good it would feel to remove the boned corset she wore under her travelling suit. The ample violet-black skirt and full petticoats, and the close-fitting lavender waistcoat and violet jacket with its high-backed collar, so smart and sophisticated when she'd boarded the train in Boston, were most inappropriate in this hot climate.

Aunt Sarah had hovered over her, seeing to every detail of her clothing right down to the white gloves and large-brimmed amber straw hat with violet ribbons. Laine had felt the most chic of travellers riding in a railcar, sipping tea and reading a novel.

Now in this almost unbearable coach she would give anything for a sip of cool water and a cotton chemise.

She stole a glance at the other passenger, a silent, dark man dressed almost entirely in black. When they boarded in Flagstaff, he had assessed her with cold black eyes that made her skin prickle.

Now her glance was caught by his sharp gaze which reminded her of the circling vultures she'd seen over the desert and how they scrutinized every inch of dust searching for weakened animals, or the dead or dying. Momentarily those eyes unnerved her. He did not move nor speak. Neither did he avert his eyes. Laine decided he was not a true gentleman.

Slowly she reached into her violet brocade travelling bag and searched among its contents for a handkerchief, grateful when her hand closed over it. She set the bag aside and blotted her temples, lightly moving the white lace over her throat and along the high neck of her ecru linen shirtwaist. Its rose scent wafted over her face like a New England spring mist, offering cool, familiar comfort.

Turning to look out the small square window, she fixed her gaze intently on the flat terrain weaving past until she was forced by the glaring sun to draw her eyes back inside the coach.

Her head leaning against the high seatback, Laine dropped her eyelids slowly, and caught another glimpse of the dark figure across from her. He appeared to be asleep now, his head nodding downward, his hands relaxed in his lap. His legs reached her side of the coach, and instinctively she drew hers closer to the door.

Laine sensed a vague recognition of this man. She wondered for a moment how that could be. Perhaps with his impeccable black clothes and perfectly manicured hands, he reminded her of the men she'd known in Boston who thought of nothing else but their appearance and how they could use it to gain more for themselves.

She had never been impressed with men like that; in fact, she avoided their company. But there was something more disturbing about this man that she sensed he kept hidden under the surface. Whatever it was caused the suspicious side of her nature to sharpen.

She withdrew deeper into her own thoughts, and dozed. Her dreams swept her back to Boston, to Aunt Sarah's comfortable home at the top of a cobblestone street. From that first night she'd felt welcome, warm and loved. Shivering with cold and fright, she'd been delivered by the railway stationmaster who found her huddled alone in one of the cars on an inbound train from the West.

Several weeks later, Aunt Sarah received word that Elizabeth had died. Later when Laine pressed her for more information about the explosion she'd heard, Aunt Sarah had replied, "I gather there was some sort of fire. It comes of no good consorting with cowboys. I told her that . . ."

But the explanation didn't satisfy Laine, and the wondering about it plagued her like the time she got a wood sliver under her fingernail. It throbbed until Elizabeth was able to extract it. Laine thought her desire to know the truth about her mother's death would throb inside her until she was able to extract it for herself.

Almost nine years of education and tutelage under Aunt Sarah's watchful eye had dimmed the memories of the night she left Silver Grande, and the shadowy figure of a tall man who took her away from the saloon and put her on the train. But her memory of Elizabeth remained vivid, and it was many years before her nightly tears ceased to flow in remembrance.

Laine's memory of Travis Mitcham had never dimmed either. She'd fought it almost too fiercely, but it grew more intense. She'd fantasized he'd returned to Silver Grande and found her gone. He'd searched the earth for her and, half-dead, at last located her in Boston as his next-to-the-last breath was drawn.

In her fantasies she'd nursed him back to health, and he'd pledged undying love for her. A fairy tale wedding followed in which she wore an exquisite gown with a train so long it was obliged to be carried by six flower girls over a trail of pink and white rose petals.

And they lived happily ever after.

No matter how often she relived the fantasy, or changed some of the story, the one remaining dream was always his searching for her, finding her, marrying her.

Laine stirred in her dozing. Would Travis be in Silver Grande now? Of course he would. And he would tell her how he'd always loved her, and they would . . .

A sudden lurch and sharp shift of the coach threw Laine from the seat and flung her forward into the dark man's chest. Her shriek was muffled in the crook of his arm. She struggled to right herself, but the coach gathered momentum in a headlong plunge that forced her body across his and jammed them both into the corner.

His arms went around her back and shoulders in a quick vise-like grip, and they were thrown as one from side to side in the pitching coach. Her bag fell open. Brushes, gloves, mirror, silken lingerie flew about them in dizzying array.

Laine forced her arms out in front to brace herself, pushing her shoulders up just in time to see a blur of dark green trees flash by the open window, and feel their spiky branches reach in and slap her face with stinging needles.

The coach gained speed, and a hard thumping from overhead repeated like crashing drums. Laine's arms gave way and she fell again against the dark coat, her ears pounding with the convoluted sounds of hoofbeats, shouts, ripping fabric, and her own heart.

When at last she could feel the coach levelling off, she forced her body up and out of the man's grip. From her knees on the floor, she reached up to grasp the side of the open window, and with the man's help hauled herself back up on the seat.

The coach slowed, and Laine steadied herself enough to look out the window as they rounded a narrow curve over a steep embankment. Far below she could see a rushing river. Then the coach came to a groaning halt, knocking Laine off balance and back onto the floor.

"Everybody all right in there?" a worried voice boomed from overhead.

Laine pulled herself up once again, and as she tried to grip the edge of the window, a man's face appeared upside down in it. She shrieked and fell back against the other door, her hair tumbling around her face and shoulders, blocking her view. She lifted it, then her eyes widened at first with terror, then narrowed in question.

"Well, I guess you'll live," the voice relaxed.

Laine felt the coach rock as the man jumped from the roof and came around to peer through the win-

26

dow. He wore a brown Stetson pushed up off his brow, and a blue neckerchief held by an ornate silver ring. A lock of chestnut hair over his forehead moved slightly in the breeze, and his brown eyes crinkled at the corners, creasing deeply tanned skin.

Laine sucked air in sharply, then fell back, her eyes fluttering closed.

"Uh-oh, maybe not," the cowboy added, then flung the door open.

Inside, the dark man was slumped in the corner nearest the open door, stirring slightly and rubbing his head, but the cowboy noticed him only in passing. His gaze was riveted to the beautiful woman propped against the other side of the coach.

Her back was against the door, her knees drawn up, revealing high-tied cordovan boots stopping above the ankles of shapely legs clad in cream-colored stockings. Pink lacy petticoats under a violet skirt were draped over one knee and pushed up over the thigh of the other leg. They settled around her like flower petals. Soft ivory hands supported each side of her body on the floor, and all around her lay combs, hairpins, and pieces of silky clothing.

The cowboy's gaze moved slowly up toward her face. Her jacket was open, her lacy blouse torn down the front. Tiny blue ribbons laced through the top of her camisole fell over softly rounded breasts. She lay so still that he was suddenly struck with the thought that she might have stopped breathing.

Quickly he crawled into the cramped coach until his arms straddled the woman's waist. He lifted the golden confusion of her hair and peered into her face, touching her peach-tinted cheek. It warmed and flushed to pink under his fingers, and he pulled them back as if he'd touched a flame. It struck him then that she was the most beautiful woman he'd ever seen.

She uttered a soft moan, and the velvety fringe of dark lashes fluttered slightly.

He slipped one strong arm around the back of her neck and the other around her waist, and drew her toward him, backing carefully out of the coach. He lifted and carried her toward a stand of cotton-woods, her legs dangling over his arm, her head bobbing against his neck. Carefully he set her down in the shade against the trunk of a tree.

He leaned back on his heels and ran a hand through his thick hair. The buckskin fringe on his sleeve swayed slightly in the hot breeze. For a moment that seemed to be the only thing moving.

Laine moaned and stirred and tried with great effort to sit up straight. Her hand moved falteringly to the back of her head, and gingerly rubbed a swelling spot. As consciousness crept into her mind, she became aware that she was not alone. She looked up and squinted at the cowboy who crouched in front of her with worried concern evident on his face.

"Hey, what do you think you're doing, hombre?" a low voice growled from the coach.

The cowboy looked over his shoulder as the dark-clothed figure advanced toward him, a derringer glinting in his hand. The cowboy stood up, tall and straight in close-fitting faded denim pants and high-heeled intricately tooled leather boots. He hooked

28

his thumbs over his brass belt buckle.

"Everything's under control here. Are you hurt?" The cowboy's voice was calm, but firm.

The dark man brushed past him with a rough push on his shoulder. "No, but I rather think that's no thanks to you. What in hell happened back there? Where's the driver? And where'd you come from?" He started toward Laine.

The cowboy grabbed his arm. "I said, everything's under control here. Put the gun away. Horses were spooked by a rattler is all. I was riding nearby and came over to help. Buck pitched off back there. I'll see to him in a minute."

The dark man wrenched his arm away, and with a disdainful look dropped the derringer into his boot and brushed off his black pantleg. He bent down in front of Laine, fanning her face with his white silk handkerchief.

The cowboy removed his Stetson and also bent down. He pulled the man's arm back.

"I guess you didn't hear me. I said everything's all right here."

Laine righted herself as best she could, leaned against the tree and breathed deeply, trying to clear her head.

The dark man smoothed her skirt around her. The cowboy straightened her waistcoat. The dark man tried to make her more comfortable. The cowboy tried to brush her hair out of her face.

"Wait, stop! Stop that!" She slapped at the air, pushing them away, then smoothed her skirt and hair herself.

They obeyed her immediately, obviously surprised by her commanding tone.

Laine rubbed her forehead. "What happened?" Her voice didn't sound to her as if it were her own.

"The horses spooked . . ." the cowboy began.

"This fool almost got us killed . . ." the dark man interrupted.

". . . and I stopped them, or they might have gone over the ravine," the cowboy finished.

". . . with his attempt at being a hero," the dark man finished.

Laine heard their voices sharpen in her mind.

Hero? Hero.

She scrutinized first one man and then the other. An interplay of emotions crossed her mind as she studied the handsome visage of the cowboy, his broad expanse of shoulders, his brown eyes, and the way his chestnut hair curled over his collar.

Travis!

Travis. Here he was, hunkered down in front of her!

Laine could hardly believe it. Any second now he would drop on one knee and propose to her. She knew it! He must have known she was in the coach and just had to stop it. He couldn't wait to see her again. He'd probably come home, found her gone, and searched everywhere for her.

She waited for his question to come. Waited to mull over her answer. She couldn't look too eager. On the other hand, stalling would look too coy. Perhaps she should just throw caution to the winds and say the first thing that came into her mind.

She stared long and hard at him. Yes, it was Travis, the hero of all her dreams.

If only he would say something!

He didn't.

Laine shook the fantasy from her foggy mind and spoke.

"Travis?" It was almost a whisper, the question tentative. "Travis Mitcham?"

The cowboy sat back on his heels as she leaned toward him, eyes fixed on his face. Waiting for him to speak, Laine tried to quiet her pounding heart. A tingling in the palm of her hands shot up to her shoulders, numbing her arms.

"Yes . . . do you know me? If I've known you, I should be shot for not remembering."

The man in black tapped his boot containing the derringer as if saying he would be happy to oblige.

Laine's hand flew to her throat, her face flushing to a rosy glow.

"I'm Laine. Laine Coleridge."

Travis Mitcham dropped forward on his knees.

"Laine?! I can't believe it! Where'd you go? When I got back from school you were gone. No one knew where you were. They said you'd disappeared one night and were not heard from again. I wondered . . ."

Laine lifted her chin, tilting her head back. So he hadn't searched everywhere. He'd simply wondered, and let it go at that. She decided to ignore the fact that he was on his knees.

The dark man looked from one to the other. "Well, what do you know? Laine Coleridge . . . and

Travis Mitcham." The two looked at him as if they'd forgotten he was there. "Well, what do you know?" he said again.

That wasn't the question Laine anticipated, nor was it the right questioner. She felt abruptly torn out of a sweet fantasy, and thrown into a less than idyllic reality.

"And just who are you?" Laine demanded of him.

The black eyes hooded over, and one corner of his mouth quivered with a smug twitch. Laine thought he was enjoying this moment of withholding his identity just a little too much.

At last he spoke. "Jamison Hadley, ma'am, and I'm most pleased to make your lovely acquaintance." He attempted a sweeping bow from his squat position.

Observing him now out of the coach, Laine judged he was roundish and soft under the perfect clothes. He probably never did one whit of any physical work in his life. He rather reminded her of the chocolate-dipped marshmallow confections Aunt Sarah made at Christmas time.

Travis gave a low whistle. "Jamison Hadley. Well, I'll be. Rumor had it you were dead." He looked directly into the dark face.

"Greatly exaggerated, I can assure you," Jamison Hadley smiled. Turning to Laine, he offered his arm to help her to her feet. "Are you hurt, Miss Coleridge?"

Laine's mind reeled with tumultuous emotion. She shook her throbbing head at Hadley's question, and allowed herself to be helped up by both of them. Her head spun. She rubbed the back of it, wincing in pain.

"Take it easy," Travis said soothingly, holding her arm. "You took some nasty bumps, but I'm sure you'll be all right."

Jamison placed a possessive arm around her waist and steered her toward the waiting coach. "I'll get you to a doctor in Silver Grande just to be sure."

Laine felt the warmth of Travis's hand as she was pulled away from the crook of Hadley's arm.

"I can take care of that," Travis said. "The doctor is an old friend of mine . . . and Laine's."

Hadley shrugged as if to concede that bit of assistance to Mitcham.

"Does anybody around here care whether I'm dead'r not?"

The coach driver stumbled toward them, brushing dirt from his denim pants and cowhide vest. He raked his wide-brimmed black hat through the air and slapped it against his leg, muttering indistinguishable phrases as he did so.

"You all right, Buck?" Travis called out to him, handing Laine up into the coach. Hadley climbed in after her.

"Wal, it's about time you noticed *me*, Mitcham," the scratchy voice shot back. "Coulda been dead'r worse fer all you cared." He clamped his hat on his wiry gray head, and it perched there oddly askew.

"C'mon, Buck, you old warhorse, nothing's gonna take you down," Travis chided his old friend warmly. "I didn't have to worry about you. Knew you could take care of yourself."

33

Buck responded as if he hadn't heard. "Lucky fer you I'm tough. You'da felt mighty bad if I'da been kilt back there." His head jerked up and down, affirmatively underscoring his words as he spoke.

He went about the business of gathering up the long reins, then checked over each of the four bay horses carefully, murmuring softly to them, rubbing a neck or patting a nose as he went. The horses pawed the ground impatiently, still heaving from their run, the smell of their blowing and sweat filling the hot, dusty air.

Buck let out long groans as he pulled his lean frame up on the high driver's box, muttering apologies to his team.

Laine leaned out the window and watched Travis handing up to Buck several bags and trunks that had pried loose and fallen off the coach during their wild ride. His shoulders and back moved fluidly under the soft buckskin jacket, and she felt a warm twinge through her middle when her eyes settled on the muscles of his thighs and buttocks straining against his worn pants.

Travis rounded up his black stallion and tied him to the back of the coach. He walked around by the window. A smile spread across his lips as he met and held Laine's gaze. She suddenly felt as if he could read her mind, just as he always seemed able to do when she was a child. She felt her cheeks flush, and quickly drew her gaze inside the coach. Travis climbed up beside Buck in the driver's box.

"Get outta here!" Buck called out the command, snapping the reins over the horses' wide flanks, and with a multitude of creaks the coach lurched forward on the direct route into Silver Grande.

"Wal, wal, whaddya make of that?" Buck held the reins in one hand and packed a chaw of tobacco inside his cheek with the other.

Travis shed his jacket, lifted his hat and wiped his perspiring brow with his forearm, leaving dots of moisture on the blue shirtsleeve.

"Feelin' kinda warm, are ya, Trav?" Buck gently urged the horses on with a muffled clucking out of the side of his mouth over the tobacco wad.

Travis looked up at the sun. "It's a hot one all right," he acknowledged.

Buck shot a sidelong glance at Travis. "I didn't mean the afternoon."

Travis leaned against the high frame of the coach and sent his gaze down the dusty hard road to Silver Grande.

"Neither did I, old friend. Believe me, neither did I."

Chapter Two

Laine tried to settle herself in the coach, but every nerve in her body battled against her. She'd dreamed often in the last few months about how she would react to her first meeting with Travis after so many years, but the actual event was as far from her fantasies as Boston was from Silver Grande. She couldn't seem to get hold of herself now, get back in control.

Oh, he was even more handsome now than in her fantasies. And her dreams hadn't allowed for the sheer masculine wide-open aroma of him, the scent of freedom, of raw excitement. It was like feeling the thrill of new adventure. She grew heady with the sense memory of his nearness.

She thought with amusement that her chattering girl friends back East would embarrass themselves to a giddy state fawning over him if given half a chance.

"Laine Coleridge," Jamison Hadley said thoughtfully, and his voice was a sobering element. He watched her as he settled back into the coach seat.

"Jamison Hadley," Laine replied coolly, not looking at him. The reminder of his presence jolted her out of her reverie.

She busied herself gathering her belongings from around the coach and stuffing them into her travelling bag. That accomplished, she set about smoothing her skirt, fastening her waistcoat, and deftly pinning her hair up into a neat coil.

Jamison watched with unbridled admiration. "Where have you been all this time?" he asked with a half smile tilting one corner of his mouth.

"East," she answered crisply. Impatiently she examined a tear in her sleeve. "And I might ask the same of you. I believe I saw you only once when I lived in Silver Grande. Where were *you* all that time?"

She worked each of her fingers into a pair of white gloves, carefully smoothing them into the vee between each finger, and did not watch his face when he answered.

"East," he echoed darkly, gazing out the window as the scenery moved lazily by. "And I hardly noticed you then," he added with an air of superiority. Then he leaned forward. "But I daresay that can change."

Laine stopped smoothing her gloves, and looked over at him. He had that disturbing look in his eyes, and she found she loathed it as much now as she had then. Only now it didn't frighten her. She was about to ask where in the East he had been, but thought better of it, deciding it was best not to ask more of him lest it prompt him to ask more of her.

As suddenly as it had darkened, Jamison's mood

brightened, and he turned his attention back to Laine.

"And what brings you back to Silver Grande, that gem in the vast wasteland of the Arizona territory?" he asked with smooth disdain.

Laine smiled briefly, then looked toward the passing land. "Vast wasteland . . ." she said distantly. This land held all the answers to her questions, she told herself. It had to. She knew of nowhere else to go for them.

She sucked in her breath and held it for a moment before releasing it in a sigh, then stared beyond the mesas, past the buttes and distant dark red mountain peaks, and reflected on her life in Boston. Disconnection. She began to realize that her time back there, while adding immeasurably to her life, had also disconnected her from her roots.

And an even greater revelation—as much as she'd wanted to run away from Silver Grande long ago, she was cautiously anxious to be going back. A mixture of anticipation and apprehension took over inside her.

Laine wasn't exactly certain when it was she began to take hold of her own life. Maybe it was in the moment she'd awakened in Aunt Sarah's bed. Or perhaps it was later when she became part of a social group who constantly bragged about family history and wealth, and who seemed to have nothing to do except travel, and gossip, and go to parties. Their example taught her exactly what she didn't want. Laine longed for more, knew there must be more that was real.

When her friends probed more deeply about her family, she fabricated a fantasy of wealth and adventure in the wilds of an untamed territory.

"My parents died of a horrible fever which swept the territory in an epidemic," she told them. "Alone, caught in a hotel fire, I was miraculously saved by a mysterious cowboy who whisked me away on the back of his white horse in the dead of night. It was he who put me on the train to Boston."

They'd listened with rapt attention and chattered about her exciting and shadowy past. But the more they talked of it, the angrier Laine grew inside, and the more restless. She wanted real answers for herself, not the fantasies she'd fabricated for her friends.

She studied and then immersed herself in designing exclusive fashions for her aunt's influential friends, and made a name for herself. She also became known for spurning every suitor who came to her door, breaking their lovestruck hearts gently, and retaining their friendships in the aftermath.

One thing had stayed painfully clear to her—she would never become close to any man. He would eventually leave, and she would suffer more deep hurt for which she knew there was no soothing balm. But always, always, Travis Mitcham lived in the dreamy garden of her heart and mind.

More and more she thought of returning to Silver Grande, even if only for a visit, but Aunt Sarah would talk her out of it. Laine would put the idea out of her mind because she owed a great deal to Aunt Sarah. She didn't want to disappoint her. But the idea would always return and nag her again.

Then the letter arrived. An attorney in Silver Grande informed her of Jackson Smithers' death, and requested her presence to go over some important papers regarding something she'd inherited from him.

That information surprised her. Uncle Jack was penniless as far as she knew. But the news reopened the old battle about going back. The strong pull toward the West at once thrilled and terrified her.

Aunt Sarah cried and cajoled, begging Laine not to go. She bemoaned the loss of a secure and dazzling life for the young beauty in Boston society.

"You're the spitting image of Elizabeth," she'd said, "and if you go to that awful place, it'll ruin you just like it ruined her, and eventually killed her. Well, *he's* the one should be blamed for her death."

When Laine's look had darkened, Aunt Sarah changed her tone. Laine begged her aunt to talk about Elizabeth and David, and tell her the truth as she knew it. Aunt Sarah refused, and when Laine declared she would go to Silver Grande and find out her own way, Sarah relented.

"Your mother, Elizabeth Laine Bradford, was a beautiful wealthy young lady. Her upbringing in Boston didn't prepare her to live in the Arizona desert. The course of her lovely life was completely altered the night she met and was smitten with a handsome cowboy who appeared in a Wild West show in a Boston arena.

"Oh, I saw him that night, too," Aunt Sarah said ruefully. "He rode a brilliant golden palomino horse past our box seat, and Elizabeth thought him to be the most thrilling man she'd ever seen. I admit he was the handsomest I'd ever seen.

"I tried to talk her out of seeing him, but, oh, she was clever. She worked out a plan to meet him, posing as the daughter of a horse breeder interested in hiring him to buy horses for his farm. David Coleridge was struck by her boldness and her beauty, and fell in love with her immediately. And why shouldn't he? He later forgave her little ruse and stayed in Boston, taking work wherever possible to remain near her.

"To our utter horror, she ran off with him one day! We were sure he'd kidnapped her and were worried sick. Then we had word from her at last. She'd moved West with her cowboy and was living in a cabin, a cabin mind you, in a sagebrush and scrub pine littered valley in Arizona. She tried to make it sound beautiful, but we knew different.

"They did have one lovely thing in their lives, dear Laine. You. I daresay you were the only good thing to come of that union. He couldn't keep money in his pocket, nor food on the table. And then he just disappeared. Elizabeth didn't tell us that, you understand. But we learned of it. Broke your grandparents' hearts. They didn't see Elizabeth again, and they never saw you.

"When you came to me that night, my heart broke all over again. And when I heard about Elizabeth, I only wanted to take care of you, give you everything the way she should have had it. I thought you'd marry someone respectable and stay in Boston. I thought I'd successfully erased every memory of that awful place from your mind.

"I don't know what happened to David. He never turned up again," Aunt Sarah had said darkly. "But I suppose there's a way of finding out . . . if you want to know."

Laine had shaken her head and waved Aunt Sarah's words away.

Sarah had begged Laine to reconsider her decision to go back to Silver Grande, but Laine had made up her mind and was determined to go.

"But," Aunt Sarah declared in one last attempt to change Laine's decision, "your artistic talent will be stifled if you go to that savage wilderness. Women there wear only" (here Aunt Sarah had grimaced) "calico, for heaven's sake!"

Two hours out of Boston on the train, Laine was overwhelmed by a sense of freedom and adventure, intuitively knowing she'd made the right decision.

She returned her look now to Hadley. "Unfinished business," she answered at last in guarded directness.

"Exactly," Hadley's black eyes riveted hers to a steady gaze. His head nodded slightly to the rhythm of the rolling coach.

Laine breathed deeply and tried to relax with the coach's rocking motion. She became aware of various aches and pains, but endured them stoically. She leaned her head toward the window and watched powdery green sagebrush and prickly pear cactus pass.

Boston seemed a lifetime past.

Travis jammed his foot into the curved railing at the top of the coach, his forearm resting across his knee, his Stetson pulled down over his forehead against the glare of the sun. He rode fluidly on the hard wood seat, letting his body move without resistance to the motion. The horses' hooves plodding an even beat over the familiar road placed him in a reflective mood.

Laine Coleridge's lovely face floated before him, suspended in the watery heat mirage on the horizon. A breeze played about a loose curl of honeygold hair over her forehead and caught it in the long curved fringe of smoky eyelashes. He lifted it so he could see into the incredible blue-violet depths of her eyes.

Travis stopped his thoughts.

Buck spat out a stream of tobacco juice into the passing sagebrush, then eyed Travis from under the brim of his ragged hat. He'd been silent for several miles, allowing his young friend to ponder. But now that the spire on the church in Silver Grande could be seen on the far horizon, he felt it was time to speak.

"Thinkin' 'bout Laine Coleridge, ain'tcha?" he asked in his usual knowing way.

"Hm?" Travis responded distantly. Then, "No, I was thinking about the shipment of lumber I'm expecting. Have to get the new feed mill started."

"Humph." A crooked smile broke into the wrinkles on Buck's leathery face. "You ain't thinkin' 'bout no lumber, son."

He reined in the horses with a firm pull. They always tried to break into a gallop at just about the same place on this road, knowing that ahead was a barn with water, food and a brisk rubdown. Buck knew they were particularly anxious at the end of this trip, the near accident having left them sore and weary.

"Buck, I guess you know me better than anyone else," Travis sat up and pulled on the brim of his hat.

"Wal, I should say. Been like a father to you since yer paw died, rest his soul."

"Yes, you have, and Molly's been like a second mother to me, too. I've been fortunate to have you as my family." Travis's mother and father had died while he was in college, and he'd been forced to return to Silver Grande immediately and take over as head of Mitcham Construction.

"And yer thinkin' nobody ever loved Laine Coleridge ceptin' her mother. That pore woman, sacrificin' ever'thin' includin' herself. Wonder what brought that child back here? Ain't nothin' left for her here now."

"I don't know," Travis responded thoughtfully. He stared straight ahead, watching Silver Grande loom larger on the horizon. "Maybe she thinks of Silver Grande as her home, although I can't imagine why. Even old Smithers is dead now. Hell, how would I know what she's thinking, anyway?"

"Cuz you always did when you were kids. I thought mebbe you had some idea . . . it don't matter none anyway."

"That was a long time ago. She sure has grown up, though, hasn't she?" Travis smiled and gave Buck a nudge in the ribs with his elbow.

"I'll say!" Buck answered, sending another squirt of tobacco juice off the side of the coach. "She's growed up real good. I didn't even know it was her. Nor thet Hadley dude neither. Didn't take him long to notice how she's growed up neither."

Hadley. Travis had almost forgotten about him. "Why do you suppose he suddenly reappeared after all this time?" He rubbed his chin.

"Whaddaya mean *why?*" Buck whispered huskily into Travis's ear. "Now that old man Hadley's ailin', he prob'ly figgered it was time to git back here and cash in on the family fortune."

In his usual canny way Buck was probably right, Travis knew. "That and all the rumors about the Southern Pacific Railroad building through Silver Grande."

"Long past the rumor stage now. It's gonna make a lotta people a lotta money, includin' you, son."

The coach was fast approaching the outskirts of Silver Grande.

"I'd say the arrival of Laine Coleridge and Jamison Hadley, together or separately, is gonna keep this town aflame with gossip for weeks," Buck mused.

"Yes, I'm sure many of them will find their arrival very interesting," Travis nodded.

"Yes sir," Buck concluded. "It's gonna get mighty interestin' 'fore it's all over."

Chapter Three

The horses slowed to a walk as they passed a new sign welcoming travellers to Silver Grande City.

"City?!" Laine couldn't keep her astonishment quiet.

"These people delude themselves," Jamison said absently. "To them a city is simply more than one dusty street."

Plank sidewalks, neat small shops and new buildings began to unfold on both sides of the coach. People bustled about their business, now and then stopping to chat, and children ran laughing among them.

"City," Laine mused again, shaking her head in wonderment.

But, then, as if to contradict her pronouncement, they passed a tavern, where cattle. drovers lounged in chairs or leaned against wood pillars smoking and talking raucously. A half-smile formed on Laine's lips as she recalled her childhood excitement at the sight of drovers guiding great herds of cattle into Silver Grande's holding pens, staying a few days before going on to California. The familiar odor of cattle now hung heavy in the air.

"I'm glad some things haven't changed," Laine said, breathing in the memory.

Jamison Hadley grimaced.

When the coach swung around a corner, Laine felt a foreboding sense of the familiar. She was almost afraid to look out the window, afraid to see the hotel, and yet at the same time anxious to see it. Instinctively she knew the moment they would pass it. She forced her head around to take a straight-on look, and a chill ran over her body when she caught full sight of it.

In this part of town all of the buildings appeared uncared for and decrepit. The old hotel, what was left of it, sat in the middle of a row of old shops, some still in business, others long abandoned. Its windows and swinging doors were boarded over, and signs issuing a warning against entry were tacked to the front posts. A shutter on a top floor window opened and closed silently in the hot breeze.

As the scene passed from her view, Laine's brow knotted in painful recollection. She drew in her head and stared at her hands, clenching the folds of her skirt. If only she could have boarded over her memories along with that dilapidated old building. She willed herself not to cry.

"Well, that place is certainly an eyesore," Jamison said evenly, watching her with a silent question in his look. "Should have been torn down long ago. Someone should do this town a favor and get rid of it."

Laine did not respond. She stiffened her back and shifted her gaze to the window.

The coach swung around another corner. Here the street was busier with people, and some of the buildings were new or recently refurbished. Laine was happily surprised that Silver Grande had grown so much in the years she'd been away. She smiled openly at a group of children who ran excitedly alongside the coach calling out to Buck and Travis as they drew up in front of the stage depot. The old depot now had a tall addition built onto one side which housed a small coffee shop on the ground floor, and a sign advertising rooms for overnight guests on the top floor.

Buck jumped down from the driver's box calling greetings to the young men who worked around the depot. Travis opened the door and, smiling warmly, took Laine's hand to help her step down. The warmth emanating from him, coupled with being back in Silver Grande, filled Laine with a mixture of anticipation and apprehension.

She didn't make a move. Descending from the coach would mean stepping closer to Travis, and stepping into her past and her future all at the same time. She'd thought she was ready for this kind of assault, but for the moment she believed she wasn't strong enough.

"Welcome home, Laine," Travis said, tipping his hat. "The place has changed a little, I guess."

"More than a little," Laine answered from far away in her mind. "It's not what I remember. Or forgot, I guess I should say."

"It's not possible to forget it all, though, is it?" he said quietly.

Laine looked into his knowing eyes. "Home," she repeated his word.

She took in a deep breath and allowed him to assist her out of the coach. Then she concentrated on viewing the changes and searching for the familiar in Silver Grande. Anything to stop her insides from knotting at the nearness of Travis, and unsettling the cool-headed Easterner she knew herself to be.

Across the street stood a new hotel with white painted clapboards and stately columns, and a wide porch where comfortable chairs and tables were grouped on the shady side. To the north beyond the roof of the hotel, the San Francisco Peaks faded in and out through undulating heat reflections in the dry air.

Just past the hotel stood the old tonsorial parlor that still boasted its red and white barber pole, but the words she remembered were still stenciled in gold and black on the window, "Rufus Drier — Haircuts, Shaves, Moustaches a Specialty — (Some Dentistry)." Laine smiled in comfortable amusement. Rufus Drier had been one of the people who was nice to her. He used to tease her with a pair of long silver scissors, brandishing them overhead like a weapon and shouting he was going to snip off one of her golden curls for a souvenir. Laine would shriek with feigned terror and hide behind the towel bin. Rufus would always act surprised when she jumped out at him and would reward her with a piece of hard candy for having bested him in the pursuit.

Next to Drier's the old candy store nestled in the same place, only something new had been added — a soda fountain. Laine recalled fond memories of the Sugar Bowl in Boston where she'd whiled away some afternoons with friends over cherry soda drinks. Thinking now that children in Silver Grande might do the very same thing pleased her.

Two clothing shops, one for men and one for ladies, stood side by side at the end of the row, but Laine thought they seemed drab and outmoded in comparison with some of the newer shops.

Noisy wagons rumbled by, horses snorting and chains rattling. Cowboys on horseback and several fine one-horse carriages passed the depot.

Laine was aware that several children and a few adults stood at a distance from her. No doubt their curiosity about the arriving passengers had gotten the best of them, she thought. She could hear the women whispering among themselves, noticeably assessing her fine clothes and wondering how they became torn and dirty, and marvelling at the number of pieces of luggage she'd brought with her.

Three little girls shyly stepped closer to Laine

and looked up at her as if she were a princess who'd just stepped out of one of their storybooks. Laine smiled and winked at them. The little girls smiled back, twisting back and forth, their starched skirts swishing against each other. Two of the women brusquely took them by the hands and led them away.

Laine felt a brief, familiar stab of pain in her chest like the prick of a needle. Could they know who she was and still treat her as an outcast? She hoped she'd read that wrong. Perhaps she'd let a little paranoia take over for a moment. She noticed how the men cautiously eyed Jamison Hadley, some of the older ones with shocked recognition on their faces.

Some things never change, Laine thought ruefully.

Buck stood with his hat in both hands in front of him, her trunks and cases spread out behind him. "Miss Coleridge, where would you like me to take your bags? Over to the hotel?"

"Buck!" Travis called, coming out of the stage depot.

He reached his old friend's side just as Buck was struggling to pick up several of Laine's bags at one time. Two young boys he'd hired were already hoisting her large trunk on their shoulders.

"Wal . . . don't jest stand there, Travis, pick up some of this stuff!" Buck motioned with his head, beads of perspiration forming on his walnut-colored face.

51

"Wait a minute, Buck. Where are you taking these?"

"T'the hotel, a'course," Buck answered with irritation, pointing with a dusty elbow in the direction of the new white building.

"Now, Buck, that seems kind of unfriendly to a lady who's been away from home a long time, doesn't it?" Travis spoke evenly.

"Whut?" Buck frowned, and set the bags down in the street with some difficulty.

Jamison Hadley had started across to the hotel carrying his own bag and one of Laine's. Travis watched his arrogant stride with repugnance, then turned back to Buck.

"I simply thought you and Molly would want to extend your usual friendly hospitality and invite Laine to stay with you until she finds a suitable place." He grinned at the older man and picked up a couple of Laine's bags. "I'll just help you load these onto your buckboard now." He turned around and started toward the back of the depot where a buckboard and horses stood waiting.

Buck took off his hat and scratched his moist wiry hair with the same hand. "Wal now, I don't know . . ." he started, but Travis turned a deaf ear.

"Oh, I wouldn't dream of moving into your home," Laine was saying as Travis walked away.

Long strides brought him to the back of the stage depot in short order to an old but well-kept buckboard, hitched to a pair of roans. Deftly he swung Laine's bags up into the small bed in the back, then walked around the depot smiling as he advanced toward her and Buck. They trudged slowly toward him laden with bags, while he swung past them in a light-hearted open-armed gait. They stopped and turned to watch his broad-shouldered figure move into the street.

The two boys with the trunk turned around twice in confusion until Travis stopped them and pointed them in the direction of the buckboard. They half-dragged their burden, tripping over its corners and their own feet.

Travis kept moving, reaching Jamison Hadley just as he was stepping up onto the hotel porch. He clamped a hand on Hadley's shoulder and swiftly grabbed Laine's bag with the other.

"Here, Hadley, let me help you with that." Travis grinned, then turned on his heels in the opposite direction.

"Hey!" Hadley whirled around. "That belongs to Miss Coleridge!"

"Right!" Travis shot back, and kept walking.

Almost three miles out of town on a straight hard road lay Buck Harmon's place. He held the horses at a moderate pace so as not to exhaust them in the unrelenting late afternoon heat, and kept his thoughts to himself.

Laine pulled the amber straw hat onto her head, and tied its violet ribbons securely under her chin. The wide brim would add scant protection from the burning rays which had already caused her unprotected skin to sting a little. Every bump and dip in the road told her nothing she wore protected her from the rough ride on the hard buckboard seat, nor from the tingling sensation of Travis's hard thigh as it brushed provocatively along her own.

A deep breath of dry desert air burned her lungs, yet still felt rather good somehow. She rode silently comparing the differences between Boston and Silver Grande. The roses would be budding in Aunt Sarah's garden, and she would miss seeing them burst into fragrant bloom. One of her favorite places to go and think had been in that rose garden with the two cats purring at her feet.

Her eyes began to sting with tears, partly in remembrance of what she'd left behind, and partly from dust particles swirling up into the air from the rolling buckboard wheels. There are no roses here, she thought as she gazed around the countryside from her seat between Buck and Travis. Maybe a clump of sagebrush here and there, or a gnarled manzanita with a jackrabbit or two scurrying by.

Out of the corner of her eye Laine saw Travis push his high-crowned hat up off his moist brow. He lounged back in the seat, his arm draped casually over the back of it. The hard edge of the seat back hit Laine just above the small of her back, and had been sending small pains up her spine. His arm softened the contact and, while she felt uncomfortable doing it, she welcomed the chance to lean against it.

The more his thigh brushed hers, the more she tensed and attempted to pull away. But there was no place for her legs to go in the cramped space. Travis did not try even a little to move away, and it disturbed her that he seemed so very relaxed sitting this close to her while she was becoming unnerved at his nearness. How astounding to learn that after all these years without contact with him, her feelings could be so intense. She fervently hoped those feelings were obvious only to herself.

"Molly don't like surprises much," Buck was muttering when his voice brought Laine back to reality, " 'specially not visitors."

Travis chuckled. "That's only because she likes to cook food enough for a three-month trail drive, and get the last speck of dust from behind the stove."

Even though Travis had been like a son to the childless Buck and Molly, she always wanted to know in advance when he was coming so she could make all his favorite foods. She chided him when he didn't prepare her, and he would appear properly guilty like a naughty little boy. Then he would sneak up behind her, hug her and plant a kiss on her ruddy cheek.

"She's gonna be frettin' that I brought a fine Eastern lady to stay, and not givin' her time to tidy up the guest room and cook a decent supper," Buck said straight into the air over the clank of harness, as if he hadn't heard Travis.

Travis laughed in amusement at the older man's

words. "Aw, Buck, you know Molly. She just likes to have something to complain about. She loves to have company. Gives her somebody to show off her handiwork and cooking to."

"Yeah, wal you kin always git around her with yer soft-soapin', but I gotta live with her, and it ain't the same." He stole a quick glance at Laine, and in gentlemanly fashion tipped his dusty hat to her. "No offense to you, ma'am," he added quietly.

"I understand, Mr. Harmon," Laine smiled at him. "I would have been very comfortable at the hotel, but Travis just took matters into his own hands and forced you into an unpleasant situation. I apologize for his rude behavior." She looked straight ahead, her chin held high.

The pressure of Travis's long leg against hers now seemed to burn through her skirts. The masculine scent of him, mingled with sun-dried denim, wafted across her face with every gust of breeze. There was no space between them that wasn't filled with part of him.

"No need to apologize for me," Travis put in with an amused quirk of his eyebrow. "Sure, you would have been comfortable at the hotel," he mocked her haughty tone. "That Hadley dude would have bent over backward to see to your every need, I'm sure."

He drew his arm away from her back and yanked hard on the front of his hat, pulling it down over his eyes. Folding his arms over his chest, he slumped down in the seat and set his jaw at a hard angle.

"Well, he appears to be a gentleman, and knows how to treat a lady," Laine shot back without looking at him. She folded her arms across her chest and sat up straight.

"Oh, Lordy," Buck muttered. The white adobe of his house could now clearly be seen reflecting in the sun. He urged the horses into a quicker pace. It would be good to get this homecoming over with fast, he thought.

"Gentleman, hah!" Travis spat out in front. "I'm sure, Miss Coleridge, that you will have plenty of opportunity to find out just what kind of *gentleman* Jamison Hadley really is."

"Oh?" Laine affected an ingenuous tone, her steely gaze fixed on the road ahead.

"Yes. I can assure you that it won't be long before the gentleman pays a call on the lady, and it won't be just a social call either."

"And what do you mean by that, Mr. Mitcham?" Laine flared.

"You know damned well what I mean by that, *Miss* Coleridge." He jerked his shoulders around, and pushing his hat to the back of his head spoke directly to her. "Men like that see a woman like you, and they know exactly what they're going after."

"And what is that supposed to mean, 'a woman like me'?" she snapped, turning her head and giving him a withering glare. She could feel his breath on her face, he was that close, and it was difficult

57

to maintain her indignant demeanor.

"Well, all right, since you asked. You've returned to a town you knew only as a child. Things have changed, people have changed. You won't know many people here now. You'll want to get settled, meet people, and someone like Hadley will be only too willing to help you. And look at you, all pink and refined, and showing your . . . assets." His eyes dropped to her throat.

Laine's slightly sun-burned skin reddened under his gaze. Her hand flew to the open neck of her blouse to be certain all buttons were fastened. She spun around to a straight position in the seat.

"Oh, Lordy!" Buck said louder.

Travis leaned forward, his voice softening. "I mean, Laine, you arrive here looking like a fine, wealthy lady. There are some men who would take advantage of that while you're adjusting to your new surroundings. I think Hadley's that kind, that's all I'm trying to say. It's just a warning, that's all."

"I don't believe I need your warning," Laine sniffed, smoothing her skirt and pulling her jacket more closely around her.

"Another fantasy," Travis said, more to himself than to her. "You never have lived in the present . . . Please excuse me. I guess I didn't realize you might welcome that kind of attention."

He turned back to the front and stopped himself from saying anything more. He wasn't sure how the whole argument got started in the first place. She seemed so vulnerable, and he was only trying to protect her from unscrupulous people, he reasoned. He was surprised to hear his voice hold more a tone of jealousy than it did protection. Jealous? He'd never felt jealous in his life.

The buckboard pulled into the dooryard of the Harmon house, ending any further speculation on either part.

"Here we are!" Buck announced, clearly relieved the trip was over at last.

Laine stared straight ahead, the heat of the moment beginning to cool. This was not the way she'd dreamed of their reunion. Travis certainly seemed to have a low opinion of her. She looked over at him, hoping for another word, a softer word, something that would put to rest the questions that now rose in her mind. But Travis kept his gaze on the road, his expression stony.

The questions whispered around her like the ceaseless desert wind. Did Travis think those things about her when they were in school? Was he like everyone else then, believing the worst of her mother, and so the worst of her?

Chapter Four

Molly Harmon stood on the front porch of her small house, a hand above her eyes to shield them from the glaring sun, watching the buckboard approach. Buck pulled the team up to the gate of the rail fence, wrapped the reins around the brake pole, and jumped to the ground.

"You do the explainin'," he whispered to Travis as he started around the back of the wagon. "I ain't claimin' this idea."

"Molly!" Travis sang out when he spotted her on the porch. He jumped down and ran toward her, arms outstretched. "How's the love of my life?" He reached her before she had the chance to say anything, and scooped up her ample figure in his arms, swinging her around until she protested.

"Travis! Now you stop that!" Molly pushed back his shoulders with her strong hands. "It's clear you've brought me unexpected company, so stop tryin' to throw me off the track." She narrowed her twinkling gray eyes at him.

Travis reached to pick up his hat which had flown off in his exuberant greeting. Holding it in his hands, he looked down at the ground like an apologetic child.

"Now, Molly, the poor lady was stranded in town all alone. No family, no friends. All alone." He stressed the last words, and looked into her ruddy open face, earnestness radiating from his eyes. "What could I do? All I could think of was how warm and welcome you'd make her feel in a strange place. I mean, we couldn't leave a frail young thing like that all alone to fend for herself, what with the drovers in town and all, could we?"

Molly planted her hands over her wide hips. She gave Travis a disbelieving look, then peered around at the young woman who sat in the buckboard with her hands folded in her lap. Her eyes shifted back at Travis with a "I-never-could-resist-you" look in them.

"Well," Travis clamped his hat on his head and made a turn to leave. "I guess it really would be hard on you to have an unexpected guest. I mean, you have so much work to do as it is, and this would only add more than you can handle. I'll just drive . . . Miss Coleridge . . . back into town and check her into the hotel. That should be safe enough, shouldn't it?" He glanced over his shoulder at Molly.

Molly's gray eyes sharpened with steely glints. "Coleridge!" she whispered. "Not . . . ?"

"Yes," Travis answered quickly. "Elizabeth Coleridge's little girl, Laine. Been in the East all these years, and now she's come back." He reached out

61

and took Molly's rough hands into his own. "Molly, dear, it would really help a lot if . . ."

"What do you mean, Travis Mitcham, more work than I can handle?" she cut him off. "I can out-work you any day of the week, and you know it! One more in the house ain't no work atall. Just an extra plate on the table is all." She broke away from him and headed toward the buckboard at a fast clip, her long brown print skirt swishing around her flat boots.

"Land sakes, come down from there, honey." Molly held a hand out to Laine as she reached the buckboard. "These menfolks ain't got no sense, let-tin' a fair-skinned girl like you set in the hot sun. Come in, come in. Got some nice lemonade made fresh. It'll cool you off."

Laine allowed the amiable woman to help her down from the buckboard. "I'm sorry, Mrs. Har-mon, I know it's a terrible imposition to have a stranger thrust on you like this, but . . ."

"Now I won't hear none of that," Molly soothed her. "It'll be no trouble atall, a pleasure to have you. And besides, you ain't no stranger. I remem-ber you when you wuz a little girl." She led Laine toward the house, an arm around her shoulders as they walked through the gate. "I don't get lotsa news from beyond Silver Grande much. You'll be doin' me a favor by stayin' a spell."

As they passed Travis, Molly made a good-na-tured face at him.

Travis caught and held Laine's violet gaze as she

passed him. He wanted to say something to her, but no words came. In any case, his voice seemed to have taken leave for some reason. He felt tongue-tied in her presence and that disturbed him.

Laine tore her gaze from Travis's face and tried to concentrate on what Molly was saying. They walked to the front door, and she turned and glanced over her shoulder at him before going inside. As he turned back toward the buckboard, she caught sight of his chestnut hair curling over his collar, and a flicker of a smile played at the corners of her mouth.

Buck had been standing stock-still, keeping the team between him and his wife through the greetings.

"Lordy," he sighed in relief. "I thought thet was gonna be a lot harder'n it was," he said to Travis, who was walking toward him with a smile on his face.

"A snap!" Travis said confidently, making a sound with two fingers in the air. "Let's get the horses watered and fed. Can't be late for supper, you know. Molly'll have your hide!"

With that, Buck threw the ends of the reins toward his young friend's chest, and set about unhitching the horses. Travis untied his stallion from the back of the buckboard and led all of them toward the barn, whistling and grinning at Buck over his shoulder.

* * *

When the door had quietly closed behind Molly, Laine sank onto the quilt-covered bed in the small guest room. She sipped the cool lemonade left with her and leaned back against the pine headboard with her eyes closed. Her heart pounded in her ears, and her stomach began to churn. She held the cool glass to her temples and breathed deeply.

The day had been physically and emotionally demanding, what with the near accident, and the return to Silver Grande. But the unexpected meeting with Travis had unnerved her, more than she ever would have guessed. She'd thought she'd prepared herself for that first meeting. Of course she'd thought it would happen when she arrived in town. She would be dressed in that violet dress that brought out her eyes and accentuated her waist, and her hair would be softly curled under the hat which she would have set at a jaunty angle. But no. He had to drop out of the blue like he did, and right back into the center of her life. How could any lady be prepared for a reunion like that?

Molly's warmth and caring made her think of her mother. And her bustling about to make her unexpected guest welcome gave Laine the same feeling she'd felt so long ago when she'd arrived at Aunt Sarah's. Her lower lip began to tremble, and she gritted her teeth hard to make it stop. In the next moment hot tears started down her cheeks.

When the wave of emotion passed, she sat up straight and placed the glass on a low bedside table, then admonished herself that she must pull herself together. Appearing at the supper table with red, swollen eyes would never do. She was determined to show that she was strong and capable of handling whatever came her way. Shaking her head, she wiped the tears away.

Rising slowly, she undressed and placed her soiled clothes in a neat pile on the floor at the end of the bed. She opened one of her bags and took out a pale blue flowered cotton dress, and a pair of blue shoes with low heels.

The mirror over the dresser reflected a sad image. Her skin was moist with tiny specks of dirt clinging to her throat and the delicate white skin above her breasts. Her hair had pulled away from the combs, and strands were sticking to her neck and forehead. Rose-colored streaks where tears had cleansed away some of the dirt made crooked trails down her cheeks, and already her eyes were red-rimmed and had begun to swell.

She frowned, then quickly set about pouring water from an ironstone pitcher into its matching washbowl on the low commode. The tepid water felt good on her face, and she bathed with a soft white cloth and a bar of French milled soap she'd brought with her. A white towel hung on a hook near the mirror, and she took it down and folded it around her body, patting gingerly over a few scrapes and bruises that had begun to show darkly through her skin.

She sat down on the bed and searched through her bag for her old doll, and the tea tin. She shook the tin as she had every night since she left Silver Grande as a child. The same money she and her mother had put in the tin long ago still rustled and rattled inside.

She drew the ragged doll to her bosom, sat back on the bed and pondered. Travis Mitcham's handsome tanned face invaded her weary mind and floated in front of her.

He was still treating her like a child, a little sister who had to be humored! The idea exasperated her. Surely he could see she was no longer a child.

At that moment she vowed to make him change his mind about her. He'd said she'd never lived in the present. Perhaps that was true when she was a child, but no longer. She was back in Silver Grande, and she had no immediate plans to leave. Whatever the lawyer had to tell her would have great bearing on her plans and her future, she knew that.

The dark visage of Jamison Hadley now crept into her mind. His eyes made her very uncomfortable, seeming to say much more than his words. She shook his image away.

She placed the doll on the pillow, and rose to finish dressing. She picked up the uncomfortable corset, and then in her first act of becoming the adult Laine Coleridge of Silver Grande, threw it on the floor with her other soiled clothes.

She pulled a pair of thin creamy stockings over her legs and stepped into a lacy petticoat, tying its narrow ribbons loosely around her waist. Then she

66

slipped into her dress and shoes. She dabbed some rose-scented cologne at her throat, and tied a blue ribbon around her head, letting her hair fall down her back in long loose waves.

She twirled around, letting the air lift her dress and hair. What a delicious feeling of freedom! No corset, no tightly wound hair. No Eastern ladylike restrictions? Those might not be as easy to shed as a corset and hair combs.

Travis's face again floated in front of her, and her hands tingled. Imagine this, she thought. As sophisticated as she'd been, socializing with the young men in Boston, and coolly keeping them at the distance she preferred, here she was now with a childhood friend, the thought of whom caused all her senses to quiver like a child's on Christmas morning.

She knew she would have to fight that as a grown woman now, for it was best to keep her head if she were to fulfill her own expectations.

Laine took a deep breath and left the bedroom.

"Now don't you look pretty as a picture," Molly exclaimed when Laine entered the kitchen. "Supper's 'most ready. The menfolks are in the parlor talkin' about Lord knows what. Never ceases to amaze me how they can find so much to talk about. 'Course Travis is like a son to us."

Molly continued to chatter as she bustled about

setting the table. Steam poured out of two pots on the big black iron stove, their covers rattling a comfortable, homey sound.

"Come set a spell while I take up supper, honey." Molly indicated a chair at the end of the table.

"May I help you, Mrs. Harmon?"

"No, no, no," Molly protested. "Jest set and tell me all about Boston. What are the houses like? Are the kitchens big with lots of windows? Always thought a kitchen should have lots of windows," she mused, pushing back a red print curtain from the small paned window next to the stove. It was the only open window in the room.

Laine followed Molly's bidding and took a seat at the table. She began by telling Molly about Aunt Sarah's house. Molly's gray eyes sparkled as the spacious kitchen was described, and as she heard of the dinners prepared there for the many guests who were in and out of the big house constantly. Molly proved an enthusiastic audience for Laine who, as usual, spun the stories with great detail.

Molly had been so rapt in attention to Laine's detailed descriptions, she was unaware of the insistent pounding of the cover on one of the iron pots as it built up a head of steam. White foam bubbled at the edge of the pot, then spilled over, pouring a steady stream down the sides onto the stove burner, sizzling furiously.

Both Molly and Laine jumped up and ran to the stove, grabbing towels on the way. In a moment it was all over as together they moved the pot to a sideboard. Steam moistened their faces making Laine's more flushed and deepening the ruddiness of Molly's. The two women looked at each other, then burst out laughing.

Molly allowed Laine to help her then, and together they dished up supper and set it on the table. Molly called the men to the kitchen. She and Buck sat at opposite ends of the square age-marked wood table, with Laine and Travis seated across from each other.

"Now fill up your plates," Molly ordered. "My mother used to say that a good hot meal in your insides on a hot day would cool your outsides." She passed a huge yellow bowl of boiled potatoes.

"Your mother said that about cold days, too," Buck said. Molly flashed him a reprimanding glare. "But, I guess she was prob'ly right," he added hastily. Quickly attempting to take his wife's focus off him, he asked Laine, "What do you think of Silver Grande City now? Changed some since you were here last, eh?"

"To be sure," Laine smiled, taking a slice of meat. "I confess I'd still been thinking of Silver Grande and the people," she sent a sidelong glance toward Travis, "as I remembered them as a child. The changes are indeed a surprise, but not disappointing."

"Nothing stays the same, except the past," Travis put in.

Molly and Buck exchanged glances, and Molly pressed the conversation further.

"Are you back permanent, Laine, or is this jest a visit?"

"I have no immediate plans to return East. If everything appears favorable, I will consider staying on permanently," Laine replied, smiling at the older woman. Then looking back at Travis she added, "I'm simply going to take each day as it comes."

"You never can tell what might come calling on any given day," Travis quipped, looking directly at her with an amused glint in his eye.

Laine knew that was a direct reference to their earlier discussion of Jamison Hadley. "True, but I'm sure I can count on my friends to warn me of any impending disaster, so that I may avoid unpleasantness at all costs. I trust I can count on you for that, Travis?"

"Oh, I wouldn't dream of overstepping the boundaries of personal privacy." He lowered his eyes. "You can count on me to mind my own business. I'm much too busy to get involved with other people's social dilemmas."

Buck stared questioningly into Travis's eyes, then reached past him for the bowl of potatoes. "Uh, Laine, do you have a place to stay? What're you gonna do while yer here?"

"Unlike my friend Buck," Travis muttered as if continuing his own sentence.

"Thank you for your concern, Mr. Harmon," Laine said, ignoring the remark. "I do have some plans which aren't complete at the moment. As for a place to stay, I had planned on using the hotel."

70

"Nonsense, we won't hear of that," Molly cut in. "This place doesn't have the convenience of being right in town, but it's your home for as long as you'd like it."

"Oh, no, I couldn't impose . . ."

"Not another word about it," Molly smiled, her hand raised to stop the protest. "We would be honored to have you with us, and it's no trouble atall. Stay as long as you like."

"That's right," Buck said, not looking up. "Thet way my wife gits somebody to fuss over and coddle, so's she'll stop botherin' me."

"Buckton Harmon!" Molly glared at him.

"That's right," Travis said, keeping his eyes on his plate. "Where do you think the word 'mollycoddle' came from? It was invented right here in this house!"

"Go on with ya'!" Molly gave him a playful pat on the arm.

Laine relaxed and enjoyed their banter. "Thank you Mrs. Harmon. I will accept your offer, and I hope I won't have to impose for very long. I have an appointment tomorrow with John T. McCauley, an attorney in town. I'm hoping he'll have information that will get a few things started for me."

Travis set down his fork. "What business could you have with that shyster? Be careful of that one."

"I see you know him. Is this my first friendly warning of impending disaster? I certainly hope your opinion of him is just that, your opinion."

"It isn't the only one like it, I can assure you.

How did you get his name? There's another very good lawyer in town, new to the area. I could set you up with him."

"Actually, Mr. McCauley got in touch with me. It seems Uncle Jack, Jackson Smithers, has died, and Mr. McCauley said he has important business with me concerning his death. Uncle Jack had no family that I know of. I think it might have something to do with the old hotel."

"Laine, it's been over two years since Smithers died. Why is McCauley just getting around to letting you know about it now?" Travis frowned and shot a glance toward Buck. Buck nodded almost imperceptibly in response.

"I had no idea when it happened. I simply thought he'd died recently," Laine said. "Now I'm wondering why he waited so long to let me know."

"Well, I don't trust him. If you'd let me, I'd be happy to go with you when you meet with him," Travis said, concern heavy in his voice. "A crook like that is liable to weasel around you and persuade you to sign papers you don't understand."

"Thank you, but that won't be necessary," Laine bristled slightly. "I can take care of things myself. My education will serve me well."

"Did your education provide you with the ability to handle crooks who've made it a lifetime business bilking unsuspecting people out of their hard-earned savings? Men like that have done it to many a seasoned prospector and rancher, and believe me, they could easily do it to a babe in the woods like

72

you. You ought to accept my help."

Laine's voice became edged with irritation. "Will you stop treating me like a child? I can handle my own affairs, and I certainly don't need you to help me."

Molly and Buck exchanged knowing glances, and the older woman slipped a soothing hand over to rest on Laine's arm.

"Now, I'm sure Travis don't mean you can't take care of things yourself, honey. It's jest that he knows the kind of man thet McCauley cuss is. He's been in his father's business a long time, and had some bad dealings with him himself."

"I'm sorry, Mrs. Harmon, I didn't mean to get so riled at your dinner table like this."

"Thet's all right. If I had sense enough I'd go to thet lawyer's office with you. We do think it would be good if you had Travis with you at least the first time. Please consider it."

Travis kept silent as Molly talked. He watched as the defiant set of Laine's chin softened, and when at last she looked at him, he could see reluctant acquiescence in her eyes.

"All right," she gave in, "perhaps all of you are right. I don't know this man McCauley, and you all do. You can come with me, Travis."

Travis nodded, and Buck and Molly showed relief.

"Sposin' you end up with thet old relic of a hotel? What would you do with it? Tear it down?" Buck wanted to know.

"That's what Jamison Hadley thought was the right thing to do," Laine answered, "but . . ."

"Hadley?" Travis cut in. "Have you discussed this with him already?"

Laine struggled to keep her resurging irritation with Travis down. "No, I did not discuss it with him. It was merely his comment as we passed the hotel coming into town."

"I'm sorry I snapped," Travis said. "What would you do with the hotel, that is, if you do inherit the thing?"

Laine sharply drew in a breath. This would be the first time she shared her thoughts about this with anyone. "Well, I do have an idea . . . I'm not sure Silver Grande needs another hotel, what with the new Black Canyon Hotel I saw as we came in today." Laine looked down shyly, hesitant to tell her ideas, yet feeling secure enough to risk saying a little. "I was thinking of refurbishing it into an elegant establishment. And, perhaps, opening a dress shop with garments of my own design and creation."

"Oh my," Molly smiled. "I'm sure lots of the ladies in town would like that. Most who want fine things order from San Antonio or San Francisco. Takes a long time to get here by freight wagon, but things are getting better now. Travis is the one seen to that."

"How's that?" Laine asked, genuinely interested.

"His business," Buck replied. "Construction, freight, all kinds. Got trade going with Texas and

74

California. Mighty big," he added, with pride evident in his voice. "Kin git a lot more shipped here now, and once the railroad comes through . . ."

"Oh, my yes," Molly beamed. "Travis, here, has done real well, he has. Most sought after man in town!"

Travis cleared his throat and looked down studiously at his plate. "Molly exaggerates," he muttered.

"No, I do not!" Molly gave him a playful push. "Why them young girls in town was all abuzz with excitement when he came home. Eligible bachelors are few and far between in this territory. 'Course he was always too busy to spend much time with them. But thet don't stop them from tryin'." She leaned close to Laine with a conspiratorial look in her eye. "A girl couldn't do better'n t'hitch up with Travis Mitcham."

Laine blushed at Molly's inference, then looked across at Travis. He cleared his throat again and begged Molly, "Ah, let's not talk about this anymore."

"Wal, it's the truth, and you know it," Molly grinned at him lovingly.

"And just how have you managed to stay the most eligible bachelor in Silver Grande?" Laine teased Travis. Trying not to show it, she added a serious question. "Or have you finally succumbed to the womanly charms of one of these excited ladies?"

"Not yet, he ain't!" Buck laughed. "Still footloose and fancy free, but not without workin' at it. Gets a lot of practice stayin' one step ahead of La-Belle Hadley."

Laine blanched visibly, but gathered her wits about her before she spoke again. "Guess you're right. Some things don't change a bit, do they?" She moved uncomfortably.

Travis sent a direct gaze to her. "Possibly. But like Buck said, I'm still footloose and fancy free."

"Coffee?" Molly asked, rising.

"I'd love some," Laine answered, grateful for the change in subject. "Did I hear you mention something about the railroad, Buck?"

"Yep, you shore did. Southern Pacific."

"I thought they'd completed their route to Texas," Laine mused. "It's been in all the papers."

"Wal, mebbe so, but talk is they want another branch. I suppose it's because of the mines."

"Oh, of course. The silver." Laine nodded.

"And gold and copper, too," Travis added.

"Well, Silver Grande has everything, hasn't it?" Laine said with a wry smile. "Silver, gold, copper, and eligible bachelors."

"Thank you," Travis inclined his head toward her.

Molly came to the table with the pot of coffee. "I was wondering, whatever happened to your father, Laine?"

Buck lowered his fork and held it hovering over his plate, eyeing Travis.

Laine's cheeks burned hot. "I don't know," she snapped. "I'm sure he's dead."

76

Travis caught Buck's agitated look as Molly pressed on. "Do you know that for sure? I remember him. He was nice. Had a string of bad luck, but that can't be held against him. Maybe he could help with your plans if you could find him."

"No, I don't want to!" Laine flared. "As far as I'm concerned I have no father."

"But . . ."

"I said no, and I would appreciate it if you would say nothing more about him . . . ever."

Molly nodded silently, and set a cup of coffee in front of Travis. Laine stood up and started clearing the dishes. Buck and Travis drained their cups silently.

"I'm sorry for being so abrupt, Mrs. Harmon." Laine turned around slowly, her throat constricting, swallowing back tears. "I want to know all you know about my mother, but I haven't thought about my father in a very long time, and I don't want to think about him ever again. Please understand. I can never forgive him for what he did to my mother. Even . . . even if he is . . . alive . . . somewhere, I want nothing whatever to do with him. He's dead."

Molly nodded. "Of course, dear, I do understand. We'll speak no more about him."

Laine expressed unspoken gratitude through her eyes.

Travis and Buck held glances for a moment. Then Travis stood up and pushed his chair away from the table.

77

"Well, I guess I'd better get back to my place. Long hard day tomorrow. Thanks, Molly, as always, for a great supper."

He embraced Molly in a bear hug, his massive shoulders straining the back of his blue cotton shirt. Then he shrugged into his buckskin jacket, and sent a look toward Laine.

Molly said the same thing she always said when his visits came to a close. "Now you come back here soon as you can, Travis. Anytime you want. You always got a place here. Jest let Buck know when you're comin'."

He kissed her cheek, then shook Buck's hand. When he turned back to Laine, she looked up slowly from washing a dish.

"Would you mind walking outside with me for a few minutes?" Travis asked her. "I won't keep you long."

She set down the dish, then nodded slightly, and followed him outside.

A sliver of moonlight cast a shadowy cream glow into the little back porch. Travis held his hat against his leg. He gazed down at Laine. Her face was breathtaking, framed by her honeygold hair in the moon's pale wash. Business, he told himself, he had to keep his mind on business, and he had to tell her about David Coleridge.

"About your father . . ." he began.

"Travis," she interrupted wearily, "I said I wanted to hear no more about him, and I meant it." She turned her back to him. "If that's why you brought me out here, I'm going back in right now." She made a step to leave.

"No, wait a minute," he said quietly, then reached out and firmly took her arm. "You sure did grow up, but you hung onto your stubborn streak," he chided, trying to lighten the moment.

"Stubborn?" She whirled around to face him. "Now, you just wait a minute, Travis Mitcham, I am not stubborn! It's just that you persist, even now, in treating me like a child. In case you haven't noticed, I've grown up. I'm not a child anymore, I'm a woman."

"Oh, I noticed all right, you can be sure of that," Travis answered in a hushed tone.

She knew he was smiling even though she couldn't see his face clearly. She could feel the warmth from his body, and it unnerved her to stand so close to him. Tilting her head back slightly, she strained her eyes to see his face more clearly. Still she couldn't see it well, but she could feel the warm mist of his breath brush the side of her face.

Watching her head drop back and the moonlight play among the long golden waves of her hair, bathing them in silver, Travis had the strongest urge to take her uplifted face into his hands and kiss her softly and fully on the tender lips he'd been watching all evening. He could feel the heat pulsating in the muscles of his upper arms, and had to will it away for fear he might crush her to him. How in hell did he get like this all of a sudden?

Laine stepped away from him, breaking the intense sensations locked between them. "Well . . . I guess I should go in and help with the dishes," she said quietly.

"Of course," Travis nodded. "I'll see you in town tomorrow. Don't forget to find me before you go to McCauley's office. Buck knows where I am. He can show you."

Laine nodded, making no move to leave.

"Welcome back to Silver Grande, Laine. I hope you'll find whatever it is you're looking for."

"I know I will. Good night, Travis, and thank you for what you did today.

"Till tomorrow, then."

Travis melted into the darkness and was gone.

Chapter Five

Laine stepped from the buckboard at the stage depot and looked up and down the already busy street. Buck gave her directions to Travis's office, and she started down a side street in the direction of his pointed finger.

She stepped smartly along the boardwalk, feeling free and strong, her gait open and breezy, so different from the demure, ladylike way young Eastern women were expected to conduct themselves in public. Although, she had to admit, she'd always resisted those constructed airs. She wondered now if that was because she'd been born here in Silver Grande where there never had been many manners.

Laine assessed the clothing of the people she passed, especially the long full skirts of the women and girls. She knew she stood out in her ankle-length dark blue divided skirt and open-necked white blouse with full sleeves and snug cuffs. The short-crowned dark blue felt hat with wide round brim and leather ties was of her own design and handmade by a Philadelphia milliner who'd worked with John B. Stetson. High polished dark brown riding boots and a rich brown leather pouch as a handbag completed her ensemble.

Passing ladies gave her a subdued nod, and she knew they talked about her once she was out of earshot. They knew who she was by now. Laine smiled to herself. Big cities and small towns had one thing in common—gossip spread at about the same speed.

She had no intention of purposely alienating the townfolk. Nor had she any intention of conforming to the kind of woman who bowed to convention so readily that her own personality and individuality became buried under corsets and layers of fabric and mannerisms just to stem the flow of gossip.

She knew these people were less than warm to women who lived and worked as men on cattle ranches or along the stage lines, and they ignored completely those women who lived and worked in the rooms above the saloons. That was simply how people were raised. Laine surmised they must be thinking of her as a combination of both those kinds of women, twice the traits in one woman to loathe. Or to be fearful of, she thought.

It was difficult enough being a woman alone anywhere, but a woman alone setting up a business for herself, especially in a place like Silver Grande, would be more than suspect. She had to be strong and independent no matter what others might think of her behavior.

Rounding the corner at the end of the dusty street, she saw a large wood sign emblazoned with red letters, *Mitcham Construction Company,* swinging overhead along the boardwalk on the opposite side. She started down the walk just as the front door of the office opened.

Travis stepped out, a tall, willowy brunette on his arm. On the walk, they faced one another, holding each other's hands. Then Travis leaned down and planted a kiss on the cheek of her upturned smiling face. She released his hands and threw her arms around his neck in a warm embrace, then walked briskly down the walk away from where Laine stood.

Laine blanched, and stepped back against a building. Was that LaBelle Hadley? Or someone else? She couldn't be certain. What little she saw of the woman's face did not afford positive identity, and besides, it had been so long since she'd seen LaBelle she probably wouldn't recognize her anyway. Perhaps Molly was right about Travis's celebrated popularity with women. Yet, last night, outside on the Harmons' porch, he'd certainly seemed interested in seeing her again . . . or so she'd thought.

She shook her head to clear her thinking, then started across the busy street, dodging several small carriages and buckboards, and narrowly missing a cowboy on horseback. A little white dog chased her, barking incessantly and snapping at the hem of her skirt. She tried to shoo it away but, undaunted, it continued barking and nipping.

She reached the boardwalk and stepped up on it. The toe of her boot caught on a broken edge of the walk, and she tripped, falling forward. She lunged out with one hand to grab a post support in front of the office door, but her reach was just short of making contact, and she fell headlong toward the walk. She let out a scream just before her fall was checked by a pair of strong arms.

"Nice going," the deep voice chuckled in her ear. "You sure do know how to make an entrance, don't you?"

Smoothly she was swept up to her feet on the boardwalk. Her hat fell forward covering her face, disorienting her mind and hiding her rescuer from view, but she could still see the dog looking up at her, still hear it barking insistently. The wind was knocked out of her, and her arms dangled from her shoulders like a rag doll's, making her feel as if there was nothing in the middle holding the upper and lower parts of her body together. The strong arms steadied her.

"There now, you all right?" the deep voice chuckled again.

Laine attempted to disentangle her arm from the straps of her bag, and at the same time push her hat up off her eyes, quick, confused movements with no results. The voice laughed heartily.

"Travis! Is that you?" she managed in a hoarse whisper.

With both hands he pushed her hat back and clamped it onto the back of her head. It framed her dark golden waves and wide glittering eyes in a halo of deep blue. He stopped laughing and gazed into the beautiful face, his hands still holding the sides of the hat brim.

"At your service, ma'am . . . as usual." He laughed, and dropped his hands, bowing deeply.

"Well, you certainly have a habit of showing up at the most auspicious times." She brushed the dirt and dust off her skirt with hard, deliberate strokes.

"Why, ma'am," he mocked chivalrously, "I live only to rescue fair damsels in distress!"

A chorus of raucous laughter broke through the dog's barking and Laine's sputtering. She swung around to face a handful of rough-clothed men who had gathered in the street in front of the office. A jab of pain seared her right ankle. She grimaced and whirled back to face Travis, her face pinched in embarrassment and pain. She slammed a small hand into his chest and pushed by him, limping into his office.

"All right, boys," she heard him laugh outside the door as it swung shut, "show's over, back to work."

Laine heard the men laughing and talking, and heard them refer to Travis as "Boss" as their boots tramped heavily down the walk. Travis flung the door open and strode into the office. His large frame filled the doorway and was illumined by the sun which was rising higher in the sky and burning almost white hot. He took another step, and closed the door behind him.

"You all right?" he asked again, sincere concern evident in his voice.

"No . . . I'm not," she answered softly, wincing and rubbing her ankle through her boot, and trying to block the image of him and the beautiful dark-haired woman in an embrace.

Travis poured a glass of water from an ironstone pitcher on the sideboard near his desk. "Here," he proffered, "drink this, and pull up your skirt."

"What?!" Her eyes snapped up to his face.

"Take the water," he ordered. "I'm not suggesting anything immoral. We've got to get that boot off and take a look at your ankle before it swells so much we can't get it off. Now pull up your skirt before I do it for you." He made a move toward her ankle.

Hastily Laine took the glass from his hand and pulled her skirt up to her knee.

Travis knelt in front of her and tried to gently slide the boot down. He had to steady his shaking hands. His lips seemed to have a mind of their own when they were this close to her shapely leg.

He tugged lightly on the back of her heel, and even though she set her jaw against the pain he could see in her eyes that just removing the boot would hurt her a great deal. The last thing he wanted to do was hurt her, in any way.

He stood up straight, then turned his back to her. "Lift your leg if you can," he said gently. She lifted it slowly. He straddled it, then took hold of the toe of her boot with one hand, the heel with the other. "Lean back in the chair and brace your other foot against my backside," he instructed matter-of-factly.

"I'll do no such thing!" Laine protested with indignation.

"You'll do as I say," Travis commanded over his shoulder. "You're going to be in bigger trouble with this ankle in short order than you are now if you don't get this boot off. Now stop letting your pride get in the way and get your other foot up there!"

"All right," she said in meek compliance, and slowly raised her other foot, carefully placing it on his backside.

"Now push," he commanded again, pulling on the boot. She let out an involuntary cry, and he stopped pulling. He looked over his shoulder at her. "Stop acting like a child and help me, or else I'll show no mercy and just rip it off. Now get your foot up there and push!"

"With pleasure!"

Contempt flamed in her eyes, and Travis grinned broadly at the sight. Clamping the hard heel of her boot against his backside again, she gritted her teeth and shoved against him with all the strength she could muster. Even through her pain she knew she'd given him more of a kick than a push.

His bent, straddled form over her leg set Travis off-balance just enough to be sent forward by the thrust of her foot. He pitched onto his knees, and the yank of his hands sucked the boot off her foot. She groaned as the pain shot up her leg and, clasping her ankle with both hands, rocked back and forth rubbing the swelling that was already appearing.

Then, the sight of Travis down on his knees, her boot clutched in his hands, elicited a deep laugh from her. He was right where she'd always wanted him to be. She curbed the urge to say so.

"I knew you could do it if you got mad enough!" Travis spun around, a satisfied grin curling the corners of his mouth. The grin soon faded when he saw the laughter leave her face to be replaced with pain. He dropped the boot, and tenderly felt around her ankle.

"Well, I don't think it's broken, but you've got a nasty bump on it. Better see Doc Fletcher. I'll take you over to his place."

"You don't have to help me anymore, Travis, I can . . ."

"Do as I tell you," he interrupted. "Why are you so darn ornery? It's all right to be dependent once in awhile, you know." He helped her to her feet.

Laine grew silent and reasoned that she did need help getting to a doctor for her ankle, which was now relentlessly throbbing. The question about the dark-haired woman and the appointment with McCauley would have to wait for the time being.

Travis swung her up into his arms easily. His face was very close to hers, but she did not look at him. He gazed at her for an instant, taking in the flawlessness of her fair skin, and breathing in the sweet scent of roses rising from the open neck of her blouse. Her eyes came up quickly to his and held his gaze, and he felt a clutching like bands across his chest.

"You're going to have to put some meat on your bones if you expect to survive out here," he said smiling and hefting her slightly while her legs dangled over his arm.

"Don't you worry about my survival," she said firmly. "I'm very good at taking care of myself."

"Yes, so I see," he laughed, then carried her out the back door of his office to a small carriage.

"Nothing major, just a slight sprain." Old Doc Fletcher finished wrapping her ankle in a bandage, and strapped a shoe-like contraption over her foot. "Not much to look at," he apologized with a kindly look in his small gray eyes, "but it'll do till the swelling goes down and you can get your boot on. Keep applying cold compresses and stay off it as much as possible." He brushed a shock of white hair off his furrowed brow, and turned his stooped shoulders toward Travis. "See she stays off it, Mitcham," he ordered.

"Me? Corral this little mustang?" Travis stepped back, his hand over his heart in mock weakness. "Please, Doc, don't expect miracles!"

"Try, Mitcham, I know you're up to the job." The doctor turned to write something in an age-worn black journal.

"I won't need Mr. Mitcham to supervise me, I can assure you, Doctor," Laine interjected in a firm voice, lifting her chin in small defiance. Gingerly she stood up and applied pressure to the injured ankle, refusing to let the pain throbbing against the bandage show on her face. "I'll do just fine, and will follow your advice as best I can."

Doc Fletcher removed his wire-rimmed spectacles. "See that you do," he said, pointing the spectacles at her. "Come in next week and let me have a look at it. In the meantime, you can borrow this cane." He reached into an umbrella holder and extracted a finely carved wood cane. "It belongs to the missus, but she won't mind if you use it."

"Yes sir," Laine complied in a whisper.

"Thanks, Doc, talk to you later." Travis swept her up in his arms against her mild protestations. "Come, Miss Coleridge, your chariot awaits!" Deftly he maneuvered Laine's slim body through the door, and headed out of the doctor's house to the hitching rail in the front where he'd left his horse and carriage.

"Buck and Molly's, is it?" Travis asked as he urged the horse away.

"No, not yet. I'd like to keep that appointment with Lawyer McCauley."

"Now, Laine, you promised Doc . . ."

"I'd follow his instructions as best I can. I'll do that later. It's best I get this meeting over as soon as possible. Then I'll ease my ankle and my mind."

"I hope you're right," Travis said quietly. "But I'd bet what's in store for you won't include ease for your ankle, and especially not for your mind."

Chapter Six

A white painted sign suspended over the board-walk on the newer side of town proclaimed the office of John T. McCauley, Esq., Attorney-at-Law. Travis reined in the horse and carriage to the hitching rail at the end of the street, then helped Laine down. He started to pick her up and carry her once again, but she stopped him.

"Thank you, no, Travis, just let me take your arm. I don't think I'll make much of an impression if I'm carried into Mr. McCauley's office."

"I don't know about that, m'lady," he smiled.

She smiled back and slipped her hand through his arm. Travis opened the glass-panelled door and escorted her inside, a tinny ringing of a bell heralding the entrance.

A pinch-faced young man sat at a small mahogany desk intently poring over a thick sheaf of legal documents. A pair of wire-rimmed round spectacles perched over the bridge of his nose, their black keeper ribbon dangling along the sides of his face. He did not look up at the sound of the bell, but made an obvious display of studying the papers, frowning and nervously adjusting his spectacles.

"Excuse me," Laine politely interrupted him. The young man did not respond. She cleared her throat, and taking note of his nameplate displayed at the front of the desk, said more firmly, "Excuse me, Mr. Boynton, I have an appointment with Mr. McCauley."

Percival Boynton stood up stiffly. He pulled his back rigid in an attempt to make his small frame appear taller.

"Your name please?" he asked in a high formal voice through pursed lips.

"Laine Coleridge," she replied, mimicking his formal tone.

Boynton's eyes blinked nervously. "I'll . . . uh . . . see if Mr. McCauley is free . . . Miss."

He pivoted quickly and opened a mahogany gate centering a low polished wood railing, then rapped timidly on the heavy door on the other side. A low command to enter filtered through the door from the inner office. Boynton opened the door narrowly and slithered inside, closing it quietly.

Laine looked around as Travis strolled to the other side of the room and inspected some of the books lined along the shelves in floor-to-ceiling cases on two walls. On a third wall over a low table hung a large map with dotted and solid lines showing the growth of Silver Grande over several years.

The office door rumbled open, and Percival Boynton scurried out, his spectacles dangling off the black keeper and bouncing against his trim brown suit coat. Behind him emerged a short, roundish man of about sixty years, pulling a gray tweed coat around his stout middle, and buttoning it with some effort.

"Come in, Miss Coleridge, come in," he beckoned in a booming voice, causing Boynton to step to one side and bump into a chair. "I hope my secretary hasn't kept you waiting long." McCauley's eyes narrowed as he shot a glance toward Boynton, who was now quaking in his small pointed shoes, and staring at Laine with little brown eyes.

"Oh no," Laine responded with a warm smile, "he was very obliging." McCauley strode toward her, his hand extended. She accepted it, and turned toward Travis. "You know, Mr. Mitcham, I'm sure."

McCauley nodded, tight-lipped. "Mitcham? I don't recall we had business."

"We didn't — until now. I'm with Miss Coleridge."

"I see." He stroked the blunt point of his heavy chin. "Well, I'm sure we won't be very long. Why don't you wait right here for her?" He turned to take her arm, then noticed the protective shoe and cane. "Have you been hurt, Miss Coleridge?"

"Nothing too serious, just a slight fall. Mr. McCauley, I've invited Mr. Mitcham to this meeting as an interested friend. I would like him to be present."

"I see," McCauley hedged again. "This is, of course, highly irregular."

"It's temporary, I can assure you, until I can secure an attorney of my own."

"Well, now," McCauley smiled patronizingly, "I don't think that will be necessary. I believe we can handle things between us. If you must have Mitcham here present for now, that will be fine."

Laine nodded a polite thank you, and McCauley

ushered them into the inner office. Travis looked over his shoulder at the quivering Boynton and spoke in a friendly tone.

"How are you, Percival? Haven't seen much of you lately. You ought to stop in at the hotel tavern now and then for a beer with some of the rest of us."

Boynton reddened visibly and sank with a nervous sigh into his hard chair.

Inside McCauley's office, Laine and Travis were surprised to find Jamison Hadley seated at one end of the lawyer's massive desk. He slouched in a heavy oak chair, one dusty boot resting on the opposite knee, one arm draped over the side of the chair, a bent elbow planted on the other side, his chin resting on folded fingers. A smirk sharply curved a corner of his mouth. With slow movement he rose from the chair, and crossed the room to greet Laine.

"It is a pleasure to see you again, Miss Coleridge." He bowed, lifted one of her small hands and kissed the back of it.

Laine held her composure and withdrew her hand from his moist grip. She felt the urge to take out a handkerchief and dry her palm, but her education in ladylike behavior wouldn't allow such a rude response.

"I see you haven't managed to shake your self-appointed bodyguard." Jamison sliced a look toward Travis and extended his hand. "Hello again, Mitcham. What are you doing here?"

"Hadley." Travis did not extend his hand in return. "I might ask the same of you."

Hadley did not respond, but returned to the chair and sat down, lounging smugly against the back of it, a sardonic smile tipping the corners of his mouth.

"Sit down, please." McCauley gestured toward a pair of high-backed dark-red upholstered chairs which were angled toward his desk. He settled his portly frame into his own oversized armchair which groaned under his weight. "Let me extend a warm welcome back to Silver Grande, Miss Coleridge." He smiled, sweeping up the ends of his thick reddish moustache.

"Thank you," Laine responded, taking a seat. Travis stood behind her chair.

"And . . . how long may we expect your visit to last?" McCauley asked with forced nonchalance.

"This isn't just a visit, Mr. McCauley. I plan to settle in Silver Grande, make it my home again." She leaned forward slightly. "I'd like to know why Mr. Hadley is here, also."

Travis had been watching the exchange of looks between the lawyer and Hadley as McCauley engaged Laine in idle chat. "I think you owe the lady an answer, McCauley. What's Hadley doing at this meeting?"

McCauley squirmed slightly, and straightened several pages and pencils on his desk. "Now if we'll all just remain calm, I'm sure we can straighten out this, uh, little problem."

"What little problem?" Laine asked with a small frown. "Mr. McCauley, is there another reason you've asked me here? It's my understanding that Uncle Jack has died, and I may possibly have inherited something from him. And by the way, I understand Uncle Jack died more than two years ago. Why did you delay so long in telling me?"

McCauley cleared his throat. "You are quite right, Miss Coleridge, you have inherited from the Smithers estate. In fact, I'm pleased to tell you that you are the sole heir." He handed her a long folded document. "As you can see in his will, he has referred to you as someone he loved as the daughter he never had."

Laine smiled faintly and lowered her eyes, remembering the many kindnesses Jackson Smithers extended to them when she and her mother were living in the hotel.

"I'm afraid what you've inherited, Miss Coleridge, is the hotel he owned on Phoenix Street. As you may know, it's in a state of disrepair, and will take rather a large sum of money to bring it to the level of structure now befitting the city of Silver Grande."

"I understand, Mr. McCauley, and I would plan to do just that, and do as Uncle Jack states in his will." She pointed to an item near the bottom of the page as Travis read over her shoulder. "I'm to use the building to establish a business, to provide an income for me and my heirs." She smiled openly. This was just the thing she needed to fulfill the dreams and plans she'd made.

"I'm sure he meant well, but as you may note in the item above that, you must first settle any liens against the property before you may take possession."

"Liens?"

"Yes, debts. You understand. The property must be cleared of all encumbrances before the deed can be signed over to you. This is routine procedure."

Laine looked up questioningly at Travis, who nodded slightly. "And, are there debts against it?" she asked.

McCauley nodded. "That's why Mr. Hadley was invited to this meeting. The debts are owed to him."

"But how?" Laine was confused.

"Yes, McCauley," Travis spoke at last. "How? Hadley has not been here for a long, long time. How could he have any claim against that property?"

"Perhaps Mr. Hadley can explain that more fully than I." McCauley deferred to Jamison. "Would you?"

Hadley sat up straight. "I believe I can. Some years ago Jackson Smithers ran into trouble with his brother, Dodge, who bought into a gold mine in California. Dodge was always involved in some hare-brained get-rich-quick scheme, and he talked Jackson into sinking almost all he had into the mine. Jackson agreed, thinking that perhaps this time Dodge had the right idea and would come out in good shape. But, like everything Dodge touched, the mine went bust. He couldn't take that last defeat, and he hung himself, leaving his brother Jackson to pay off the debts."

Jackson Smithers's weary features crossed Laine's mind. She'd had no idea he'd been through such an ordeal. Was Hadley telling the truth?

"Smithers had nothing but that old hotel and saloon," Jamison continued. "The other partners in the mine threatened to take that away from him, too, if he didn't pay up. But you see, Miss Coleridge, by that time you and your mother were living there, and Jackson Smithers didn't want to lose you in the deal as well."

Hadley rose and went to stand at the end of McCauley's desk. "At that time, my father was about the richest man in the Arizona territory. He held much in property, cattle, and businesses. Smithers went to him and begged for money to pay off the mine debts . . ." He stared toward the window over McCauley's shoulder and paused for a moment, a faraway look in his eyes. "My father never could resist anyone in trouble . . ." Laine saw the muscle in his jaw tighten. ". . . which is why he lost almost everything we had."

He jerked his head back toward Laine. "Smithers signed an IOU for the loan, with the agreement that my father would own the hotel if he failed to pay the full amount." He softened his tone. "Of course, then there was the fire. Jackson never did recoup his losses. And then he died. And that's the whole story. Except for one thing—not one dollar was ever paid toward the loan."

"That still does not explain where you come in, Hadley," Travis cut in. "Are you representing your father?"

"My father is a sick man, Miss Coleridge," Jamison went on, ignoring Travis's remark. "Money lent to Jackson Smithers came from my father's business, not from personal funds. Since his illness has become worse, he has signed the business over to me. Unfortunately for you, that includes the debt against the Smithers property. Thinking from a business standpoint, I'm sure you can understand, Miss Coleridge," he shot a glance toward Travis, "as I know you can, Mitcham, that I must request immediate payment."

Laine was struck speechless for a moment, then gathered her thoughts together. "How much is repayment of the loan?"

McCauley consulted a ledger. "Including interest, right around forty thousand dollars."

"Forty thousand . . . ? I'm not sure I could even borrow that much money." Laine's spirits dropped. It appeared that all of her hopes and dreams for her future, and Uncle Jack's desire to help provide that future for her, might be dashed forever. Not only would she not have the money to put into building repairs, would have nothing with which to begin her business, she would also owe Jamison Hadley forty thousand dollars.

"Now, Miss Coleridge," McCauley stood up and came around his desk. "I know this is difficult news to accept, but Mr. Hadley and I have discussed the situation, and while I don't believe it's entirely fair to him, he has agreed to release you from the debt that you, as an innocent party, had not contributed to, by accepting the property, as is, even though its value is far less than the combined debt and cost of repair. I'm sure you can see that you would be relieved of any further debt if you were simply to sign the property over to him." He produced a set of documents and pushed them toward Laine. "I've taken the liberty of drawing up such an agreement, because I knew you'd see the value to yourself in handling the matter this way."

Laine leaned into the chair. She felt the warmth of Travis's hands at the back of her shoulders. Thoughts tumbled around her mind. If she signed the agreement Hadley and McCauley were proposing, she'd be exactly where she was before she left Boston. Without money, but also without an inherited debt. Should she just sign the agreement, and forget the possibility ever existed of owning the property? Try to think of another way to begin her business? No. That was unthinkable. She would find a way through this dilemma. Uncle Jack meant for her to have his hotel, and have it she would.

Something about this whole meeting unsettled her. Something about McCauley and Hadley and their tone and remarks left her with more unanswered questions than ever. But they also left her with more determination than ever to find the truth and claim her independence.

What Laine needed now was time, and she had to think of a way to stall.

"And to show good faith," McCauley's voice broke into her thoughts, "your expenses for travelling all the way out here from Boston . . . and back . . . will be reimbursed. I do hope that will help to ease your mind."

Laine's mind was far from easing. It was spinning. She'd believed this transaction would be a simple act of signing papers that granted her possession of Uncle Jack's hotel. She regretted she wasn't prepared for this turn of events. She'd wanted to handle everything herself, but now had to admit she might need help. She turned to look up at Travis, grateful for his presence.

Travis had been listening to the proceedings, waiting for Laine to make the decisions he knew she wanted to make on her own. When McCauley and Hadley had succeeded in confusing her with the story of a debt owed to Hadley, and then sweetened the pot by offering to pay her travelling expenses with a not too subtle urge for her to return to Boston, his suspicions rose more sharply than before.

He didn't like the way Hadley was looking at Laine, either. There were more than dollar signs in his eyes. It was time to get her out of there. He hadn't wanted to interfere too much, but now he thought he saw in her eyes a silent plea for assistance.

"Miss Coleridge has had a long and difficult journey, and a nasty fall today." Travis took Laine's arm and helped her to stand. "I'm sure you'll understand that she should not be pressured into making a final decision on such an important matter right now."

Laine swallowed hard, regaining momentary lost strength. "Yes, that's correct. I must have a few days to think over your . . . generous offer. Naturally, I want to be fair to all concerned." She looked directly at Jamison, then took Travis's arm. "Thank you for your time, gentlemen."

"But, Miss Coleridge . . ." McCauley began.

"I'll be in touch, Mr. McCauley."

Travis walked her to the door, and they stepped into the outer office. He closed the door behind them.

"Don't worry, you did the right thing," he told her calmly.

"Travis, I can't believe it. I had no idea Uncle Jack was in such trouble," she whispered.

"I'm not so sure he was. Something tells me we haven't heard all the details where Hadley and McCauley are concerned."

"Even so, where would I get that kind of money? It will be difficult enough for me to borrow the money to repair the hotel and get my business started. I had planned to use the building as collateral. I had such hopes . . ."

"Don't give them up yet," Travis cautioned.

They walked out of the office and were on their way down the boardwalk to the carriage, when Percival Boynton rushed up behind them. He stopped them as Travis was settling Laine into the seat.

"Mr. Mitcham, Miss Coleridge, wait, please." He was breathing hard from his rush to catch up with them, and his spectacles swung across his chest on the black ribbon. "I . . . I feel I must violate a confidence and tell you something."

"What's the matter, Percival?" Travis drew him around to the other side of the carriage away from the passersby on the boardwalk.

"Please understand, I would never, never do this . . . I mean, I would never divulge anyone's private business, or anything I learned in the performance of my duties in the law office, but . . ." His face flushed and he sucked in a hard breath.

"Mr. Boynton, are you all right?" Laine leaned down from the carriage and placed a gloved hand on his arm.

"Oh yes, Miss Coleridge, thank you. It's just that I . . . I couldn't in all good conscience let you . . . that is, I think . . ." He looked first at one and then the other with troubled brown eyes that reminded Laine of a puppy.

"It's all right, Percival," Travis reassured him. "If you have something you want to tell us, you can trust us not to let McCauley know."

Boynton let out a relieved sigh. "Thank you. I need this job, you know. Mr. McCauley would dismiss me if he knew. But, it's just that you've been a real friend to me, Mr. Mitcham, the only one who was nice to me when I first arrived, putting me up at your place and everything."

"Don't mention it, Percival, I know you'd do the same thing if situations were reversed," Travis said.

Percival blushed and looked down at his shoes. "It's just that I . . . I think Mr. McCauley and Mr. Hadley aren't telling Miss Coleridge everything. I think they might be trying to . . . to cheat you somehow. I mean what with the railroad contracts and all . . ."

"Contracts? I thought this business about the railroad was just talk." Laine looked at Travis.

Travis nodded in thought, but did not look at Laine. "Yes, Percival, you could be right."

Boynton smiled, and sighed nervously. "I'd better get back into the office before they miss me. I just thought I should say something to you. You can handle it however you wish."

"Thanks, Percival, you've been most helpful." Travis shook his hand. He helped Laine into the carriage and started to climb in, then turned back to Boynton. "Would you be willing to kind of keep your eyes and ears open to see if you can find anything out that would be of more help to Miss Coleridge? I mean, only if it wouldn't jeopardize your position, or make you feel uncomfortable doing it."

Boynton smiled proudly. "I'd be happy to try to help you and Miss Coleridge. I've seen many more underhanded dealings in that office than I ever wanted to know about, and I've never said anything. I've never had the courage before. But I just couldn't ignore it this time."

"Thanks, Percival, and I meant what I said about stopping over at the hotel now and then."

Travis climbed into the carriage.

"Railroad contracts?" Laine asked again.

Travis didn't answer. He slapped the reins over the horse's flanks, and he and Laine drove away, leaving a beaming Percival Boynton standing in the dusty street.

Chapter Seven

•

"I really don't see how this can work out," Laine said to Travis over lunch in the Black Canyon Hotel's cozy dining room. "I guess I thought Uncle Jack might have left some money to me. I admit the hotel was in the back of my mind, but I thought he might have sold it or left it to someone else, and I was to have part of the money."

Travis half-listened, his mind turning over the events that had rapidly twisted a simple act of love by Jackson Smithers into a whole scenario of greed and deception.

But what worried him more was the uncertainty of how long he could continue to carry on his own deception.

"In any case," Laine continued, interrupting his thoughts, "I don't see yet how I can avoid signing over the property to Jamison Hadley, no matter how much I don't want to do that. I can't pay the debt, but I owe it to Uncle Jack to at least clear his name." Thoughtfully, she sipped a cup of tea. "And if I have no business and no money, I'll have to consider returning to Boston," she added sadly.

"Don't start packing yet," Travis said quickly. "I have an idea. You don't have to make a decision on it right away, if you don't want to. Take some time to think about it. We need time to find out what's really going on with Hadley and McCauley. It's quite possible Smithers did get himself mixed up with Reed Hadley somehow. From what I understand, Smithers was a good sort, liked to help people, and I did hear about a brother he had who went to California because of some gold strike. Their story isn't completely out of the realm of possibility." He stirred his coffee absently.

"If their story is true, then I have lost the hotel. But, what's your idea?"

He set his spoon down. "I'm offering you a partnership . . . with me. I'll pay off the debt—if it's legitimate—and back your business to get you started. What do you think about that?"

Laine's eyes widened, and her mouth opened in genuine surprise. "I . . . I don't know what to think about that." She turned her tea cup round and round in its saucer.

While Laine thought over his proposition, Travis fell into his own thoughts. The Panic of 1873 had wiped out his father's Eastern railroad connections, and the business started to decline. He sometimes believed his parents died of broken hearts over it.

When Travis returned to Silver Grande he'd vowed to rebuild and succeed for his parents. And he had, by sheer determination, grit, his own back and sweat, and that of the crew who stayed loyal. But he'd had to prove himself to those men.

The men who had worked with diligence and loyalty for his father were skeptical of leadership in the form of a freshfaced college boy, as they called him, but his fairness and respect for their knowledge and ability won them over, and they returned to him as much loyalty and respect as they'd shown his father.

He employed a core of ten, and at varying times swelled their number to more than twenty. There would soon be a need for more.

Travis was determined to bring the railroad track through Silver Grande yet, and to realize his father's dream. His help had come from a surprising source in California, a source connected with the Southern Pacific Railroad. Together they became instrumental in forging bonds for a transcontinental link. The benefit to people across the country, and especially to Silver Grande, would be immeasurable, and Travis was thrilled and thankful to be a part of it, thrilled to build the dream for his father.

And it was quite possible he couldn't have done it without the valuable assistance of his California source.

"How can you do that?" Laine's voice seemed to come from far away. "That would take a lot of money. I couldn't let you . . ."

"I can do it," he answered quickly, "don't worry about that. Think of it as a loan. As soon as your business is established and operating in the black, and I have no doubt that it will, given that Coleridge determination and grit, then you can start paying me back. If you continue to let me stay a partner, then your loan will be wiped out, of course."

She smiled at his compliment, but was still unconvinced that she should accept his offer. "I don't know, Travis. I hadn't anticipated being in debt to anyone, except possibly a bank."

"Think about it. In the meantime, I think you should find your own attorney and not leave everything in the hands of McCauley. He can't possibly strike a fair deal when he's representing two clients with separate claims on the same property. Possibly he can't strike a fair deal no matter who's involved," he added wryly. "There is a new man in town. So far he seems honest and fair. I used him once for a sticky contract negotiation, and found him to be quite thorough. Name's Anson Daniels, and he's in that little storefront next to Rufus Drier's place. Will you speak to him?"

Laine thought about the wisdom in his suggestion. She felt he seemed also to be suggesting that he didn't want her to return to Boston, and she liked that feeling. Still, there had been the dark-haired woman in his arms this morning. Why hadn't he spoken about her at all? Perhaps all this business with McCauley and the Smithers property truly did occupy his mind to the degree that it didn't occur to him to mention her. Or perhaps he wasn't about to mention her at all. Perhaps he enjoyed his role as Silver Grande's most eligible bachelor.

Funny how she'd somehow always thought of him as belonging to her. Well, maybe not belonging, exactly. A little girl's fantasy. And she was not a little girl any longer.

"Laine, what do you say to that?" His voice sliced into her musings.

"What? Oh . . . yes, you may be right. I'll think

about seeing . . . Mr. Daniels, is it? I'll think about seeing him as soon as possible."

"Good. I hate to leave you to take care of all this on your own, but I have some pressing matters back at my office. You can have the carriage. I'll get Manuel from Buck's place to come over and drive you around. Would that be all right?"

"No, it most certainly would not be all right. I can drive a carriage myself." She smiled, chiding him for intimating she would need that kind of help. "I have a few other errands I'd like to take care of as well."

He smiled back, and they stood to leave. "All right. Stop by my office later and let me know how things went with Daniels if you get to see him today, and . . . think about my offer."

Outside the hotel, he helped her into the carriage and untied the reins, then placed them securely in her hands. His own hand lingered a moment, and the combination of her soft skin and the hard straps gave him the sensation that he was holding an unbeatable combination of satin and leather, softness and strength. It rendered him motionless for a moment.

She pulled the carriage away from the walk, and Travis smiled at the picture she made, back straight, head high. He cocked his head to catch a last glimpse of her as she rounded a corner, her golden curls fluttering on a breeze.

Laine drove the carriage feeling a renewed sense of control of her own life. Regardless of the difficulties she would be facing, she believed she was up to the battle. And she had Travis on her side.

Lost in thought and enjoying the freedom of her drive, Laine hadn't been paying attention to where the horse was taking her. The Smithers Hotel was already in her sight before her mind had focussed clearly. She reined in the horse and stopped in front of the crumbling building.

Her thoughts turned somersault back to the last night she'd been in this hotel, and her eyes filled with hot tears. She cleared them and made herself take a hard look at the place. It didn't look too bad from the front. The facade. How appropriate a word, she thought. It's behind the facade where sorrow always lies.

She steeled herself and walked carefully and slowly around to the back. The charred frame, now bleached with ashes, and years of sun and weather, loomed like a gaping mouth ready to swallow weak and vulnerable prey. Laine's eyes filled again, and this time they spilled over.

"Oh, Mama, why? Why did you go back into there? Why did you leave me?"

She wept like the child who still lived in her heart had wanted to for so long. Then she stopped herself like the woman whom she'd become demanded. A cold fact remained: there was no grave to visit, no stone engraved with Elizabeth's name to cry over. This was her grave, this building her only monument.

"Ah, Miss Coleridge," a hard voice startled her.

Laine turned slowly, dabbing at her tears with the backs of her hands. Jamison Hadley stood a few feet from her.

"I'm sure this is difficult for you," he continued smoothly, "knowing your dear mother's ashes are mingled there with those of the other whores in that dreadful hole."

"Please, Mr. Hadley," Laine started wearily.

"Oh, I know, I know," he said, making his voice sound full of sympathy, "you must want to turn your back on it all and walk away, just forget this whole sad part of your life."

Laine held up her hands in a gesture meant to stop him from speaking more, but he ignored her.

"And you can do just that, rather easily. And rather handsomely, too, I might add. I'm prepared to double my offer to you, pay you more than twice as much as this old place is actually worth."

Laine drew in her breath. Anger was taking over where sorrow had been in her heart. "And just why would you want to do that, Mr. Hadley?"

"Let's just say I want to help an old friend of the family."

"Your family was never a friend to me or my mother."

"That's not the way I understand it."

"However you understand it, you're wrong. No member of your family was close to either one of us."

"Perhaps not to you, but I've heard your mother and my father were, ah, extremely close, shall we say? Closer than family, if you grasp my meaning."

Laine grasped his meaning all right, and she didn't like it. She had an overwhelming urge to grasp his throat and choke his lying words back into his mouth.

"You're wrong," she said quietly, with a hard edge in her voice, "and further, I resent your disgusting inference."

Hadley's bottom lip twitched slightly, letting her

know he felt he'd successfully undercut her strength. "Hardly an inference, although I gather my father wasn't the only one. My mother wrote me about everything. LaBelle told me all about it as well."

"LaBelle!" Laine flared. "Mr. Hadley, I will refrain from speaking about your mother, but whatever makes you think your sister isn't capable of telling lies for the sheer perverted pleasure of it? She always enjoyed saying things to hurt other people."

"I know my sister is capable of many things. She can be very persuasive when she wants to be. Ask Mitcham sometime."

Laine turned abruptly, intent upon leaving. Twisting her sprained ankle, she stumbled over a board. She winced in pain, and Jamison caught her arm and broke her fall.

"Be careful, you might get hurt," he muttered in a threatening tone. "Let me help you."

"I don't need your help," she shot at him, wrenching her arm free.

"I know you will soon see that you will need me, Miss Coleridge. There are truths of which you are unaware. I didn't mean to hurt your feelings. I merely sought to help you make the right decision. You could say we're almost brother and sister." He gave her a meaningful look. "I find that rather disturbing, myself. I'm not feeling a bit brotherly toward you at this moment. No, I couldn't say what I'm feeling is brotherly at all."

Laine cast him a look full of the loathing she was consumed with at that moment. She limped around the front of the hotel toward the carriage. Hadley followed closely behind.

"Once my sister is married to your friend Mitcham, why, we'll all be one big happy family, won't we?"

Laine spun around. "Travis marry LaBelle?! Don't be ridiculous. And as for your fondness for the word family . . ."

"Don't be so sure, Miss Coleridge. One can't depend on much of anything anymore, can one?"

With some difficulty, Laine got into the carriage and urged the horse away.

"Good day, Miss Coleridge," Hadley called behind her. "I'm sure we'll meet again soon. Perhaps at the wedding feast!"

Laine slapped the reins over the horse's flanks, and the carriage lurched forward. She took a quick look over her shoulder, and saw a last glimpse of the hotel swimming crazily through her angry tears.

Shaking them away, she drew the carriage around and headed toward the office of Anson Daniels.

Chapter Eight

Behind his massive oak desk, Travis sat motionless, his jaw set in a hard angle, neck muscles tensing, contemplating the purple mountains in the far western distance framed in the back window. On his knee lay a neatly written letter.

Of all the damnable timing! He dragged his gaze away from the mountains and forced it back to the letter, studying the familiar signature. His association with the writer was mostly conducted on paper since the two were many miles apart in the vast Western country. Travis sat in his Silver Grande office in the Arizona territory, pondering a letter from someone in a similar office in San Francisco. He studied the signature again, then slammed a fist down on the letter.

David L. Coleridge.

Of all the damnable timing!

David Coleridge wrote about his plans for a trip to Silver Grande. It would be only a matter of days before he arrived. His letter was full of excitement about the linking of the railroad system with California through Silver Grande. Mitcham-Coleridge Trackage was on the brink of sealing a partnership with two of the railroad companies, an arrangement that would make them richer than they could ever have imagined.

Travis turned over his quandary in his mind. He needed more time before he could tell Laine about her father. She wasn't ready yet. She thought him dead, or, without proof of it, tried to heal the raw emotion of his abandonment by symbolically burying him in the past. He suspected there was more to her suppressing her father's existence, but he hadn't been able to figure that one out yet, and she offered no overt clues.

He would certainly have hoped for more time for her to accept the idea her father was alive before the man actually appeared. That would be difficult enough, but then to explain to her his connection with Mitcham Construction. . . .

Travis glanced at a calendar. There was not enough time for communication to reach David Coleridge before he would be on his way to Silver Grande. Travis would somehow have to bite the bullet and simply tell Laine the truth. He ran his hand through his hair. God, he didn't look forward to that now.

But what about David Coleridge? How would Laine's arrival in Silver Grande affect him? He didn't know she was here either. Oh what a tangled web we weave, he thought.

Travis searched the far reaches of his heart for a way to tell her about her father, and about so many other things. Her abrupt reentrance into his life had swirled his mind from the moment he recognized her after the near-accident with the stagecoach. He had difficulty concentrating on anything now. Except Laine.

He recollected their childhood, and the skinny little girl

dressed in secondhand clothes. He remembered how the other girls taunted her when she arrived at school wearing something they'd thrown away, and how proud he was of her for holding her head high and ignoring their teasing.

He remembered how Laine's big dark blue eyes reflected the hurt of the treatment she suffered, but she never once shed a tear. Instead she would set her little jaw into a hard line and seek him out to regale him with stories about life in a big mansion in Boston. She was his best friend, and he was hers. He knew the other girls were jealous of that, but that wasn't the reason he'd been friends with her. He genuinely liked her, enjoyed her company. Hell, it was more than that, wasn't it, even when they were children?

The teasing subsided a little once Laine discovered she could take their discarded clothes and refashion them for herself into something quite different and pretty. He'd found that to be very appealing about her, and sometimes at college when he'd noticed a girl in an ill-fitting dress, he would think of how Laine might have changed it.

College. Travis smiled to himself at the thoughts. He'd flung his first wild oats back then. He'd been surprised when he discovered he had something those refined young ladies were interested in. All those Eastern girls had been drawn to his rugged good looks and loved calling him "Cowboy." He never did anything special to attract women; it just happened naturally.

He'd seen some lovely girls there, and he'd enjoyed himself with a few of them, but not one claimed his heart. Something always seemed to stop him from making serious plans with anyone. He was never quite certain why, but it was almost as if an iron door clanged shut over his heart the moment he sensed a growing attachment by any of them. Then his college career was cut short by his parents' deaths.

When he returned to Silver Grande and took over the business, the flirtatious LaBelle Hadley began the first of many overtures to him. He'd heard all the rumors that she would one day come into a rather substantial inheritance, and she used those rumors to her advantage. She would give him coquettish looks and hint at the idea of a possible partnership which, in her mind, meant marriage. Travis would only smile and evade her suggestions and hints, but he'd had a devil of a time doing it. She was persistent, and becoming relentless. She, and everyone else, knew she would be an unbearable spinster if she were forced into that undesirable fate.

"Travis?" Laine's melodic voice emanating from the front office crept into his contemplations. Her uneven footsteps drew nearer his office, and the door opened slightly.

Travis twisted and quickly deposited the letter in an open desk drawer. He stood up to greet her.

"Travis? Are you here?" The door swung wide open, and she stood framed in its oak casing, one arm outstretched with an open palm against the crosspiece.

"Laine . . . all finished with your errands? Did you see Daniels?"

"Yes," she answered quietly, and Travis thought she sounded distracted.

"Did he say something that upset you? You look . . . did he frighten you?" Travis went around the desk toward her.

She put up her hand to stop him, then seemed to transform back into the determined woman he'd seen earlier.

"Yes, I did. Mr. Daniels says he'll get to work on it right

117

away, and he advised me to take you up on your offer."

"Good," Travis said and went back to his desk chair. "Well, it appears we have some planning to do now." He motioned for her to sit down in the armchair opposite his desk.

"First," she said, pausing before taking a seat, "I want it understood that this is strictly a business deal between you and me. Mr. Daniels says he will draw up the necessary papers for us." She sat down. "Then we'll begin the enormous task of rebuilding . . ."

"Don't worry about that. Remember you're in business with a construction company now." He smiled.

"Yes, but I have big plans. For one thing, they're working with electricity back in the States, you know. It's time Silver Grande modernized, and I think Elizabeth's Grande Hotel should install all electric lighting. I'm surprised the Black Canyon Hotel doesn't have it. And a telephone is an absolute necessity."

"Elizabeth's Grande? So that's what we're calling it, are we?" He smiled approvingly. "In case you haven't noticed, partner, Mitcham Construction has a telephone," he gestured toward the back wall to a brown wood box with its double brass bell and long mouthpiece.

"I see. But it isn't connected to any telephone lines."

"One thing at a time, you know. I suppose next you'll want Arizona to annex the States, and then decide you'll be president!"

Laine smiled. "As you say, one thing at a time."

"Anything else?" Travis teased, but he didn't ignore the shadow in her eyes despite her enthusiastic planning.

"I believe the hotel should have a large elegant dining room," she rushed on, "and a small tearoom, as well as comfortable sleeping rooms. On the wing that borders the

118

side street I will have my fashion design shop. We can have an office in that wing as well."

Travis wrote rapidly on a long sheet of paper as she spoke, smiling and nodding as he wrote. "Well, I can see *we* won't have to make any plans at all; you've made them already."

"I'm sorry. I guess I should have waited for you. It's just that once the ideas started coming to me, and it looked as if they might be possible, I . . ."

Travis shook his head and stopped her. "I think your plans are exactly right for the place, and I'll be glad to get started on them, when it's possible."

"What's wrong with right away? The sooner we get started, the sooner we'll be able to see a return on your investment."

"You've forgotten about McCauley and Hadley. We have to work out all the legal entanglements first. I'm sure you've noticed they're not willing to simply hand it over to you."

Laine sighed. "No, I haven't forgotten. I had a rude reminder of it earlier. Why don't we go over there right now and tell McCauley I have the money." She started to push herself up with the cane.

"Wait. Let them stew a little longer. The more they wonder about you and how you're going to manage this feat, the more they will be insecure about what they think they have. And I think it's a good idea to give Percival and Anson a chance to gather more information. Give it a day, and we'll go there together."

Reluctantly she agreed. "This *will* work out, Travis, and I guarantee you will not lose any money. I don't intend to let them get the better of me, but if for some reason they do, I will find the means to pay you

119

back. I hope you understand that."

He nodded, understanding more than she knew.

"We have a deal then, do we?" She stood up, holding her right hand out to him. Withdrawing it quickly, she removed her glove, then extended it once more.

He reached out and enveloped her small hand in his own. The mutual warmth and strength in the handclasp held their eyes locked in a long gaze.

The warmth spread through Laine to her fluttering stomach and heart, and almost unnerved her. She couldn't have that. She had to be strong for herself. She was the only one she could believe in right now. Aside from the fact that Travis had agreed to a business partnership, that was all she could be sure of.

Her senses had been turned upside down from the moment she'd seen him again, and if indeed he was as interested in women in general, and LaBelle Hadley in particular, as she'd seen and heard, then she would have to keep her emotions in check and her thinking unclouded by feelings and fantasies. This was no time to lose her heart. Perhaps there would be no time to let him know that she'd lost her heart to him long ago.

She gave his hand a small squeeze, then slipped hers from his clasp. Her eyes fell on a bottle of brandy and some glasses in a glass-front cabinet.

"Good! That's settled," she said, working to keep her voice steady. "Shall we have a drink on it, then?"

"A . . . drink?" Travis was so surprised at her request he could hardly get the word out. He pulled himself together when he saw she was dead serious and in a crisp tone replied, "Drink on it, of course, that's the way men seal all their deals. Right?"

"'Right,'" Laine said with forced certainty.

He opened the cabinet and took out the brandy and two small glasses. Filling each to about half, he handed one to her, and clinked his glass against hers.

"To our partnership."

"To our partnership," she repeated, raising the glass to her lips.

She paused for a fleeting moment, then downed the entire contents of her first strong drink ever in one swallow. Travis's eyes widened in astonishment. Setting the glass down on his desk, she turned quickly, and without speaking, pushed through the office door and limped quickly with the cane into the front office.

"Wait a minute, Laine!" Travis ran after her. She had the door to the building open when he reached the outer office.

"Are you going home with Buck?" he called after her.

She nodded silently, and left the office.

Laine hurried around the building as fast as she could, given the tenderness of her ankle and the use of the cane. Turning a corner into a narrow alley, she stopped and leaned against the back wall, her breath coming in small gasps. Then she doubled over, nearly collapsing in a heap. The heat of the brandy seared through her chest and stomach, and made her knees weak. Or maybe it was the effect of the charged moments she'd spent that afternoon.

Whatever the outcome, she was now in partnership with Travis, something that even her fantasies hadn't created. From now on she would brazen everything out, be the mistress of her own destiny, hold onto what was rightfully hers whatever the cost. Hadley and his family be damned!

Whether or not her destiny included Travis Mitcham, not even she could dare to fantasize about any longer.

Chapter Nine

Laine left Doc Fletcher's office several days later feeling much better physically. The sprain had healed rather easily, considering how little she rested her ankle. It still felt tender, but she was back to wearing her boot and walking on it without aid of the cane.

Patience was a virtue Laine had never learned to cultivate. She was anxious to move, move on with business plans, move on with life. And while it was pleasant at the Harmons', her interest in finding a place of her own remained strong.

Staying with Buck and Molly, however, had afforded her the opportunity to see Travis every evening. Molly had remarked at supper the evening before that never had they seen so much of him in so short a time. Laine was inwardly pleased hearing that, hoping his frequent visits meant he'd wanted to see her as well as the older couple.

As often as they'd been together with Buck and Molly, and alone on walks after supper on the pretext of helping to strengthen her ankle, never had Travis mentioned the woman she'd seen him embrace the first morning in town. Why did it seem he wanted to keep it from her? And he hadn't mentioned LaBelle either. Laine marvelled at her good fortune in never even catching a glimpse of the Hadley woman when she was in town. She knew it was inevitable that happy state couldn't last much longer.

Laine felt she and Travis were growing closer. Was it only a friendship from childhood that carried into adulthood? Was it her imagination? Her childhood fantasies about sharing a life with Travis now bloomed into full flower, and what to do about them, wondering what might or might not happen, left her too often full of uncertainty where he was concerned.

But she was very certain about everything else, and anxious to get on with the legal work of Uncle Jack's property. If she were to inherit, then she wanted to waste no more time in getting things finalized. She was itching to get to work, to reconstruct the hotel, to begin to show her dress designs. It was time, more than time.

This morning she approached the office of Mitcham Construction feeling strong, resolute. Just as her hand grasped the handle, the door opened and Travis stepped out. The sleeves of his blue plaid cotton shirt were rolled above his tanned forearms, and his faded soft denim pants molded to his long muscular legs and tapered snugly over the high heeled boots. His hair curled over a turned up point of one side his collar, and Laine curbed the urge to reach out and turn the point down. She steadied her racing heart to speak.

"Travis, good morning. I was just coming to see you," she called, smiling openly and wondering if her look betrayed her feelings too much. As Aunt Sarah had often said, it was not to a lady's advantage to let a gentleman feel secure.

Travis dragged in a deep breath. She was as brilliant as a desert sunrise, clad in a soft doeskin divided riding skirt and deep rose blouse open at the neck. As a wayward breeze played about her shining sun-kissed hair, brushed out long and loose as he'd remembered, it carried the scent of roses to sweep delicately over him, and rocked his senses.

His desire for this vibrant woman she had become mounted each moment he spent with her. Every time he thought about her the rest of his thinking spun dizzily away, and he was finding it more and more difficult to concentrate as the vision of her persisted in his mind.

"Good morning to you," he managed to respond lightly. "You're out and about early."

"Just got a cautious clean bill of health from Dr. Fletcher, and I'm ready to take on McCauley and Hadley. Wish me luck."

"I'll do more than that. If you'll give me a few minutes to finish some business," he tapped the packet of papers he was holding against his thigh, "I'll go over there with you."

"No need for that," she said briskly, "I can handle it myself."

"I've no doubt about that, but we are partners and the sooner they know that the better. I'm coming with you. Wait here. I'll be right back."

He ran across the dusty road into an office on the other side. Laine watched his long legs stretch out, and that tingle in her hands returned, and her pulse beat rapidly. His affect on her was becoming more and more profound.

Laine knew she was in love with Travis, irrevocably in love with him. She'd fought it in her heart, harder than she'd ever fought her Eastern suitors. Waiting for him now, she was reminded of how her mother had waited forever for her husband to return to her. He never had, and Elizabeth's heart wouldn't heal from the loss. Laine had suffered her mother's loss with her, and then lost Elizabeth as well in the end. She couldn't feel that kind of loss again. She had come to realize Elizabeth loved more deeply than Laine had known it was possible for a woman to love a man. And he'd left her.

Laine couldn't, wouldn't, let that happen to her. She was afraid, she knew it, afraid to love a man deeply, afraid to end up as Elizabeth had.

What was taking Travis so long? Laine frowned and kept her eyes pinned on the door he'd entered. Then she saw him, and her rapid pulse settled. He came back on a run across the street and took her arm.

"Shall we proceed, partner?"

Laine let out a small relieved breath. "We shall proceed, partner."

When they walked into McCauley's office accompanied by the sound of that tinny bell, Percival was not at his desk and the door to the inner office was ajar. They could hear two voices locked in verbal combat, but become subdued at the sound of the bell. McCauley's round face emerged around the door.

"Why, Miss Coleridge . . . and Mitcham. This is an unexpected surprise." He leaned his head back inside his office for a moment, then opened the door and came out to greet them. "I don't recall that we had a meeting today, and Boynton seems to be away at the moment."

"We didn't have a meeting scheduled, McCauley,"

Travis spoke firmly. "Miss Coleridge has some news for you that she thought you'd want to know about right away."

"I see," McCauley stroked his thick chin. "Well then, I think I could, that is, I think I could see you now. Step this way, Miss Coleridge. Have a seat out here, Mitcham." He gestured toward the open door of his office to Laine, and toward the waiting area to Travis.

"Actually, Mr. McCauley," Laine said sweetly, "I've requested Mr. Mitcham to attend this meeting."

She stepped into McCauley's office. Standing behind the door was Jamison Hadley. She noticed that his hat was thrown carelessly across several documents on McCauley's desk. How easily he makes himself at home here, she thought suddenly, as if he owns the place and the man in it.

"Why, Mr. Hadley, how fortunate that you're here also. This will save so much time," Laine's voice took on an air of business. Confidently, she took a seat near the desk, smiling at Jamison as she did so.

"Good day, Miss Coleridge. And I see Mitcham seems to be trailing you once again."

Travis said nothing. He nodded toward Jamison, then stood near Laine's chair. McCauley squeezed his portly frame past them to sit behind his desk.

"Now then, Miss Coleridge, what is the news you have for us . . . me, that is so important?"

"I'm pleased to tell you, Mr. McCauley, that I have secured the funds necessary to pay off the debt against the Smithers property, once, of course, you produce proof of that debt. I will be happy to do that just as quickly as my lawyer has had the chance to look over the will and other papers."

McCauley's heavy jaws dropped open. His eyes shifted to Jamison then back at Laine. Jamison said nothing and his emotionless face did not change, except for the small rippling of a muscle along his sharp jawline.

"You . . . you've found the money? But how did you manage that, Miss Coleridge, so soon? And what made you engage another attorney? Surely we could have saved time and money by handling everything through this office. May I ask who you've hired?" Small beads of perspiration popped out on McCauley's forehead, and he stroked the ends of his thick moustache as if it too had suddenly become moist.

"I've secured the services of Mr. Anson Daniels, on the advice of my new partner."

Laine watched McCauley's face redden to almost purple, and eyes bulge with anger. "Inexperienced pup," he muttered. "Doesn't know when to speak and when to keep quiet."

Laine ignored his remark. "Mr. Daniels tells me the circuit court judge will be in town at the end of this month, and that we should be able to finalize everything at that time."

McCauley squirmed in his chair which groaned under his weight. He glared at Jamison for some response, but Hadley continued to remain silent. Moving Hadley's hat to the side and shifting several papers on his desk, he cleared his throat, uncomfortably searching for words.

"Uh, Miss Coleridge," he began, tapping a pencil on the edge of the desk. "The will states nothing about your taking on a partner. I believe Mr. Smithers was indicating that you solely were to be the one . . . May I

127

ask, who is your partner?"

"I am," Travis answered evenly.

McCauley slid a look of panic toward Jamison. Jamison didn't move. "Yes, well, of course this will take much more investigation before any papers will be signed. There's Mr. Hadley to think of here, too."

Jamison rose slowly, a half smile on his face. "Now, John T., don't worry about me. If Miss Coleridge can work out things to her advantage and pay off the debt, why, I couldn't be more pleased. All I want to see is justice done, and Smithers' wishes carried out of course."

McCauley smiled nervously. "Yes, of course, Mr. Hadley. I was only thinking of your best interests."

"I appreciate that, of course. Now, Miss Coleridge, why don't we just have a nice quiet lunch together, get acquainted, and discuss some other possibilities you may not have thought about." Jamison smiled down on her and offered his hand.

Travis stepped between them, his eyes set in a steely glare at Jamison. "Sorry, Hadley, Miss Coleridge has a prior luncheon engagement with me. So much to discuss about our business. You understand."

Hadley glared back, his black eyes blazing. Laine, taken aback at first by Travis's announcement of their luncheon engagement since he'd not mentioned it to her earlier, was warmed by the kind of possessiveness he displayed.

"Shall we?" Travis offered his arm, and she rose and linked her hand through it.

"Jamison," Laine turned to face him directly. "I hope you'll give my regards to your father, and tell him I'll arrange a visit with him, whenever it would be convenient."

128

"My father is a very sick man, and is not up to receiving visitors. His heart is weak."

Laine was momentarily discouraged. She thought Reed Hadley might have some answers for her about the hotel fire, and possibly about the mysterious man who saved her life that night. She was most anxious to see him.

"I don't wish to disturb him if he's not feeling well, but perhaps when he's stronger? Would you ask if he'll see me, even if it's only to say hello?"

"I'll relay the message. And I hope you'll let me call on you another time. I'm sure there's much we could discuss as well."

He peered directly into her eyes with a gaze that made her feel uncomfortable, then he lifted her hand and kissed the back of it, lingering just a little too long.

Travis applied small pressure to her arm and drew her away from Jamison's hold. Laine said nothing and followed him out of the office. He closed the door securely behind them.

Percival Boynton was back at his desk, and rose sharply when the door opened. He nodded to them just as McCauley's door was opening. Laine and Travis turned quickly and left the office, the tinkling of the door chime echoing behind them.

Away from the law office, Laine looked up at Travis, a small smile playing about the corners of her mouth. "I was unaware we had a luncheon engagement today."

"So was I. But it seemed like a good idea at the time." He gave her a smile with an amused quirk of an eyebrow. "In fact, it still seems like a good idea to me. What say you, fair lady?"

"Agreed, but isn't it a little early?"

"A bit. Why don't we meet at the Black Canyon around noon? That will give me time to take care of a few things, and give you time to do some shopping or whatever it is fine Eastern ladies do on a lazy hot morning."

She gave him a playful grimace. "We ladies usually buff our nails, or brush our hair the requisite one hundred strokes, or perhaps sit together in groups reboning our corsets." She put an open palm to her hair, fluffing it and preening with overly deliberate actions. "What do Western gentlemen do on a lazy hot morning?"

He leaned close to her, whispering secretly, "Oh, important things like sitting together in groups wondering how those corsets might be undone."

"Oh!" she feigned embarrassment. "How utterly shocking, sir. I'm not certain a lady with my kind of education in corset study should share a meal with you. But, perhaps if I do, I might teach you to mend your errant ways," she added sweetly. "Yes, I shall meet you for luncheon at the Black Canyon. However, I think one o'clock is a much more civilized hour. Till we meet again, then?" She lifted her hand demurely and offered it to him for a kiss.

He took her hand in both of his own, held it closely, and gazed down intently into the violet depth of her eyes. He patted her hand lightly.

"I believe the hand-kissing gesture is much more suited to Jamison Hadley, my lady. This is more my style."

He dropped her hand and quickly slipped both of his around and to the back of her waist, then pulled her gently but firmly against his body. Before she could speak, he lowered his head and captured her full rose lips inside his own and kissed her for a long moment.

Laine was so completely taken by surprise, she did not have time to think to push him away or struggle against him. Nor did she have the inclination. Her breath went out of her as he crushed her against the length of his body. She could feel every hard contour of him as her yielding form molded into his. She felt the strong shield of his chest through her blouse and chemise, and her nipples hardened as they moved against him, a new sensation she wasn't shocked to learn she enjoyed.

His tongue parted her teeth to explore the inside of her mouth with a sweet heat that travelled along her nerves and settled throbbing below her stomach. The more her body's curves melted into the hollows of his, the more she experienced a blended oneness with him, and the more she gave in to her own mounting desire until she was kissing him with as much fervor as he was enveloping her mouth with his hot, moving lips. A sense of one of her old fantasies coming true crashed around her with blinding truth.

Then reality insinuated itself into her desire-fogged mind. Remember you are standing in the middle of the street in Silver Grande, kissing the city's celebrated most eligible bachelor. She stopped kissing him, her lips still burning against his, and her eyes flashed open.

Somehow she found the strength to push hard against his chest. She looked around nervously to see if anyone watched them. Suddenly a more disturbing thought than being observed hit her. He didn't think she would be another of his conquests, did he?

Travis released her and her lips pulsed to the rhythm of her heartbeat, her cheeks burned. He looked down at her, his hands at her waist, smiling with laughing eyes that creased up in a fan at the corners. Was he mocking her?

Laine brought herself to her senses, and expressed the perfunctory outrage at his action. "How dare you embarrass me publicly!" she exclaimed hotly.

He leaned into her face and squeezed his hands at her waist. "Ah, I see. You'd rather I did it privately." He nodded his head in overstated understanding.

"I would not!" she said indignantly, the hint of a lie in her voice. "But, you . . . you kissed me right on Main Street!"

He leaned back in feigned surprise. "I did? I must have been out in the hot sun too long. I thought I kissed you right on your beautiful mouth." He turned abruptly and started down the boardwalk on a half-run. "The Black Canyon at one it is!" He tipped his hat.

"Travis Mitcham, come back here!" she commanded in a loud whisper.

"Why?" he called back. "Do you want more, right on your . . . Main Street?"

"How dare you . . . ?"

"It was easy," he called over his shoulder, "and I dare to do it again as soon as I get the chance!"

He rounded a corner and disappeared, leaving her standing on the boardwalk, mouth open, face flushed.

Chapter Ten

Laine drew in a deep, steadying breath of hot dry air, then let it out slowly, and felt her nerves begin to relax. The events of the last few days unsettled her more than she wanted to admit, and she had been feeling tense from holding things inside, keeping herself together.

Travis's kiss, brashly bestowed right in the center of town, still burned on her lips, and had all but shattered her self-control. Her senses had reeled under his kiss, and left her defenseless to resist him. Betrayed by her own lips!

What would she do now to defend herself against his advances, if indeed there would be more? His parting words told her there might be, and when she least expected them. And would she want to defend herself anyway? If he were involved with someone else, then defend herself she must. Loving him under those circumstances would serve only to break her heart in the long scheme of things. And if any one man could break her heart it was Travis Mitcham, and

133

she feared her own body and emotions would help him.

She started down the boardwalk slowly, no definite destination in mind. As she crossed a side street, the dark-haired woman she'd seen embracing Travis came out of a shop and passed a short distance from her. She climbed into a small carriage, and deftly pulled the reins on the horse, heading down the street toward the outskirts of town. Women waved to her and men tipped their hats and smiled, and she gave a cheerful wave back.

Laine watched her, and with a twinge at the bottom of her stomach acknowledged that the woman was strikingly beautiful and obviously known and well-liked in Silver Grande. Determined to know her identity, Laine walked down the side street toward the shop she'd seen her leaving.

The display window of Ella Cooper's Apparel Shop was filled with an array of female clothing, and Laine's brow creased in critique of the garments and accessories gathered there. A dress of blue lace with a wide neckline hanging on an antiquated form was well made, but had long been out of style. The accessories placed around it were a mixture of hats, gloves and scarves for a woman, and small laced boots, petticoats, and a thin white nightdress all to fit a young girl. All of the things looked clean and cared for.

So much was crammed into the window space that one peering in from the outside could not see into the shop. Laine visualized what she would do with it if the shop belonged to her. The first things to go would be the items in the display window, replaced by the latest fashion, crisp and new, changing every week.

Laine turned the loose handle on the shop door and stepped quickly inside. The only sound was that of a squeak from the door as she swung it open and closed it behind her. The still air inside made the dry, musty odor all the more oppressive. Stiffly she looked around the tiny shop, feeling closed in by its smallness and by the great number of frocks and shawls and other apparel which seemed stuffed together in tight, restricting lines. No one seemed to be about to attend to any customers, if any had been there, and she wondered how Ella Cooper could afford to stay in business.

She touched the sleeves of a few dresses. She did not have to walk far to effect a browsing attitude; rather she could simply turn this way and that and have looked over most of what hung there. Toward the rear of the shop she noticed a narrow door frame covered by a faded chintz curtain, and she walked toward it.

"Hello? Is anyone here?" she called as she turned her body to slip between two rows of hanging dresses. "Hello, Mrs. Cooper?"

A small woman emerged from behind the curtain, a dark full-skirted dress draped over one arm. Her hair was pinned neatly all around her small head, and Laine surmised it might once have been a light chestnut. It was now cast with a silver gray, almost as if it had been painted with light brush strokes.

"Hello," the light voice greeted her. "I was so busy in the back I didn't hear you come in. May I help you find something?" When she looked Laine full in the

135

face, her beginning smile faded.

Laine's eyes darted quickly around the cramped shop, and rested on a pair of white lace gloves which lay crossed over each other in a small etagere by the sales counter.

"Gloves," she said abruptly. "I'm in need of a pair of white gloves for a social engagement I will be attending this evening." She walked toward the counter.

"Yes, ma'am, perhaps these . . ." From a side table the woman picked up a pair of ivory kid gloves with several pearl buttons at the wrists, and turned to place them in Laine's open palm.

"Actually, I was thinking of the lace pair over there." Laine gestured toward the etagere.

"Those are not for sale," the woman said quietly. "I keep them only for display. These will be quite appropriate, I'm sure." She smoothed the kid gloves in Laine's hand. "Will you be in Silver Grande long?"

"I'm not certain. I was born here, but left when I was very young. I've only recently returned." Laine smiled. Perhaps if she seemed friendly, Ella Cooper might be more relaxed. "I don't remember this shop being here when I was a child. Have you been in business long?"

"Long enough," Ella Cooper answered, busily adjusting the neckline of a dress draped over a form.

Laine turned toward the etagere once again, then turned back. "I'm sorry, I didn't introduce myself. I'm Laine Coleridge." She smiled and held out her hand to the small woman.

Ella Cooper nodded, then flushed slightly. "Ah yes," she acknowledged through a tight voice.

Laine caught the response. "You know my name?" she asked urgently.

The woman avoided Laine's eyes and busied herself with the dress. She nodded slightly. "I believe I may have heard it some years ago."

"What . . . what do you remember?" Laine asked quietly.

"Oh, I really couldn't say," the woman answered brusquely, moving to a rack of dresses and studiously straightening them. "Is there something else I might help you with? A shawl perhaps? Or a bag?"

Laine was made sharply aware that the subject had been changed. She scanned the cramped shop. "I don't think so." Then she remembered that Travis's dark-haired lady friend had been in this shop earlier. "Oh yes, Mrs. Cooper, shortly before I came in, a rather attractive woman left here, dark hair, green dress. I thought I recognized her, but she was on her way out of town before I could catch up with her. Would you tell me her name?"

"Why yes," the small woman smiled, only slightly able to conceal her relief that the conversation had changed. "That's Kate Hardy."

Laine nodded thoughtfully. "Kate Hardy," she repeated. "Does she live around here?"

"Not far, just out of town."

"Does she have a family?"

"Just a young son, twelve or thirteen, I'd say. Quite a handful, I hear tell."

"Yes, I suppose it's a difficult age. But I'm sure her husband must be able to handle him," Laine ventured into the subject of her greatest concern.

137

"Doesn't have one. He died a year ago, pneumonia, I think. She's had to make do with running a small ranch herself and bringing up that boy. It hasn't been an easy row to hoe."

"No, I suppose not," Laine replied sadly. But it looked as if Travis had been helping her out, she added silently.

Kate Hardy was a lovely woman, a woman with a difficult son to raise, and a home to keep together. No wonder she gravitated toward Travis, and no wonder he was drawn to her, Laine thought. They would make a lovely family.

"Well, thank you for your time," Laine said, turning to leave and starting toward the front of the shop.

As she turned, her eyes fell once again on the gloves lying in placid repose in the etagere. They seemed to draw her to them, and cautiously she moved toward them. They were old, she guessed, but perhaps not as old as they looked to be at first. They were somewhat yellowed, and when she picked up one she noticed brownish discolorations along a couple of the finger seams. Upon closer examination she thought they looked as if they might have been burned. Perhaps whoever wore them had come too near a candle flame.

Laine mused for a moment about an elegant lady wearing white lace gloves at an intimate dinner for two. They touched their champagne glasses in a toast to each other, and the lady's hand brushed too closely to the candle flame. Laine shook her head to remove the fantasy from her mind.

She turned the delicate lace over in her hand.

Something showed through the lace on the inside wrist, and she brought it toward the front window for more light. Gold thread had been used to delicately embroider two initials at the pearl button and loop which held the glove closed. *E.C.* Laine smiled slightly. If these belonged to the shop owner, that meant Ella Cooper might have once been a wealthy lady. She allowed her imagination another small flight.

Ella Cooper stood away from her and watched for a few moments as Laine turned the lace gloves over and over in her hands. She stepped closer to her.

"You may have those, if you like," she said quietly from behind Laine.

"Oh no," Laine replied, turning around quickly and replacing them in the etagere. "I couldn't take them. I understand now why you have them for display only. They're yours personally."

"No, they aren't mine."

"But the initials . . ."

"The same, but not mine. Just a coincidence." She took some tissue paper from the counter and painstakingly wrapped the gloves in it. "I truly would like you to have them. Think of them as a welcome home gift." She smiled and pressed the small package into Laine's hands.

Laine smiled in genuine appreciation. "All right. Thank you very much. You're very kind." She moved to the door, then sensing something questioning inside of herself, she turned back to the small woman watching her intently from the counter. "I'd like to talk with you again sometime. Perhaps you might remember something about my family. Would you consider talking with me again?"

"We will see each other," Ella Cooper replied matter-of-factly.

Laine arrived at the Black Canyon Hotel shortly before one o'clock. There was no sign of Travis outside, so she went in to see if he was already in the dining room. She didn't find him there either, and asked a waitress if Mr. Mitcham had arrived yet. The waitress checked at the desk and withdrew a folded note addressed to Laine. She opened and read it.

"Laine—sorry, I won't make it for lunch today. Pressing business. If you'd like, have lunch anyway, and tell the waitress to put it on my bill. See you tonight at Molly's. I'm sorry about lunch. T."

Disappointed, Laine refolded the note and placed it in her bag. Why not? she thought. I might just as well have some tea at least. Wouldn't Aunt Sarah have a lecture for this one? A lady dining alone. It looked bad. Maybe in Boston, but who would care in Silver Grande?

The waitress seated her, and Laine sipped tea while studying the bill of fare.

"Lunching alone, Miss Coleridge? How dreary. And to think you could have accepted my invitation. Mind if I join you now?"

Before Laine could answer, Jamison Hadley pulled out the chair opposite and sat down.

"Mr. Hadley, if you don't mind, I . . ."

"Ah, but I do mind, Miss Coleridge. You have your

140

reputation to consider. It's not proper for a lady to dine in a restaurant alone."

"I'm sure in Silver Grande, propriety is not an issue," Laine sniffed, "and I'm certain you're more interested in your own reputation than you are mine."

"Well taken, Miss . . . shouldn't we be on a first name basis by now? I mean, as close as we've become in the last few days and all. And here we are sharing luncheon together. Do call me Jamie, and I'll call you Laine. Unless you have something a bit more personal you'd prefer."

"I'd prefer that you call me Miss Coleridge, Mr. Hadley. And we are *not* sharing luncheon! Now, will you please leave? I'd much prefer the company of myself alone."

"I'd like to accommodate you, Laine," Jamison ignored her demand, "but since my sister is fast approaching this table, I couldn't tear myself away from what I'm sure will be a very interesting reunion between the two of you."

Laine's nerves leapt under her skin. LaBelle Hadley. Well, she supposed it was inevitable they would meet. She steeled herself, but knew she was up to this. Bring on LaBelle, she said in her mind.

"LaBelle, dear," Jamison stood up as his sister flounced over in a full-skirted gown that Laine noted was more appropriate for evening wear.

"Jamie," LaBelle snapped, "where have you been? I've been looking everywhere. Daddy's had one of his heart spells, and that shrew of a housekeeper expects one of us there to watch him. I have things to do. What . . . ?"

LaBelle looked directly at Laine, then froze.

"Sister, love, may I present . . . ?"

"Laine Coleridge," LaBelle breathed. "I heard you were back."

"LaBelle."

All the usual polite comments Laine had learned were correct at the time of introduction like, "how lovely to see you again," or "it's a pleasure," or "you're looking wonderful as always," rushed to her lips, then stopped cold. None of those things would be the truth, so Laine decided to dispense with them.

"How lovely to see you again," LaBelle said, barely concealing the frost in her voice.

One down, thought Laine. "It's good to be back," she said without emotion.

"Why?" LaBelle asked and let Jamison seat her. "I wouldn't think you'd find anything left for you in Silver Grande."

Laine sipped her tea calmly. "Really? On the contrary, everything I left behind was still here waiting for me when I returned."

"Wonderful," Jamison said with a laugh, shifting his eyes between the two women.

"What?" LaBelle snapped.

"Wonderful," Jamison answered quickly. "I was just saying that Laine looks wonderful, doesn't she, sister, dear?"

LaBelle frowned and gave Laine fleeting narrow-eyed scrutiny. "Yes, wonderful, as always," she said, seeming to find no comfortable position in the chair.

Two, Laine thought. And LaBelle's nervous. What for? She hadn't done anything to make her feel uncomfortable. At least not purposely. Certainly not the way LaBelle had always made her feel. She had to admit that watching LaBelle squirm a bit was making the little girl in the hand-me-down clothes in her heart feel even. More unfinished business.

"Why, thank you, LaBelle," Laine said. "Seeing you again is . . . interesting."

"And you're wearing an interesting ensemble," LaBelle said, assessing Laine's riding clothes. "But then, you can wear something like that. I simply couldn't."

"Oh? And what makes you think that, LaBelle? From my observation, you'd wear anything."

"Oh ho!" Jamison lifted his napkin, and Laine knew it was to hide his amusement from his sister.

LaBelle shot him a withering glance. "Actually, it looks too . . . loose. But then, I'm sure you're used to that. Makes you look so much like your mother."

"I'll take that as the compliment I'm sure you meant," Laine smiled, but she'd sustained a small stab wound in the heart with LaBelle's last remark.

"I'm sure *you* would take it that way. Although I'm sure your mother wouldn't be caught dead in that outfit, would she? Oops, I didn't mean to bring up an unpleasant subject. Can you ever forgive me?"

No, Laine said to herself. Never. "Unpleasant subject? I don't know what you mean, so I can't possibly forgive you."

LaBelle squirmed again as Jamison watched her face. He took out a pocket watch and noted the time.

"Oh dear," LaBelle stood quickly. "If I don't hurry, I'll be late for my appointment with Travis. We have so many plans to discuss. Have you seen him since

143

you've been back?" She looked directly at Laine.

"Every day."

"How nice."

"And every night," Laine added as a quick afterthought.

LaBelle's eyes darkened. She looked at Jamison. He shrugged. "Yes, well," LaBelle's voice constricted, "he did indulge you when you were the little saloon girl. I'm sure he still feels, shall we say, brotherly toward you? He's like that. Always charitable to visitors."

Laine cleared her throat. LaBelle was certainly working hard to put her on the defensive. But she knew she was holding her own in the imaginary arena of LaBelle's design.

"Visitor? Oh, I guess you didn't know. I've moved back to Silver Grande permanently."

"I see. Then you simply must come to our party."

"Party?" Jamison asked. "We're giving a party?"

"Of course, you ninny, in honor of my engagement to Travis. Remember?" A corner of LaBelle's mouth tipped at a hard angle.

"Oh, of course," Jamison said, picking up where LaBelle had left off. "Your engagement. I don't know how that could have slipped my mind. You'd best run along now. As you said, you and Mitcham have so many things to talk about."

"Yes, well, I'll be off then. It's been a pleasure seeing you again, Laine, and do have a safe trip back to Boston. Oh, I'm sorry, you said you were staying permanently, didn't you? Well, then, I'm sure we . . . Travis and I will see you rather often."

She turned and flounced away. Three, Laine

thought with a catch in her throat, and a fourth she didn't expect.

"Isn't she something?" Jamison asked lightly, his eyes following his sister's retreating form.

"Oh yes," Laine concurred, "she's something, all right." She took in a breath and asked what she was burning to know. "How long have LaBelle and . . . and Travis been planning to be married?"

Jamison settled back in his chair and lit up a cheroot, taking his time in letting out a column of smoke. "Always, I guess. It's always been understood they'd marry. Mitcham will have so much to gain by their union, aside from the obvious charms of my sister."

Laine moved away from the smoke that curled toward her. "Yes, I see. But, I'd heard that Travis enjoyed being unattached."

"Well, what man wouldn't? But, even he couldn't escape the long loop of Belle's lasso for very long!"

The last thing Laine wanted to do was believe La-Belle Hadley's words and her brother's corroboration of them. Neither of them were to be trusted. Yet she did listen to them, and the heaviness in her heart weighed her down. Should she believe them?

She rose and picked up her bag. "Well, I must be leaving now. Will you excuse me, Mr. Hadley?"

"So soon? Well, now, I truly am sorry. I thought we were just getting to know each other. Perhaps another time."

"Another time," Laine said absently, and left the dining room.

Chapter Eleven

Laine was helping Molly prepare supper when Buck came through the back door with Travis. The older man dropped his hat on a wooden peg near the door and kissed his wife's plump cheek. Travis sent a silent greeting in his eyes in response to Laine's questioning smile.

"Anything happen in town today?" Molly asked her nightly question as she busily dished up supper.

"I'll say," Buck answered quickly. "Seems old Reed Hadley died this afternoon," Noisily he dropped down in his chair at the table as he always did.

Laine spun around to face Travis. Before she could speak, Molly motioned them to be seated.

"Wal, I guess his heart finally took him," Molly said with a small measure of compassion. "I suspect livin' with that Elvira all those years quickened it some." She passed a platter of meat to Travis.

"Yep," Buck said, "with Elvira gone more'n a year now, I heerd him say he was gonna start some real livin'. Then that no account son of his shows up and ended that idee."

"I'm sorry I didn't get to see him," Laine spoke dully. "There was so much I wanted to ask him about . . ." her voice trailed off. "I should have tried harder to see him, I guess, but Jamison said he was too sick for visitors."

"Didn't look that sick a few days ago when I saw him," Buck threw in. "But, I guess you never know with a heart condition. Set his black horse big as life jest a day or two ago. Talked about some new medicine he was takin'. Said he was feelin' like a new man. Funny thing, you know?"

"Sure is," Travis concurred.

"Didn't seem it wuz his time yet," Molly added.

"Funny thing about time, too," Travis mused.

"What do you mean, Travis?" Laine asked intently.

"Oh, probably nothing, I guess. I suppose there's a time for everything."

"Everything has a season," Molly said knowingly, looking first at Travis and then at Laine.

"Sorry about missing lunch with you," Travis said, trying to hold Laine's gaze. She dropped her eyes. "You got my note, didn't you?"

"Yes, I got your note. Did your 'pressing business' work out satisfactorily?" Still she didn't look at him.

"Time will tell," Travis responded, cocking his head to try to get her to look at him.

"Did it take long?" came her even question.

"Not this time. Sometimes things just all fall into place, don't they?"

147

She nodded, then got up quickly to pick up a dish from the sideboard.

"Buck didn't think so the first few hours, but then even he had to admit the way the new grain chute is constructed on an angle makes more sense for unloading. Right, Buck?" Travis gave his old friend a jab in the side.

"Grain chute?" Laine turned around slowly. "You were working with Buck on a grain chute?"

"Yes. Don't worry, I don't expect you to get real excited about it."

"Oh, but I am! I mean, grain chutes can be fascinating, can't they?" Laine sat down at the table with renewed spirit.

"I never thought so," Buck interjected, looking up from his plate. "But, say, the young miss here has turned into quite a rider. Now that's exciting."

Laine laughed lightly. "Once every muscle in my body stopped aching long enough for me to enjoy it."

"Is that right?" Travis was genuinely surprised. "It was my guess you'd be buying a landaulet or some other elegant carriage once you settle in."

"Well, it seems you guessed wrong," she laughed. "Buck's been running me out early almost from the first day I arrived. I do know how to ride, you know. I learned at school."

"I suppose you learned to ride like those uppity Easterners, sidesaddle with your pinky finger in the air," Travis chided her.

Laine had to laugh at his almost correct assump-

148

tion. "True, but Buck's taught me to ride Western, and I hardly ever use my pinky now."

"I'd sure like to see that," Travis laughed. "You'll still use the pinky for tea drinking, no doubt."

"Listen, Mr. Mitcham, sir," Laine shot back, good-naturedly, "tea drinking and English riding aren't the only things I learned at school."

"Oh, really? Did I leave out needlepoint?"

"For your information, I'm an excellent book-keeper, better than any in my class, and I've designed some of the finest fashions in this or any other country, not that you'd ever be aware of anything like ladies' fashions." She gave him a sidelong glance, and put in a light-hearted jab of her own. "Or, perhaps you would, providing they were on certain ladies in Silver Grande."

"I knew I'd find a needlepoint in there somewhere," Travis murmured, "and something tells me I can find it in my side right now." He narrowed his eyes playfully at her. "And just what did you mean by 'certain ladies'?"

"Oh, come now, Travis, don't be so modest. It's common knowledge that you're Silver Grande's most sought after young bachelor. Isn't that so, Molly?"

"Most certainly is," Molly agreed cheerfully.

"Wal, it's clear at least one's after him," Buck laughed.

"Never mind about that, Buck," Travis sent a look to Buck, but the older man was busy scraping his plate.

"You two shoulda seen LaBelle Hadley today."

Laine's smile faded. "I did."

Buck continued. "Comes out to the grain chute dressed fer a party, stands there sashayin' in front of Travis like a flag. Travis didn't notice till she started in t'callin' him. That's when his crew set up t'laughin' so's I thought they'd pitch right off the top! Funniest thing I ever did see!"

"Ah, Buck, I think this story was only funny because you were there. I don't think Laine wants to hear about it," Travis jabbed Buck in the arm.

"A girl'd take a word to the wise to snap Travis up as soon as she could." Molly sent a knowing message to Laine in her smile.

Laine was struck momentarily speechless, her face burning from a quick flush.

"And the way I see it," Buck put in, "t'won't be long afore Laine becomes the belle of Silver Grande anyway, judgin' by the way the menfolks been eyein' her."

"Buck! Now you be careful what you say," Molly warned him. "No need to embarrass the girl. Everybody knows she's the purtiest thing to hit this town in a month o'Sundays. Ain't that right, Travis?" She gave him a playful poke on the shoulder.

"Laine," Travis said quickly, "how about a ride after supper while it's still light? We could probably get as far as Table Mesa."

"Good idea," Molly answered for her. "You

150

young folks run along. Buck'll help me with the dishes."

"Who me?" Buck answered, taking the last slice of meat from the platter. "That's women's work. I got better things to do than that."

"Not tonight you haven't," Molly pronounced, sending him a meaningful glare.

Buck stared back at his wife, motionless. Then a look of recognition spread over his face, and he nodded vigorously. "Oh, you're right, Molly dear. It is my night to help with the cleanin' up, ain't it? I musta fergit." He turned toward Laine and Travis. "You two git along now. Be dark shortly."

"Well, I don't need a shove," Travis said, standing up. "Laine?"

Laine had watched the conversation move around the table wondering where the final word would land. Apparently it landed with her, and it was difficult for her to conceal her mixed emotions at the outcome.

"Well, if you're sure, Molly . . ."

"I'm sure, now git fer the barn."

The amiable woman started clearing the table, starting first with snatching Buck's plate out from under his nose. Travis and Laine rose and walked out the back door leaving the older couple arguing over who was to wash and who was to dry.

Travis helped Laine saddle a gray mare, then they rode out beyond the sparse rangeland along the rim of a rock canyon. The deep brown-red shades of massive monolithic rock formations gleamed with burnished brilliance in the glow from the burning globe of setting sun. Laine marvelled as she always did, knowing they'd been there since time began, and she often wondered if her mother had once gazed upon them with as much wonder as she did now.

They stopped near the rim of Table Mesa. The only sound around them was the ceaseless whispering of the desert wind, and light clink of bridle tack as the horses flicked their heads at evening flies. The wind carried the scent of someplace wet and green that they couldn't see, but knew was out there beyond the rocks. The desert floor stretched far beyond them in waves of soft-colored sand, starkly beautiful. No matter how often she'd viewed it since she returned, Laine drank in the scene as one with a long thirst.

"The only things missing are roses," she mused quietly, as they sat astride the horses, gazing out toward the jutting ghostly stone shapes.

"Roses?" Travis turned to her.

"The things I miss most about the summer in Boston are the roses. Aunt Sarah had so many of them in the garden. Their fragrance on a dewy morning was so powerful it would wake me sometimes, it was that heady. Oh, I did love the roses."

Travis was silent for a moment, thinking and scanning the horizon. "I doubt roses would grow in this country," he observed. "Scorpions, snakes, cactus, but this is no country for anything delicate to survive."

Laine snapped her head around toward him. "If you're referring to me, I assure you I'm not delicate, and I will survive."

"I meant nothing by that, Laine. It's just that you've been leading a rather pampered life in the past few years, and I doubt it has prepared you for life in this country."

"You forget I was born here. My childhood in Silver Grande prepared me for more than you know, Travis." She gazed back to the horizon, lost in memory for the moment.

"I didn't forget, Laine." He took a deep breath. Maybe the time was right now. "Do you ever wonder where your father might be?"

"I told you before, I don't want to talk about that. He's dead. I don't wonder about him; I don't care about him. He has nothing to do with my life."

Travis pressed on, hoping she would change her mind about discussing David Coleridge, wanting so much to tell her her father was alive. He could only tell her everything if she were willing to listen with an open mind. Somehow he had to get her to do that.

"But, surely you have questions about him. Isn't it possible, if he's still alive, that he has questions about you?"

"If he's alive, why didn't he come back to help? My mother wouldn't be dead if he hadn't left us! It was all his fault!" Tears burned behind her eyes, but she fought them back with a strength she'd learned in childhood.

"Perhaps he's not dead, and if you were to find him, I'm sure he could answer those questions for you. There must be so much you'd like to know, so much he could tell you."

"Travis, why do you keep pushing this at me? What makes you so sure my father would have any answers to anything—if he were alive, I mean? I wouldn't have any questions for him anyway," she rushed on, "because I don't care what he'd have to say. The only question I'd like answered is, who was the man who saved me from the burning hotel that night, and sent me away? Whoever it was saved me, but my mother died. If he hadn't done that, maybe I could have gone back and helped her. I'd like to tell him what he robbed me of. Why can't you leave me alone about this?"

Her voice rose until she was almost hoarsely shouting at him. And then the tears broke free and spilled down her face in fast, hot streams.

She spurred her horse away from him and ran off toward a stand of faint green aspen in the far distance, snapping the reins on either side of the mare's neck in rapid succession until the horse's legs were straight out in a full gallop. Travis took off after her. She wasn't that experienced a rider yet to handle that kind of run. He reached her side, and stretched out until he caught the leather straps, and reined the mare in close to his own black horse.

"Let go!" she shouted, pushing at him and trying

154

to control the mare at the same time. She snatched the reins out of his hand.

"Don't be a fool!" he shouted back. "You'll get yourself killed and the mare, too!"

The mare lunged across a narrow dry creek bed, unseating Laine who grabbed the pommel in an attempt to right herself. One foot fell free of the stirrup, and Travis knew that it was just a matter of time before the other foot came out, and she would take a nasty fall.

He reined in close to her once again, reaching out with a powerful arm and grasped her around the waist, pulling her off the mare and seating her across his thighs. She bounced hard against him, and he slowed his horse and reined him in, until they came to a stop near the aspen grove. The mare continued off into the distance, and Travis slid down off the black pulling Laine with him.

"What do you think you're doing?" Laine cried out breathlessly, pushing her small hands against his hard chest.

"Stopping you from breaking your neck," he said, trying to get a grip on her strong enough to stop her struggle.

"It's not up to you to do that." She struggled harder.

"Then I'd have had to pick up the pieces, and I'd have hated that," he replied, trying to break her mood with lightness.

"Why don't you just leave me alone?" she sighed.

He took hold of her arms, and with a strong grip

held her still. "I can't," he whispered.

"Why not?" Her storm-tossed gaze now flashed with lightning.

He could say nothing for a moment, holding her gaze, his eyes reflecting an ocean of thoughts. Then he swept her up in his arms, carried her toward the trees, and sat down cradling her in his arms.

"You're my partner. I could never desert my partner." He pulled her head down against the softness of his sun-faded shirt.

"I'm sorry," she said quietly. "I didn't mean to fall apart like that." She dragged a hard breath. The smell of sun and wind and earth drifting up from the neck of his open shirt floated over her like a gossamer veil, and soothed her raw nerves.

"Tell me about it, Laine. Tell me about the night you were taken away from the hotel."

"No," she said, quietly. "I never talk about that. It's best left where it is."

"I don't think so. I think that's why you've begun to ask questions about that night. I think it would do you good to get it out of you," he urged. "It will help you a lot if you tell me about it. I know it will."

She looked up at him, wide eyes glistening in the brilliant orange-red of the setting sun. Sighing deeply, she closed her eyes, and her small shoulders fell against him. She gave in and told him what she remembered, including the part about the man with the soothing voice who swept her away from the burning building and sent her to Boston.

When she'd finished her story, Travis searched her face. "Are you sure you'd never seen the man before? I mean, did he frequent the saloon?"

"I . . . I don't think so. At first his voice sounded sort of familiar, but then I didn't think I knew him."

"Did you see his face?"

"No, only shadows of him. He seemed very tall, and I remember when he picked me up his shoulders felt very wide. That's all I know." Her voice grew weary in the telling.

Travis pulled her slim body closer to his chest. His mind tore apart into a thousand fragments. David! The man who saved Laine might have been David. But, he couldn't say that yet. After all, it was only an assumption. If he told her he thought it might be her father, she might reject that entirely, or worse, believe it and hate him all the more. No, he'd better ask that of David directly, if he could. If Coleridge's letter was accurate about when he would arrive, he wouldn't have to wait very long to ask that question.

Travis knew he would have to tell Laine soon that David was his partner. But when? How? He had to admit it, his feelings for the lovely woman in his arms were growing so rapidly he could not imagine living without her. When he'd kissed her, he knew he'd turned down a road to a box canyon. If he turned around to leave he would run right into himself. If he told her about David, he might

157

lose her completely. No, he would have to wait on that for now. But when? When?

"It's all right," he murmured softly through her moist hair, "you don't have to talk about it anymore."

Her small hand lay lightly against his chest, and she buried her face more deeply into the softness of his shirt. He smoothed her hair back from her face. Her translucent ivory skin showed moist trails where tears had flowed down its smoothness.

She moved to sit up, and the delicate scent of her rose cologne drifted up over his face from where it had been trapped by the heat of their bodies pressed close together. Golden tendrils of hair moved in the gentle evening breeze and brushed across her swollen eyes. She looked at him, her fine features reflecting the wistfulness of the child he remembered, and the passion of the woman she'd become.

Wordless, he searched her gaze for some sign that he should let her go, but he did not find it. Desire burgeoned within him and surfaced with searing strength. His arms went around her like bands of steel, crushing her against his chest. Her hand crept around the back of his neck, the tips of her fingers lacing through small wisps of hair that curled over his collar, then she gripped the back of his neck with surprising strength.

Travis pressed her slender body against his, stroking her back, her hair, under her hair to her

158

neck, tracing the side of her face, caressing her shoulders.

He rained soft kisses over her hair and forehead, over her closed eyes, and tenderly over the smoky moist lashes that curled against her cheek. He murmured her name over and over, his eyes closed, knowing his reality only through the tips of his fingers and the soft pressure of her body against his chest.

He slid both of his hands up over her shoulders to her throat, and cupped her exquisite face in them. Her blue-violet eyes seared directly into his heart like liquid flame.

His thumbs tracing her cheekbones, he lowered his eyes to her pale rose full lips, then lifted his gaze to meet hers. Her face was so close to his that he could feel the barest mist of her breath. His eyes lowered to her lips again, then closed as he brought his own down to tenderly enclose hers for a long sweet kiss.

He drew back and saw that she held her eyes closed, the dark lashes curling upward in a velvet fringe. Her full lips were parted slightly, her small chin tilted up toward him. A wave of passion welled inside him, and he slipped his hands quickly to the back of her head, entangling her golden curls in the grip of his fingers.

Again his lips sought hers, moving over them slowly, sensually, tasting their soft sweetness. He moved her head gently with his hands, and pressed her mouth deeper into his own. She did not resist, and when he thought he felt a warm response to his kisses, his mouth grew more insistent. His hands held her face, thumbs gently parting her lips to allow his tongue to explore the inner reaches of her mouth.

Laine fell against his chest, supported only by his hands which held her face pressed to his. Slowly she sensed that his large hands, although rough from hard work, caressed her more tenderly than she remembered ever being touched, sending tingling shock waves down her back and arms. His breathing became quicker, his lips more deeply demanding, and his tongue flicked over her teeth sending shivers through the tense knots in her shoulders.

He held her face with his thumbs touching the corners of her mouth. She breathed deeply, her breasts rising and falling against his chest. He slipped his arm around her shoulders, lowering her toward the soft earth under the trees, his lips branded into hers.

She clung to him, her fingers at the back of his neck pressing his lips even closer to hers. He lowered his chest over her and, running a hand along her ribs, over her waist, and down to her hips, he gently urged her over to fit underneath him.

Her breasts ached in the straining against his chest. She slipped her arms down over his shoulders to grip his back and pull his chest hard against her. The dark sky overhead had just begun to twinkle faintly with a dusting of stars, and she felt as if she were floating, drifting up toward them.

And then she felt the hard heat of his need pressed against her inner thigh. Her eyelashes fluttered several times, and then her eyes opened wide. She tore her lips away from his, and he leaned above her, breathing hard.

"Travis, wait . . ." she breathed, her breasts pushing hard against his chest. "I can't . . . not yet."

Every fiber in her body screamed out against the denial. She wanted him, wanted him desperately, completely. She loved him, had always loved him. But still, she was not ready to share this kind of intimacy, it was too soon, wasn't it? Yes, she told herself, it is. What about the other women? What about LaBelle Hadley?

"Travis," she whispered.

He pushed up from her at first, then dropped down to bury his face in her hair. He wanted her, and he wanted her here and now, but he wanted her to want him as much when it felt right to her. He would not push her, and he never wanted to hurt her. He sighed deeply, then moved slowly away from her.

She started to get up. He jumped up quickly, then bent down to lift her to her feet. She searched his face, as if hoping to find answers to her questions.

"I'm sorry . . ." she began.

He placed a finger over her lips. "I'm not," he whispered, and took a leaf that was caught in her

161

hair, and dropped it into his shirt pocket.

He lifted and carried her to his horse, set her astride it, then swung up behind her, his legs fitting snugly around her hips.

He urged the black over the hard ground toward the Harmon house. Somewhere from atop a high butte, the lonely cry of a coyote drifted poignantly up to the moon.

Chapter Twelve

"Good afternoon, Mr. and Mrs. Harmon," Jamison quietly greeted them at the door of the Hadley home the day of his father's funeral. "Very neighborly of you to stop in to see us in our hour of grief." He motioned a servant to take the wrapped pan from Molly's arms.

He was just about to show Buck and Molly into the front parlor, when Laine stepped into the open doorway. He reached out and took her elbow, drawing her into the high-ceilinged foyer.

"Laine, how very nice of you to come by. You must have known my father well to take this trouble."

Laine sensed a menacing edge in his voice. When he helped her out of her dark blue cape, he looked over her dark blue skirt and jacket with glittering eyes that made her uncomfortable.

"How lovely you look, even in mourning," he said huskily.

"I did not know your father well, Mr. Hadley, but I remember from my last years here that he was kind to my mother, and that's the reason I came." She brushed past him to join Buck and Molly, and the three went into the parlor.

John McCauley came to the door, pushing his portly frame inside, and removing his tall gray formal hat. Percival Boynton came in behind him.

"Tough luck, Hadley, losing your father," McCauley said out of the side of his mouth, and shook Jamison's hand.

"Not really," Jamison said coldly. "Dead men don't talk."

"What are you saying?" McCauley frowned, shrugging out of a coat that was too heavy for the heat, and letting Boynton take it for him. As was his usual manner, he ignored the little man.

"I'm saying Father knew too much. He was once sweet on the Coleridge girl's mother, and when he knew Laine had come back to town, he was all excited about seeing her again."

Boynton busied himself near a coat rack, taking in as much of the conversation as was possible.

"You're afraid he'd have talked to her," McCauley nodded thoughtfully.

"Oh, he'd have talked to her all right, and then she'd have brought that new lawyer over to talk to him."

"Why would that matter? They couldn't prove anything."

"You're forgetting about certain signed documents in your safe. If we were forced to produce

164

those, and my father saw them, he'd know those weren't his signatures, that he never signed anything regarding that property or debts owed."

"Maybe we could offer the Coleridge girl a large enough sum to make her decide the whole thing isn't worth it, and send her packing out of Silver Grande."

"No, her sentimental attachment to the place is too strong. And Mitcham would never let her accept that. He has an interest in the property now. He knows about the railroad company moving in. But I don't think he knows yet about the vein of silver that edges it. I think it's going to take more than money this time, John T. Now, if the lady found herself married to me, I would have control of the property, and you would have cash against the so-called lien. Even her smart young lawyer could do nothing about that."

McCauley laughed under his breath. "Hadley," he grinned, "you are the devil to end all devils. But it's a foolproof plan if you can pull it off. I've seen you with the ladies. Perfect, perfect." Turning to look behind him, he poked Percival on the shoulder. "Boynton, what are you doing over there? It's time we paid our respects to poor Miss Hadley."

They started around to the parlor when Jamison grabbed McCauley by the arm. "Well, do you believe this?" he muttered. "Here comes Mitcham. Why would he be here? He's never had much use for my father or this family." He frowned.

"Probably here to protect his interest," Mc-Cauley whispered, "and I don't mean the property either. You'd better act fast with the Coleridge girl." He disappeared around the corner.

"Mitcham," Jamison said, opening the door for Travis. "What brings you here?"

"I believe there's a wake for your father, Hadley, but I'm not surprised you didn't notice."

Travis stepped by him and entered the parlor. He spoke to an acquaintance, then moved to stand in the back of the room.

Laine saw Travis come in, and she nodded toward him, then sat down in a hard-backed chair next to Molly and Buck. The large room held a faint odor of mustiness, and she thought it might be coming from the shelves of old books along the east wall. Heavy gold and red drapes closed the room against the heat of the sun.

She noted sadly that there was a distinct lack of natural light in the room. Even though it was not yet sunset, an oil lamp was lit on the dark wood table next to what had been referred to as Reed's chair. Several small brown medicine bottles were clustered at one end of the table. The room was sparsely furnished, and a faded Oriental carpet showed threadbare beneath their feet.

Laine leaned over to Molly and whispered, "Look, there's the dress shop owner, Ella Cooper.

Who's the young girl with her?"

"That's her daughter, Ada," Molly whispered a reply.

"Are they friends of the Hadleys?" Laine asked with skeptical curiosity. "Ella Cooper's dress shop hardly seems the kind of place Elvira Hadley would patronize, or LaBelle either."

Molly leaned closer to Laine. "Yer right about that. They're not friends of the Hadleys, as such, and those women would never shop there. Now I'm not one to gossip you understand, but old rumors had it that Reed used to frequent that saloon where your mother worked. Ella worked there. Seems it's possible Ada's his daughter."

"Oh my," Laine was shocked, then immediately pitied Ella Cooper and her plain, quiet daughter. "Why did they stay here?" she whispered. "I'm sure if Elvira had heard those rumors, she'd have made their lives a living hell."

Molly nodded knowingly. "Must jest burn La-Belle's and Jamison's hides no end to see them two women here, representin' the wrong side of town'n all."

Laine grew thoughtful for a moment, then leaned toward Molly again. "If Ella Cooper worked at the hotel, I never saw her that I remember. But then, I never did see very many of those women."

"I think your mama tried to shelter you from bein' too close to anyone there," Molly said softly, patting Laine's hand. She looked around the room. "Say, I haven't seen LaBelle yet."

Buck turned toward the two women. "Jest as well. She's an awful terror."

From across the room, more than once Travis caught Laine's gaze and held it. She blushed and looked away, but then again and again her eyes would seek him out of the crowd just to know where he was.

As the afternoon wore on, Jamison made his way to Laine's side as often as possible, engaging her in meaningless conversation, and complimenting her at every turn. After awhile, he drew her aside to speak to her privately.

"My dear Laine, I had hoped that we might spend some time together discussing possible solutions to our business difficulties. But, I must say I've grown more interested in knowing you personally, discovering more about the charming and lovely lady from the East." He took her hand to kiss it. "Will you grant me the honor of having dinner with me one evening very soon?"

"I'm afraid that won't be possible, Mr. Hadley," Laine answered coolly.

"If you're concerned about waiting an appropriate mourning time for my father, I assure you . . ."

"No, that's not it at all. I simply don't want to be unfair to you. I couldn't consider seeing you socially, because . . . well, because I'm interested in someone else." Her eyes travelled over his shoulder to the far wall where Travis stood watching her.

Jamison turned in the direction of her gaze, spotted Travis, then turned back to her with a half sneer playing at the corner of his mouth.

"Mitcham? My dear, you'd be wise to give up that notion. I gather he has neglected to tell you one small piece of information."

She looked up at him, a question tightening her delicate features. He leaned close to whisper in her ear.

"Mitcham's formally engaged to my sister. They were forced to put off announcement because of Father's death, you understand."

Laine's face blanched. How could that be? She and Travis had grown so close. At the Harmons' table they'd joked about LaBelle's appearance at the construction site. And then when they'd gone out for an evening ride, he'd wanted her, she was sure of that. Then how . . . ? No, Jamison must be lying.

"Travis!" A shrill voice came from the doorway.

Laine turned in time to see LaBelle Hadley in a long black gown sweep across the room to where Travis stood, and throw her arms around his neck.

Travis's arms went around LaBelle in a loose embrace, but his gaze sought out Laine. She stood paralyzed, her eyes full of pain. Her face dropped, and Jamison Hadley grinned at her side. She put down her teacup and started toward the door.

Travis disentangled LaBelle's arms from around his neck, and followed her. "Laine, wait!" he called after her. He reached her side just as she was leaving with Buck and Molly. "Wait for me," he said quietly, "we can leave together."

Laine walked briskly down the walk to the Harmons' carriage. "Oh, I wouldn't dream of tearing you away from your fiancée," she retorted over her shoulder, and climbed into the carriage. Buck slapped the reins, and the carriage pulled away.

Jamison came up behind Travis and clamped a hard hand on his shoulder. "That's the trouble with women, Mitcham, they're so fickle. But, don't you worry. The little lady has consented to let me help her forget her disappointment in you."

Travis wrenched his shoulder out of Jamison's grip. "Don't count on it, Hadley," he spat, grabbing his hat from the coat rack. He left the house at a run to where his horse waited.

On the way out to the Harmons', Laine rode silently behind the older couple. Her heart ached with the hurt she felt from seeing LaBelle Hadley in Travis's arms. She'd trusted him, thought he might be growing to care for her, and she was certainly growing to care for him. No, that wasn't exactly true. She wasn't just growing to care for him. She was already in love with him, completely, totally in love with him.

Was the intimacy they shared just a ploy on his part to have his way with her? Did he think that just because people unfairly thought her mother sold her favors to men, that she would behave in the same manner? Or did he think because she'd lived and gone to school in the East, her morals were looser than the local women's?

Laine's eyes stung with hot tears, and her mind whirled. Molly must be right. Travis is very popular with the ladies, and he enjoys that status. She was just one more in his long line, and even LaBelle, who it seemed had finally persuaded him to marry her, did not have him all to herself.

Inside the Harmon home, Laine went to her room after bidding Molly and Buck a quiet good evening. A few moments later, a light knock came to her door. She opened it to Molly standing in the hallway.

"Honey, Travis is here. Says it's very important that he talk to you."

"We have nothing to say to each other," she said, wiping her eyes.

"He said to tell you that he insists you see him, that you owe that to your partner."

Partner. Laine drew in a deep breath. Yes, they were partners, she would grant him that. He had been kind to her, possibly out of the memory of their childhood friendship, helping her out with the whole legal mess her inheritance of the Smithers property had brought.

She did owe it to him to be civilized. She would do that, and then she would get over her childhood fascination with Travis Mitcham. It was probably pure infatuation, and not love at all that she felt for him.

"Very well, Molly, I'll see him."

She came out of her room and followed Molly down the hallway. Travis stood in the low light of the kitchen, his hat in his hand. Molly and Buck discreetly left the two and retired to their room.

"Laine, I'd like to explain a few things to you," Travis began.

"There's no need to," she replied over the knot in her throat. "You're quite right, we are partners, and anything personal is none of my business."

"That isn't true, we're friends, and besides you've got it all wrong. LaBelle is not my fiancée. I have no intention in this world of marrying her, or being involved with her in any way. It's all been her idea, this thing about getting married. As soon as she started talking that way, I told her we could be friends, nothing more. I thought she'd given up the notion."

"But, you were at the Hadley house today."

"That was strictly a courtesy call to pay my respects. And besides, I knew you'd be there, and I didn't trust Jamison to leave you alone, even during his father's wake. I wasn't sure you could handle a snake like that."

Laine searched his face. Perhaps she'd misunder-

172

stood Travis and LaBelle after all. And he was right, Jamison did indeed make overtures to her.

"Please believe me, Laine, I'm not engaged to LaBelle Hadley or to anyone else." His eyes pleaded with hers for some sign of understanding.

She twisted her handkerchief around her fingers. If Travis were telling the truth, she would be overjoyed. She decided to give him the benefit of the doubt.

"All right, Travis, I believe you. I'm sorry for running away like that."

His quick smiled warmed her. "Thanks. I know it's been a tense time for you, and I can see why you might misread certain things. You need some relaxation. I have an idea. There's a dance in town on Saturday night, the last one until next autumn. Would you go with me? Buck and Molly always go," he added quickly. "It would be good for you to just get out and have a good time. What do you say?"

Laine smiled warmly, her tightness relieved. "I would like that very much. Yes, I'll go with you!"

"And, there's something else, Laine, something I'd like to show you," he said carefully.

"What?"

"I think I'd rather surprise you," he said, not altogether happily. "I'm afraid if I tell you in advance, you might be reluctant to let me show you."

"Perhaps you should tell me," she replied shyly.

173

"Is it something I'm going to like?"

"I'm not sure, we'll know soon enough. I'll show you on Sunday, all right?"

She nodded.

"Good night, then. I'll see you Saturday."

He clamped his hat on his head, and left the house, leaving Laine wondering.

Chapter Thirteen

The dance was well underway in the ballroom of the Black Canyon Hotel when Laine and Travis arrived with the Harmons. Couples whirled on the dance floor, the sound of their laughter rising above shuffling feet. Swatches of blues, greens, golds, and reds swirled by them like paint strokes as the ladies twirled in their most sparkling finery, while the gentlemen moved stiffly in their unaccustomed formal suits.

A breeze floated through opened French doors, and although slight, was enough to keep the room from feeling stuffy from the otherwise warm, still night. Lamps and candles lent a golden glow to the room. A small orchestra played from one corner, the sharp notes of the violins standing out from the rest of the instruments.

Travis stood back and watched as several people made a point of greeting Laine with an official welcome to Silver Grande. Stunningly beautiful in a long deep blue gown, she accepted their welcome graciously, basking in the attention she received.

When she turned toward him, the vision made him think of a cameo portrait of an aristocratic lady. Her off-the-shoulder low round neckline was set off with pale blue lace ruffles and deep pink rosebuds at the center, repeated just above the lace bordering elbow-length sleeves.

The glow in the room enhanced the softness of her skin, tanned lightly under the Arizona sun. Her honeygold hair was caught up at the sides and piled at the top, secured with a deep pink satin rose, then twisted at the nape with the long ends fanned out on her shoulders and over the low vee back of her gown, held with another satin rose at the twist. Framed with wispy curls, her oval face was set off by long tendrils along her cheeks.

She was breathtaking, and it was all Travis could do to keep himself from sweeping her off her feet and carrying her away on the back of his horse to some stone castle on the other side of the mesa.

Together they danced, sipped punch, danced with Molly and Buck, and danced together again. Laine's face grew flushed with the complete enjoyment of the evening. Her smile, and the way her violet eyes changed in depth and hue as the evening wore on, dazzled Travis to the point where he was losing himself in the pure joy of the moments shared together.

"You were right, Travis, this is just what I needed," she laughed.

"It's a good time for me, too," he laughed back, swinging her around.

She loved feeling her hair floating out in back as

she floated over the floor in Travis's arms. Her skirts swung out and in, wrapping and slipping for an instant around her ankles as he swept her around the room in a waltz.

She saw Jamison Hadley watching them, his black eyes narrowed. What was he conniving now? She didn't want to know, and she averted her eyes lest he think she was purposefully looking at him.

The music stopped, and Laine and Travis stood applauding with the rest of the merry crowd, and then the strains of a slow beat began. Travis was about to slip his hand around her slim waist once again, when a voice came from behind.

"Time you stopped monopolizing the company of Miss Coleridge, Mitcham," Jamison clamped a hand on his shoulder and turned hooded eyes on Laine.

Before Travis could speak or Laine could refuse, he'd taken her hand and drawn her onto the dance floor, shooting a look of conquest over her shoulder toward Travis.

"Mr. Hadley, do you always just take what you want without asking?" Laine glared at him.

"If I think it's worth taking, yes. And if it isn't being cared for properly."

"And what do you mean by that?" She pushed away from his body as his grip tightened.

"I think you know exactly what I mean. Don't be coy with me, Miss Coleridge. Your face too clearly reflects what you want from Travis Mitcham. And it's quite obvious he's reserved that for someone else." He pulled her back to him and whispered close to her ear, "I understand how he's hurt you by being dishonest."

Laine flushed hotly and stiffened in his arms. "That's despicable!"

"I'm so glad we agree, Miss . . . Laine, my dear."

"Agree? *Mr.* Hadley," she breathed, her throat tight, "you lied to me about your sister and Travis. Why?"

"Me? Lie to you? I don't know what you're talking about." He swung her around sharply.

Laine caught her breath and continued. "Travis tells me he has never had any intention of marrying your sister. Apparently it's been all her idea, but he wishes for them only to be friends."

Jamison laughed, and his black eyes snapped with hard glints. "And you believe that?"

"Yes, of course. Why shouldn't I?"

He pulled her closer to him until she could hardly catch her breath, then placed his lips close to her ear, and breathed hotly into it. "I think if you'd let me share an evening with you, I could enlighten you somewhat. There's a lot more you could learn from me, Laine, and I think you're afraid of that."

She pushed hard on his chest and forcefully stopped dancing. "Really . . . Jamison, I've told you before that I don't wish to see you socially. There is nothing I want to learn from you. Now, please loosen your hold on me this instant."

She strained away from him, and at last he stepped back from her. Laine became uncomfortably aware of other couples watching them,

178

curiosity evident in their glances.

"Still holding out for Mitcham, are you? Well, listen to this, and then decide. I didn't want to have to tell you this way," he snarled, "but you give me no choice. The only reason Mitcham is snuggling up to you is so he can get his hands on that Smithers property himself. Has he bothered to tell you that the railroad will be coming through Silver Grande, and the tracks and depot are to be laid directly across the back part of that property? Oh yes, that property stands to be worth a goodly sum of money, and you can bet Mitcham wants to be on the receiving end of that little venture."

Laine's breath caught in her throat. Travis had briefly mentioned the railroad to her some time ago, but nothing was said in relation to the Smithers property. She pushed her way out of Jamison's hard grasp.

"Well, the same thing could be said about you, couldn't it, Jamison? I mean, you've been pressuring me to sell to you, spend an evening with you, and whatever else, almost from the moment I met you, haven't you?"

"I was merely trying to protect you, that's all."

"Protect me? You were trying to protect the claim you say you have on that property."

"Well, of course I thought about that, but that was secondary to your welfare. After all, my father knew your family, and he'd made the transaction with Smithers. The fact that the debt is now owed to me is not of my doing, surely you can understand

179

that. If only my father hadn't died, poor man . . ."

"I'm not exactly certain what I should understand, Jamison," Laine spoke through tight lips, "but you can be very sure I'll find out."

Hadley grabbed her arm. "While you're at it," he hissed, "ask him about his other partner in this deal?"

"Other partner?"

"Yes, *other* partner."

"I'm not certain who you mean."

"Ah, I see Mr. Honest Travis Mitcham has failed to give you yet another piece of valuable information. As I told you, there's a lot you could learn from me."

His fingers dug into Laine's arm, and he leaned into her face. She could see the perspiration dotting his upper lip, smell the acrid scent of too liberally applied cologne.

She wrenched her arm free and stormed away, leaving him standing in the center of the dance floor. Travis was instantly at her side when she left Jamison, having never taken his eyes off her from the moment she'd swung off with him.

"Travis, did you know the railroad coming through Silver Grande wants to buy the Smithers property to lay track through it?"

Travis's eyes widened, then narrowed. He remained still for a moment, then touched her arm. "Yes, I know something about that."

"How long have you known? Who told you?" she demanded.

180

Travis paused. This was not the time nor the place to tell her that her father had told him about those plans. If he'd been able to talk to her about David before this, it would have made the moment that much easier. Now he would just have to get around it temporarily until he could tell her properly about David. This was all becoming too complicated. The more he cared for her, and the longer he put off telling her about David, the more entangled everything became.

"Well," he began, "I don't exactly remember when I heard about it. I was going to tell you, but then we were going through all that with McCauley, then Hadley died, and well, it just never came up again, that's all."

Travis knew that was a weak excuse. He would have to think of something stronger than that soon. He'd received another letter from David Coleridge telling him he'd been delayed in leaving California because of details in the building of a school. But it was to be only a short delay.

Laine scrutinized his face skeptically. There was nothing more she could say now. Out of the corner of her eye she could see the Harmons making move to leave, and she waved to them to wait for her.

"I think it's time for me to leave, too." She started for the cloakroom for her cape.

"Let me take you home, Laine," Travis offered.

"No. I have a lot of thinking to do. I'll ride home with Buck and Molly." She threw the light cape over her shoulders.

"Don't forget about tomorrow, and what I have to show you."

"I haven't forgotten. That's one of my problems. I remember too much."

"I'm glad you do," he said meaningfully.

She searched his eyes. Was she fantasizing again, or did see she something more than friendship in them as he looked at her now? Was it love for her? Or was it desire for wealth through her property, if she secured it, and the railroad? And who was the other partner, if indeed he had one? LaBelle?

She watched him turn and walk back into the room, his broad shoulders squared, his muscular legs taking long strides. She wanted to run back to him, throw her arms around his neck, and shout to the crowd that she loved him. But no, she couldn't do that. She needed too many answers first.

She stopped. That was no way to leave him, with things hanging in the air like that. They'd spent a lovely time together before she'd danced with Jamison Hadley. She owed him thanks for that.

She decided to go back into the room to say a kinder good evening to him. She rounded the corner to search for him, just in time to see him swinging around the room in a spirited waltz, the elaborately coiffed and gowned LaBelle Hadley in his arms, gazing provocatively up into his eyes.

Chapter Fourteen

Sunday morning Laine took her daily sunrise horseback ride around the Harmon's ranch. She was almost back to the corral before she stopped to watch the sun steaming steadily upward. Illuminating the harsh beauty of the panorama, it cast a subtle bronze and gold wash over the dusty flatlands, then rolled up the mesa to sit atop the red-brown rocks as if on a pedestal.

Her mare whickered at the sight of the other horses in the corral noisily munching a breakfast of grains and hay, comforting sounds to Laine. She was so caught up in the intrigue of the sunrise that she was unaware of soft footfalls behind her.

"Never ceases to amaze me, too," Travis said quietly.

Laine jumped, causing the mare to react as if spurred for a run. She deftly drew her around with a firm pull on the reins, gently patting the sleek neck and speaking in soothing tones.

"Say, you're getting good at that," he said brightly, admiring her equestrian skills.

His eyes made a slow sweep over her, appreciative of her appearance. The evening before she'd been a stunning lady in blue taffeta, and this morning she was as warm and bright as the sunrise in a blue plaid shirt, buckskin divided riding skirt with matching vest, and brown riding boots. He sucked his breath in sharply.

"Thank you," Laine replied evenly. "You startled me, and Lady, too."

A rush of heat spread over her face. The early morning rides always exhilarated her, leaving her flushed and full of energy. Seeing Travis this morning heightened that exhilaration, yet caused a heaviness in her heart. She hadn't slept all night because she couldn't get the picture out of her mind of him holding LaBelle in his arms at the dance. And she hadn't been able to erase Jamison's words either.

Travis reached out and grasped the mare's bridle while she dismounted. They fell into smooth strides side by side as they led Lady toward the corral. Each was silent, appearing to wait for the other to speak, as if this meeting might be different from all the others. The memory of the evening before lingered in the minds of each of them, but for different reasons.

When they reached the corral, Laine released the bridle and carefully removed the bit from the mare's mouth. She seemed so small and vulnerable to Travis, no match for the wiles of that pair of coyotes, McCauley and Hadley. Yet, she'd surprised him with her cool head and calm determination in the meetings with them.

Laine went around the mare and opened the cinch on the saddle, then reached up to grab the pommel. She was about to slide the saddle down, when Travis moved in and lifted it off the mare's back, and flung it up to straddle the fence. Laine pulled the saddle blanket off Lady's back, and with a light tap on her rump sent her into the corral with the other horses. She shook the blanket and flung it over the fence.

She was the first to break the heavy silence. "I thought if Percival had uncovered something important that might be helpful to us, we'd have heard from him by now," she said without looking at Travis. "I haven't heard a word from him. Perhaps he was worried about what McCauley might do to him, and changed his mind."

"Boynton!" Travis ran a hand through his hair.

"What? Have you heard from him?" Laine's eyes were wide with flecks of golden fire jetting through their blue-velvet depths when she looked up at him.

"Boynton has been sneaking up on me in the damnedest places, skulking behind buildings and lurking in alleys, making sign language at me." Travis waved his arms through the air describing Boynton's gestures.

"Strange little man," Laine affirmed, "but I think he genuinely wants to be of help to us."

Travis nodded agreement. "He'd say your name in a loud whisper, look over his shoulder, then dart into the nearest doorway as if McCauley were just a step behind him," Travis went on, laughing. "I figured if he had something important to tell me, he'd come out with it sooner or later. Then, last night . . ."

"What happened last night?" Laine pressed him.

"I stopped at my office after the dance. When I was leaving, I went to get something out of the buckboard, when this claw came out and grabbed my arm. Damned near gave me heart failure! I reached in and grabbed at whatever it was and yanked hard. It was Boynton, crouched down in back of the seat. I banged his head, I'm afraid. All he could do was clamp a finger over his mouth and whisper, 'ssh, ssh'." Travis chuckled at the memory.

"What was he doing in your buckboard?" Laine was getting impatient.

Catching her glare, he cleared his throat. "Well, he shoved a package into my hand, pleading for me to 'give it to Miss Coleridge, and get it back to me as soon as possible,' and then he bolted out of the buckboard and was gone."

"What package? Where is it? Did you bring it with you?"

"Yes, I did bring it. It's in the house."

Laine's impatience jumped out of control. She slammed and locked the corral gate, and started on a run toward the back of the house, Travis close behind. She reached the door quickly. He marvelled that she was not out of breath at all, and seemed more charged with excitement than he'd seen her in days.

"Where is it?" Laine asked with anticipation high in her voice.

Inside the kitchen, Travis snatched the brown

186

package from the table, and snapped the string with a nearby knife. Inside was a packet of papers tied neatly with a blue ribbon. Quickly Laine drew off the ribbon. She opened the papers and spread them out on the table, scanning them rapidly. Travis peered over her shoulder.

"This must be what he was trying to tell us about. Oh, that sweet little Percy," she murmured.

"Sweet . . . *Percy?!* Let me see those!"

Laine pushed the papers over so Travis could have a better look. Percival Boynton had painstakingly gone through and extracted or copied by hand what appeared to be every document he could find in Mc-Cauley's files that contained the name Coleridge or Smithers. A half-sheet document showing Reed Hadley's scrawled signature, and describing the nature of a debt against the saloon owed to him, was next to the last. On the bottom was a copy of Smithers' original will dated three years earlier.

"That's funny," Travis scratched his head.

"What's funny?" Laine said absently, looking over several of the papers.

"Unless there are a few things missing, Smithers mentions nothing about the debt supposedly owed to Hadley."

"What about these?" she produced the half-sheet, and one other document. "They're signed by Reed Hadley and state that any debts owed to him should be paid to his son, Jamison."

"But there's nothing here with Smithers' signature to support claims or debts against that property."

"Too bad Reed died so soon after I got here. I'm

certain he could have told me a lot about Uncle Jack, my mother . . . everything. I had no idea he was so gravely ill."

"Neither did anyone else, not that ill, anyway. His death was certainly a surprise and untimely, in more ways than one."

"What are you saying? Somebody may have . . . killed him?"

"No, I'm not saying that . . . yet. I think I'll stop in and see Doc Fletcher in the morning. Maybe he has some information he's willing to let out."

Laine began to fold each document and place it back in the brown paper. "We have to get these papers back to Percival today, or early tomorrow. He certainly did us a big favor in securing them. So thoughtful of him, and he took a big risk doing it. Everything was done so carefully." She sighed deeply.

"Almost lovingly, one might say," Travis added with playful mockery close to her ear.

Laine reddened visibly. "I guess he does like me a little."

"A *little!*" Travis dropped his head back and roared with laughter. "To get all this out of him? He's probably blind by now. Probably had to do it in the middle of the night, with only a small flicker of a candle for light!" He mimicked with squinted eyes and pinched fingers holding an imaginary pen.

"Stop it, Travis." Laine was slightly embarrassed. She looked back at the papers. "Percival has done a very important thing for me, for us. I owe a lot to him."

"Well, next time you see him, just plant your pink lips on his bowed head of thinning hair, and he'll rush right out and rob Wells Fargo for you!" he baited her. He folded his hands under his chin in angelic fashion, and blinked his eyelashes rapidly. A wide grin spread across his face.

"Darn you, Travis!" She snatched up a towel from the sideboard, and attempted to swat him with it.

"Whoa!" he laughed, dodging her reach and lunging around the table, ducking as the towel raked through the air over his head.

Laine's face was flushed with frustration at her inability to connect with her fast moving target, and the chase became more serious. He laughed heartily and sped out the back door leaving the screen to spring back in her face as she came after him.

"Travis! You get back here and take what's coming to you," she laughed.

She flew out the back door and ran after him, her boots making little clouds of dust as they came down hard in the dry earth. She could hear his laugh echo as he ran around the barn, and it intensified her chase. Hot on his trail, she ran into the barn. Spinning around right, and then left in the scattered straw, she could not see him anywhere.

"All right, Travis, come out, come out wherever you are! I give up," she lied, laughing lightly. No response. "Travis, come on out," she called sweetly, but her voice betrayed her frustration.

She crept around a huge pile of straw, then behind a small storage area. He wasn't there. She walked back toward the middle of the barn again, her chest heaving for breath in the dry, still air, her pulse pounding in her ears.

From above her head came a mocking chortle. Looking up, she caught a glimpse of Travis overhead in the haymow, laughing from behind a pile of hay. He pushed on the pile, and it descended in a tumble to land directly on her head, covering her hair and shoulders. It wasn't heavy, but in her surprised reaction she fell to the floor under the heap of it.

Kicking and spluttering, she fought her way out of the loose hay, the towel still clutched in her hand. Now she was spitting mad in her frustration, and more determined than ever to get her hands on him and . . . what? She wasn't sure yet.

His face appeared once again from over her head in the haymow. "There you are!" she pointed up at him, and he fell back in convulsed laughter.

She drew herself up to her feet quickly and ran to the wood ladder leading up to the mow. Swiftly she went up the flat rungs and dropped to her knees at the top. Travis apparently had not heard her, for he was flat on his back in the thick hay, still chuckling to himself.

Laine leapt up from her crouched position, shrieking and kicking hay up to cover him. Travis froze, astonishment plastered on his face, as the hay momentarily obstructed his view of her. She had caught him unaware for a moment, but in the next he reached out as a child would to catch the back of her leg. She tripped and landed stomach down across his chest, her face buried in the hay.

Kicking and flailing her arms and coughing from the fog of hay dust stirred in the air, she pushed into the unresisting hay trying to propel herself backward off him. He kept laughing and held her down so that she could not wrest herself free. Weak with laughter, she managed to loosen one arm, swing it around, and grab a handful of his thick hair. He reached around and playfully caught a handful of hers.

He pushed himself up, taunting her with childlike teasing, and grabbing at her hand in his hair. She grew stronger with his teasing, and turned herself around to face him, her smile brilliant, her eyes glittering.

And then their wrestling stopped abruptly, hands still caught in each other's hair. Lungs burning with the dry heat in the haymow, they breathed deeply, panting for fresh air. His sea blue eyes pierced into the blue-violet depths of her gaze, and playful teasing turned to hypnotic seriousness. He moistened his lips.

Slowly he lifted his shoulders and moved toward her, slipping an arm lightly around her waist and sliding his hand up the middle of her back. His fingers sought the back of her neck, and he lowered his eyes to her mouth, caught and held by the rose-pink fullness moving closer to his lips. The air around them crackled with electricity.

Tenderly his mouth descended upon hers, bringing her softness into his warmth. The searing meeting of their lips, and his fingers on the back of her neck, sent shock waves down to her stomach. She swayed against him, wanting him closer, yet knowing they should stop.

Using every ounce of strength she could muster in her weakening surrender to his touch and kiss, she pulled herself away. She searched his face, longing to find confirmation in it for the feelings she was experiencing inside herself. She loved him, no doubt in her mind about that. And if he loved her as well, why shouldn't they make love? Convention forbade it, never allowing for the passions that love fired. Yet, in her heart she knew she could not let it happen. What would he think of her? What would she think of herself? And, she had to admit, if he loved her, wouldn't he have begun to speak of marriage by now?

"No, Travis," she whispered, moving away from him.

He closed his eyes, and shook his head slightly. When he opened them, his heart pounded loudly in his ears at the sight of her. Her honeyed hair was tousled all around her face, with bits of straw and hay clinging to several strands. The soft swelling of her breasts, visible in the open vee of her shirt, rose and fell with her breathing, and her eyes were wide and luminous, smoky with denied desire. Everything in him ached to hold her; his hands ached to know every inch of her satiny skin.

He calmed himself. "I know. I'm sorry. I lost control, wanted you . . . too much. Please forgive me."

He rose up and helped her to her feet. She brushed her clothes and attempted to straighten her hair.

"Now then," he said quietly, taking a deep breath. "I promised to show you something today, and I think this would be a good time to go. Is that all right with you?"

She nodded silently, grateful for the change in mood, then followed him down the ladder.

Chapter Fifteen

Travis hitched up the Harmons' buckboard while Laine went into the house to leave a note for them. They pulled away from the house as the sun climbed higher and hotter.

The scenery differed little from what Laine had seen in other rides around the ranch, or between there and Silver Grande. The same sun-scorched labyrinth of barren mesas stretched out before them, while farther ahead jagged summits pointed to the stark blue and cloudless sky. A border carpet of dry brush and an occasional clump of prickly pear cactus lined the edge of the dusty gray road.

Laine silently wondered how anything lived on this parched land, but every now and then a stand of twisted pines or faintly moving aspen seemed to spring out of the gray-cream desert floor in green surprise. She remembered how thunderstorms had split the sky, then caused flash floods to rush through scoured stream beds. When she'd lived here as a child, she'd grown to hate what this uncompromising land represented. She'd never recognized the supreme strength of it, nor of the people who might tame it. She turned toward Travis, regarded him for a long hard moment, then drew her eyes back to the land stretched before her. A shiver ran up her spine and spread over her shoulders.

"How does it feel to be back now that you've settled in?" Travis broke the silence they'd fallen into since leaving the ranch.

"I've been too busy to think about it," she answered distantly. Then, turning to look behind the buckboard and then around to the side, she asked more pointedly, "Where are we? I'm beginning to feel as if I've been here before."

Without answering, Travis tugged on the right rein, guiding the horse in a northward direction. He wondered how she was going to react to this little sojourn today. And then he decided she would probably react the way she'd reacted to everything else since the first day she'd come back to Silver Grande — head on and able to handle it. At least he hoped so, and wouldn't be hurt or angry with him for what he was doing.

He smiled, remembering her spunk when he removed her boot after she sprained her ankle her first morning in town. That, and everything else since then, made him think she hadn't lost that passionate will for life lived her own way, the thing that sustained her long ago when they were childhood friends. That was one of the things he admired about her back then, even though he'd chided her about romantic fantasies. She had more spunk than any of the other girls he'd ever known.

Laine moved restlessly about in the hard seat like an excited child, twisting side to side and around. The land turned greener as more stands of trees sprung up thicker and larger than the others they'd passed.

"I *have* been here before . . . I think," she said, trying to focus a memory.

The buckboard leaned back as the horse led it up a rise, higher and wider than any yet. They reached the pinnacle of the rise, then started a descent following the road to the left. As the buckboard started downward, Laine sucked in her breath, filling her lungs with sun-hot air that carried the faint scent of moist earth. The land around them moved up and down in a never-ending maze of gentle slopes.

They bore northward again, and then began a downward trek around to a butte that had been hidden from view by the slopes. Travis hauled the horse to a stop. The dust had become shallower as they'd travelled, until at this point the road was smooth as rock.

Laine held her breath, awed by the beauty in the landscape spread out before her like a vast canvas. The butte overlooked a wide mesa which was fitted under the rim. Below that the green and gold slopes melded into a nutmeg-colored valley corridor which slowly widened in the far distance, met at the horizon by the stark blue of the sky. To the left of the widest part of the valley lay an arroyo carved by a running stream.

Laine was rooted to her seat, not a muscle moving in her body. Travis sat silently watching her watching the living land beneath them.

"Where are we? What is this?" she begged him.

Again he did not answer, but urged the horse forward in the direction of the valley. Laine rode without speaking then, absorbing as much as she could of the splendor as it washed over her in constantly changing motion. Every now and then she cast a questioning glance at Travis, but he drove in silence.

As they drew nearer the arroyo, a grove of trees formed a lazy, soft curve. It seemed to Laine that they had not grown in wild abandon, but rather had been carefully placed by a sensitive painter, an inhabitant of the valley with an eye for art and beauty. Again she felt a vague sense of recognition, and looked to Travis for the answer. He stared straight ahead.

"Travis, please, what is this? Where are we?" she implored him, grasping his sleeve with both hands.

At last he offered, "You'll see in a minute."

They rounded the tree grove, and came upon a drive flanked by huge century plants and red-brown pock-marked rocks. He looked over at Laine, but she did not see him. She was locked in a gaze toward the end of the drive, straining to see what lay at the end of it. The horse snorted impatiently, the smell of water in her flaring nostrils, perspiration glistening on her coat. Travis let her move into the drive.

Slowly they rounded the bend, the buckboard creaking in the silent air as it moved past tall saguaro cacti in long columns standing sentry on either side of the drive. At the horizon of the next rise, red tiles gleamed in the sun, a heat mirage floating over the tops of their curves. The tiles seemed to move out of the earth as they neared, and with them rose the pink-hued adobe walls of a Spanish hacienda.

"This is where I live, Laine. This is my home," Travis said, pulling the horse to a stop.

Laine's hand flew to her open mouth, as her memory became clearer . . . this had been her home, too, a long time ago. He helped her down from the buckboard, and she stood still, leaning against it, just looking at the house.

At last she found the strength to move away, and started to walk around the house, touching the adobe walls, and looking in the windows. Travis opened the front door and ushered her inside. She moved shyly at first, then resolutely as she headed to the inside rooms of the fourplex. Wandering purposefully throughout the house, she paused briefly in each room, then moved on to the next. Travis followed a discreet distance behind her, watching her. Whenever her face was turned toward him, he tried to read her eyes, but they were expressionless.

The sun had long passed its peak and was moving westerly across the steel blue sky, its lowering rays casting lacy shadows through low pines onto the veranda in back of the house. Laine leaned against a cracked wall in the middle of the veranda, at the edge of which grew tall grasses and gnarled roots that provided homes for reptiles. She was so lost in deep thought, their scurried slitherings escaped her view.

Travis stood silent at the far end of the veranda. Every now and then he raised his eyes to read her face, hoping he hadn't made a mistake bringing her here to her childhood home. She'd been born here, had lived here with her parents until they'd lost everything they had and were forced to move into town.

At last he spoke to her. "Laine, are you all right?" he whispered. She didn't move. "I thought you ought to see the house, and I wanted to be the one to show it to you before someone else mentioned it to you. Do you remember it very well?"

She pushed herself away from the wall and walked toward him, her boot heels making a muffled noise on the flat stones of the veranda.

"Yes, I'm all right. I don't remember it vividly . . . I was very young. But some of it I do remember, and I can feel it. This is your home now?"

He nodded. He wanted to add that he owned only half of it. The other half was owned by her

199

father who couldn't bring himself to relinquish all rights to it. But he couldn't tell her that yet; it wasn't the right time. When, oh when, would be the right time? He was beginning to think there would never be one.

"I think I must have been happy here," she smiled at last. "I feel as if that were so. Maybe it's memory, or maybe it's because you've made it a home, but it feels comfortable." She walked to the end of the veranda, and, leaning on a white pillar, looked down across the valley to the table rocks beyond. "I'm glad you brought me here. So much of my childhood seemed dark, but being here now makes me believe that there was once a lot of light, a lot of happiness." She sighed. "My mother must have adored it here."

Travis dragged in a hard breath. "Yes, and I'm sure your father did, too," he ventured. "It must have been very difficult for them to leave it."

"It's his fault we had to leave it," she responded sharply, and Travis knew not to pursue the subject for the moment.

She walked back inside the house, and he followed her. Her footsteps echoed slightly on the tile and stone floors.

"It's a beautiful house," she breathed, touching huge ferns in terra cotta pots, running her fingers over polished wood doors and casings, and taking in the earth tones and desert colors of the mats and rugs strewn under wood and leather furniture. "And you've made it a beautiful home." She

200

started down a narrow hallway dotted with recessed hollows where thick candles or short round cactus plants nestled. "What is in the back wing?"

"Those are the bedrooms," he said, following close behind her.

She peeked in each of three, smiling. "I don't remember details, but I do have vague pictures in my head. Do you know which one might have been mine?"

He took her into a sunny room with a wide window overlooking the stream in the back. "This one looks as if it would be the perfect room for a little girl," he laughed, opening the door wide. He knew this room had been hers; David had mentioned it at the time they'd settled the financial agreement on the house.

She stepped into the middle of it. The lowering sun streamed into the room through the wide window, bathing her in a glowing column. Travis thought she looked as if she belonged in this room.

"I think you're right. A little girl could be very happy in this room. This little girl could have been happy in this room." She turned round and round. "Is it ever used now?" Her question was timid. If he were not the kind of man who wanted to be married, did he invite his lady friends to visit him here in this lovely house? If he did, did they sleep in one of the guest rooms, or . . . ? She thought of the lovely dark-haired woman close in his embrace, and of LaBelle Hadley floating in

201

his arms at the dance.

He shook his head. "Not since I've lived here." Laine wasn't certain how to take his response. "Down this way is the last of the bedrooms," he said, leading her down the hallway.

He pushed the door wide to reveal a spacious, open room with wood ceiling beams, and a gleaming wide planked floor. A massive bed with a high dark wood headboard dominated the white walled room, and two high windows side by side framed the stand of cottonwoods just beyond them outside. A low white stone fireplace occupied the wall opposite the bed, and in several wall niches sconces held thick candles.

"Ah, the master bedroom," she declared, not stepping inside.

"Yes, sometimes it seems too luxurious for a man like me. I should probably have a bunkhouse with a cot or something," he laughed.

"On the contrary," she said, thoughtfully, "it suits you, I think."

"I think it would," he responded quietly, "with the right woman in it."

He stepped into the room and drew her in with him. Her heart thumped wildly against her chest, and his hand over hers generated a heat she'd never known before.

She withdrew her hand slowly. "I . . . I think perhaps we should start back now. The sun is already setting, and it gets dark so quickly out here."

"That's the wonderful thing about this room," he said lightly.

"What is?"

"Watch."

He went over to the windows and pulled on a long white rope first on one window, then on the other. Bleached muslin shades rose in deep folds to stop a few inches from the casing tops where the ends of the ropes were wrapped around hooks. An expanse of sky above the trees was opened to view, showing a light dusting of stars in the early evening sky.

Striking a long wooden match against the inside of the fireplace, Travis moved around the room with its flame and lit the candles in all the niches and alcoves, and the room was bathed in a soft glow.

"It's beautiful," she whispered. In fact, it's magical, she thought, the kind of room that cast a spell over a person and made her feel ethereal, awake inside a fantasy. She walked to the windows to gaze out at the mauve-shadowed twilight.

"And you are beautiful," he whispered from behind her.

Slowly she turned to face him. He drank in the loveliness of her face, the soft curves of her body, and took a step closer. When she didn't back away, he came still closer, until he stood tall above her, gazing down into the dark depths of her violet eyes.

A piece of hay still clung to a wave in the hair

at the side of her face, and he reached out to gently take it away. The backs of his fingers grazed her cheek, and the sense of its softness stayed with him. He turned his hand over and placed the palm lightly over her cheek, the tips of his fingers resting in her hair.

He drew her face closer to him as he bent his head. He lingered a moment, his lips hovering above hers, and then lightly kissed her. She did not resist, and he felt encouraged to continue. He lifted his lips away, then lowered them and kissed her again. Once again he lifted his lips from hers, opened his eyes and drew in her beauty. Her eyes were closed, lips parted slightly.

He gazed at her lovely face, desire mounting with every moment she was this close to him. It surged along his nerves, heated his blood, and settled in his pulsing desire. He wanted to crush her to him, fill his senses with the very essence of her, fill her with the heat and power of his feelings and desire. Yet in the back of his mind echoed his own voice, cautioning him to move very slowly.

She parted her lips slightly, and moaned faintly, slipping her arms around his neck. Her mind swirled dizzyingly. She wanted him as she'd wanted no other man ever in her life, and she knew there would be no other man she would ever want in this way.

If that were so, then she longed to give him her ultimate gift of love, and she would have this moment for herself, forever. The echoing voice of her desire fought and won over the insistent voice that warned her against such behavior. She melted into his arms, entwined her fingers in his hair, and pulled his mouth down to hers, her lips trembling at the burning touch of his against them.

Travis could take no more. His resistance crumbled, and scooping her up in his arms, he carried her to the massive bed, and laid her down gently on the blue coverlet, never taking his lips from hers. Then slowly he lifted his mouth away from hers and held her head in his hands. Her eyes were closed, lips parted, breasts rising and falling.

"God, I love you, Laine," he whispered huskily. "I think I've always loved you. And you've probably always known that in your incredibly intuitive mind, haven't you?"

Laine gazed up at him, knowing her heart was in her eyes, her passion fueled by his words. "I only know I've loved you all my life, and dreamed you'd fall in love with me and want me."

He kissed her deeply, reluctant to release her lips. "I think we're about to make both of our dreams come true."

Fierce hunger boiled up and out of him like a hot spring. He dragged in a deep breath, lowered his body over hers, his fingers closing on the thick softness of her hair, entangling golden curls in his grasp. His mouth came down hard on hers, devouring her lips, his tongue probing the inner moistness of her mouth, his hands moving her head with the intensity of the kiss.

Laine arched her back, matching the strength of his relentless desire as her hands rubbed up and down along his spine. His tongue probed deeper, sending streaks of lightning pulsing through her stomach down to her thighs, setting them afire. Her own tongue responded to his, meeting it, circling it, then pushing insistently into his mouth, flicking enticingly behind his front teeth.

His hands released her hair, travelled down her back, and below to cup her firm round buttocks. He pulled her hard against him, and she felt the taut muscles in his thighs, and a pulsing hardness burning against her.

Travis drew his lips away from hers and gazed down into her eyes now filled with desire. He whispered her name over and over, traced her cheekbones with his thumbs, lightly kissed her eyelids, her hair, her forehead, the tips of her ears as he murmured to her.

His lips and tongue floating over her ears as he spoke sent a shudder through her throat and a tingle down her arms. His lips moved over her skin. She uttered a low moan, closed her eyes and let her head fall back, offering her throat to the touch of his lips and tongue. Her insides burned as if licked with constantly moving flames.

Carefully he removed her clothing with a combination of hands and kisses, his breath cooling then heating her skin in small circles until she felt she could take no more without erupting into a million fiery embers. His movements were intuitive and so subtle that it seemed to her he was motionless until the sensation of his actual touch inflamed her skin.

Slowly he slid his hands up to cup her softly rounded breasts. His thumbs hovered over the budded tips, and she shuddered lightly, her breath catching in her throat, as her breasts swelled to fill his hands.

A small sprig of green-tipped hay, trapped inside her blouse during the tussle in the haymow, lay in the moistness on the curve between her breasts. Slowly he lowered his parted lips, stopping for a brief moment over it. His light breath over her breasts sent a chill through her, and her nipples pushed longingly against the pads of his thumbs. He dropped his lips over the feathery branchlet, and with a light flick of the tip of his tongue, lifted it gently from her fevered skin.

He raised his face to hers, the green leaf held between his lips, his eyes fired with passion. She reached out a hand and removed it. With the other she caressed his lips with one finger, then two, then gently parted them to receive the moist warmth of her mouth. Placing both hands on his face, she gently tilted it upward and pulled his bottom lip between hers, breathing in the masculine scent of him.

When he disengaged his lips from hers, he leaned above her. A delicate scent of roses radiated from her body and saturated his senses, pushing his passion to its limits with tumultuous strength.

Lifting her upper body with the pressure of his hands under her breasts, he bent his head to the rise and fall of their softness, licking the salty moistness from her skin, softly kissing the rising mounds. She strained her aching breasts to his hands and mouth, and he kissed and nuzzled first one firm tip and then the other.

His lips moved between her breasts, then down to her stomach. His hands slipped down and closed over the soft roundness of her hips.

He stood up and tore off his clothes, and the moving candlelight danced lightly over his magnificent golden muscled body. Laine thought she could never get enough of gazing upon him in his supreme masculinity. His startlingly blue eyes burned over her, and her body began to tremble.

She wanted to beg him to claim her now, but no voice came. Instead she was sent to an even higher plane of private ecstasy as his hand moved down to caress the soft moist folds between her legs. With a low moan Laine tilted her head back.

Her unspoken need for him radiated out of the violet depths of her eyes, and when she reached out her arms, inviting him down to her, the pulsing urgency in his mounting desire exploded in a sweep of hot demanding kisses over her face and yielding body.

In aching response to her own desires, she matched his demanding body and mouth with demands of her own. His eyes closed in abandon as his hard warmth moved slowly along the inside of her thigh toward the moist vee between her legs, then thrust gently but insistently against the heated barrier. She arched her back and met him tentatively at first, then with equal strength, and his second thrust brought them deeply together.

Arching higher to bring him deeper, she cried out in the exquisite pain and thrill of it. He pulled away, then thrust again. Instinctively she wrapped her legs over his back and strained to him until their waves of emotion brought them to dizzying heights, spreading through each of them like silken connecting threads.

Slowly their mutual passion subsided until he lay sprawled alongside her body, their feverish skin still clinging together, their breath slowing. He pulled her into his arms. She rested her head in the hollow between his neck and shoulder, and sighed against him as his lips brushed the top of her tangled hair.

"I love you, Laine. God, how I love you," he whispered into her hair.

"I know," Laine whispered, "and I know now what it feels like to have a fantasy become real. I love you, my prince, my hero."

Slipping an arm over his ribs, she slid her palm up the middle of his back. Silently they held the moment locked between them.

The frantic pounding of his heart slowed to a comforting hypnotic whisper in her ear, and she drifted into a half sleep as the even rise and fall of his chest lulled her with a rocking motion. He curled a protective arm around her shoulders, and the tension in her muscles released, allowing her body to mold into his hard contours.

And together they drifted away into the deep sleep of lovers.

Chapter Sixteen

A warm, bright light fell across Laine's eyelids, rousing her from a deep sleep. As consciousness slowly rose to the surface, she stretched her body's length, unfolding like a sleepy cat. Her hands trailed over smooth white sheets, and the smell of coffee drifted into her senses. She moved her hand along the sheet until it rested on another pillow and nestled into the deep impression left from a sleeping head, not her own.

She bolted upright. Forcing her eyes open and blinking them to focus, she suddenly remembered where she was. This was Travis's house, his bedroom, his bed, and . . . she was naked in it! Pulling the quilt up under her arms, she whirled her head around to the expanse of bed next to her. It was empty except for rumpled bedclothes and the pillow with the round impression in its feathery plumpness.

Had she dreamed last night? Had she and Travis made exquisite love in this big bed? She ran her hand over the sheet. It was cool. She remembered coming here yesterday afternoon, remembered discovering this house had once been her home. And she'd come into this bedroom with Travis on a tour of the house. He'd carried her to his bed, and they had shared lovemaking more beautiful than she'd ever fantasized. Closing her eyes and sighing, she dropped back down on the pillow.

"Well, it's about time, sleepyhead," Travis's rich voice penetrated her sharpening consciousness.

Her eyes flew open and she sat up in the bed, pulling the quilt up quickly under her chin. He came farther into the room, barefoot and naked from the waist up, wearing only his denim pants. His dark hair was still tousled from sleep, and several strands curved down over his forehead. He sat down next to her on the bed and set a tray across her knees.

"I thought you might like some coffee," he said cheerfully. "Sorry there are no roses, but I hope you won't mind a few Arizona wildflowers," he added, making a production out of fluffing a small bouquet of yellow and dark red blooms in a low vase on the tray. He held out a mug of steaming coffee to her.

She accepted the mug as if in a trance. He drank from his, watching her with a bright blue light in the ocean depths of his eyes. She sat holding the mug, staring into the flower petals.

"Go ahead, try the coffee, it's pretty good. In fact, I'm a pretty fair cook, so if you'll rouse out of that bed, I have breakfast almost ready." He sipped the coffee silently. "Well, I guess you're one of those people who never talk before breakfast. Never been one of those myself, but . . ."

"It's morning," Laine said suddenly.

"Oh, you do talk before breakfast, and with a fair measure of brilliance, too, I see. Yep, you're right, it is morning. Sunrise was gorgeous. If you get up right away, you can see the last part of it."

"I stayed here all night . . ."

"Right again."

"And we . . . we . . ." Laine scanned the bed, then looked at Travis questioningly.

Travis was silent, containing his quips. He wasn't sure how she might react to the night before. He had awakened with a sense of being fully alive and happy, more than he'd ever been before.

"Yes, we did, we made love," he spoke at last, and watched her face for her reaction.

Her eyes widened. It wasn't a dream! She had stayed in his bed with him last night, and they'd made love. And she'd willingly given to him and taken from him with all of her senses, and she'd felt glorious afterward, and completely comfortable falling asleep in the crook of his arm.

Sipping the coffee that was surprisingly very good, she searched his face. Was he different? Had she changed? Were either of them steeped in regret in the morning light? She couldn't answer the question for him, but she certainly knew she was different now. She'd given him her ultimate gift of love. It could be given to no other man ever, no matter what happened in her life.

213

Regrets? There were none, at least not on her part.

Travis watched her watching him. What was she thinking? Was she regretting what they'd shared the night before? He hoped not. He had been thrilled by it. He drained his mug. No matter what the consequence, he was determined to tell her the truth about his association with her father as soon as possible. This morning.

He'd felt that way from the moment she'd reentered his life like a blazing star. But he wanted no barriers between them. She had to know what she wanted, and he wanted only truth to be their foundation. He never wanted to stand in her way of achieving her dreams. He wanted her to know that he believed her to be a completely capable woman, all woman, the only woman he could ever want in his life, forever.

Suddenly, her eyes sparked with dark flashes. "Oh, no, the Harmons! They must wonder where I've been, why I didn't come back to the house last night! They'll worry. Oh, dear, what must they think of me?"

She set down the mug and moved the tray off her lap. He took it from her to keep it from spilling over. She leapt out of bed, sweeping the quilt around her.

"I've got to go, got to get back . . ." She spun around searching for her clothes.

"Wait, Laine," he stood up, his voice soothing. "Buck and Molly knew you were with me. They won't worry. I know them."

She stopped twisting about. "That's probably worse! They know I'm with you, and I didn't come home all night . . . they'll probably think we . . . oh dear."

"No, they won't think anything like that. Their major concern would be for your safety, and since they knew you were with me, they won't worry. And, they won't think anything bad about you. They're much too fond of you for that." He walked close to her, and put both hands on her small shaking shoulders. "There's nothing to think badly about. Is there?" He leaned down and placed his lips in the top of her wild mass of hair.

The feel of his hands warm on her bare shoulders sent Laine's mind spinning. As he leaned down to kiss her hair, his naked chest and the earthy, masculine scent of him sent her senses reeling. Her eyes fell on the dark hairs curling on his chest, and the tingling in her hands told her she wanted to touch them, feel them between her fingers.

She let out a small sigh, releasing some of the tension she was feeling. He slid his hands gently around the back of her shoulders and drew her inside his embrace. She dropped her head against his shoulder, her cheek resting on his chest. Lightly he stroked her back, then ran the tips of the fingers of both hands up along her spine to the back of her neck, and felt her shiver.

Closing her eyes, she rested her lips against his chest. He lowered his head until his lips, buried in her hair, lay just over her ear. His breathing sent

215

chills along her veins, warming her blood in their wake. She pressed her lips against his chest and kissed the muscle flexing there. The taste of his skin brought a desire to taste more, and she turned slightly, raising her palms to rest on his chest, and lightly pressed her lips into the curling hair over the muscles, skimming the brown points on each side.

His blood heated under her touches and kisses, and his desire mounted to the explosion stage. He leaned away from her, and she tilted her head back and opened her eyes dreamily. He slid his hands around her neck until he cupped her face. Leaning down slowly, he caught her lips inside his own and held them gently.

Slowly she slid her palms up over his chest and shoulders, and her arms encircled his neck. The quilt, draped loosely about her body, fell to the floor. She stood close to him, naked, and filling with desire to know his body intimately once more.

He slipped his hands from her face, held her lips still locked in his own, and let his palms float gently down in a mist of a caress over her breasts to her waist, over her hips, and around to cup her buttocks and pull her tightly to him. As her breasts pressed against his chest, her head tilted farther back letting her hair fall down her back in a cascade of golden waves. His tongue sought the inner sweetness of her mouth, tantalizing the tip of her tongue as it swept more frantically over and around it.

He released her and, his eyes burning with desire into hers, knelt down and spread the quilt out in a wide circle around her feet. Still on his knees he gazed up at her, took hold of her hands, and placing a light kiss on the front of each of her thighs, he pulled her down to stretch out on the quilt.

There, in the first flush of a new day, bathed in the early rose glow, their bodies sought each other hungrily, until they were spent, locked together in a complete embrace.

"I guess this breakfast might have tasted better earlier," Travis said, his eyes glittering with amusement as he bit into a less than tender biscuit.

Laine smiled shyly, pulling his borrowed blue shirt more closely around her. Her eyes flashed up once to meet his, then lowered quickly to the scoop of fruit preserves she was spreading on the biscuit on her plate. The act seemed to be the most perfectly natural thing to do in the morning.

"They're really very good," she said quietly. Better than what I could do, she added silently.

"I have a plan for today," he said evenly. "When we get into town, I think you should go over to Anson Daniels' office. I'm sure he's heard about Reed Hadley's death, but perhaps he's heard more. The circuit judge should be here soon, and you should find out what Anson wants you to do to prepare for his arrival."

She agreed. "Perhaps I should see Percival, too.

He may have found out more."

"If you do, be very careful. Don't go into Mc-Cauley's office alone. I don't trust that old buzzard one whit."

"Where will you be?"

"I'm going to stop in at Doc Fletcher's office to see if he can tell me anything about Reed's death. Maybe it was just a coincidence, and maybe not."

"Do you think Doc will tell you if he suspects anything other than a natural death? I mean, what about violating confidentiality?"

"I think he'll tell me. He's not a vengeful man, but he's certainly had his share of raw deals with the Hadleys over the years. I heard once that they never paid him a dime when he helped Elvira birth both those offspring."

"Why not? It doesn't appear they were destitute."

"She said Doc botched the deliveries or something." Travis grinned wryly. "Maybe he did, and that's why they've got such sour dispositions."

"Travis, really," Laine admonished him properly.

"Sorry. Anyway, I'll meet you at Anson's office. Will you wait for me there?"

"Yes. But I really should see Buck so he'll know I'm . . . all right."

"I can do that for you," he said, sensing her embarrassment. "That is, if you want me to."

"No, I can take care of it."

"Shall we get started?" He stood away from the table placing dishes on the sideboard.

"I'll be ready soon," she said, standing up and

making a move to leave the kitchen. She stopped and turned around slowly, an impish glint in her eyes. "That is, if I can find my clothes."

He grinned, and watched her leave, the long tails of his shirt tapping lightly on the backs of her bare legs. He sucked in his breath deeply.

Once again he hadn't told her about her father, and he didn't like it.

Chapter Seventeen

Laine sat on the other side of the desk in the tiny office of Anson Daniels as he sifted through several documents. Laine noted his youth and thought he'd grown the sandy brown moustache to make himself look older. But listening to him made her believe his youth did not alter the facts of his honesty and forthrightness.

"Your friend Boynton slipped these to me in the hotel tavern last night. He's taking an awful chance. He must be a real friend to you, Miss Coleridge."

"I believe he is, Mr. Daniels, and very honest as well. I think it's been difficult for him to work in McCauley's office once he began to learn about some of his illegal activities. But Percival needs a position that fully utilizes his abilities. He dearly wants to become a lawyer himself."

"I know. I wish I could afford to hire him, but I'm just getting started myself and couldn't afford to pay him enough to live on, let alone what he's worth."

"You will one day."

"I hope so. If what he has discovered here is legitimate, he would be an invaluable asset to this office and to any client."

"What is it?"

"Take a look at this." Daniels pushed a paper closer to her.

Laine read it carefully. "It looks like a document naming Jamison Hadley owner of his father's business interests. It encompasses everything pertaining to it. And . . . it's signed by Reed Hadley." Her heart sank. This document could mean she would indeed have to pay Jamison for the debt owed by Jackson Smithers.

"Yes, but look at this." Daniels produced another document. "This is an old deed to the property the Hadley home stands on, legitimate and verified, also signed by Reed Hadley."

Laine took the document, not comprehending yet exactly what the lawyer was trying to prove. Then she looked at the signature, and the full impact of it began to take shape. The capital letters were very much the same on both documents, but the rest of the letters in the signatures were quite a bit different.

"I see what you're trying to point out, but isn't it possible Mr. Hadley's illness may have affected his handwriting?"

"Not in that way. It might have become shakier, less pronounced, but generally the letters would keep their shape. This is firm, deft, and might suggest the signature of a much younger person than Reed Hadley was at the date of this document."

"What are you saying?" Laine asked, just as Travis entered the office. "That Jamison Hadley may have forged his father's signature?"

"I'm suggesting that it's quite possible, and in the not too recent past, as well. Percival says these documents were not in the files when he extracted the last set of papers he gave to you. If we can prove it, we have a clear case of forgery against Jamison Hadley, and sworn to by John McCauley."

"And," Travis interjected, "add to that the possibility of murder."

"Murder!" Laine swung around in her chair.

"Yes. Doc performed an autopsy on Reed, against the family's wishes and without their knowledge, and says there was enough nitroglycerine in his body to blow up a mine."

"Nitroglycerine!"

"Yes, Doc says it has some use to people with heart problems, but hasn't been completely proven yet. Apparently it was working with Reed Hadley to control his heart spasms or something, when given to him in mild doses. But a massive dose is poisonous, can kill a person, give him what appears to be a fatal heart attack from what Doc indicated."

Laine's face went ashen, and her hand fell over her own heart. "Poor Reed. But how can Doc be sure that someone, Jamison, administered an overdose?"

"He can't yet. He doesn't know who gave it to him. I guess Reed usually did it himself."

"Could it have been suicide?" Anson wanted to know.

"I asked Doc that, and he said absolutely not, that Reed was feeling positive about the way the nitroglycerine was working for him and had real plans to set about trying to right some of the wrongs he'd committed over the years. Kind of feeling repentant late in life for being given a second chance, I suppose."

Anson scratched his head. "Well, we've got to find out what really happened there. The timing couldn't be more crucial, what with the judge arriving soon. We have a lot to do and little time to do it in."

"What can we do?" Laine asked with a hint of disillusionment in her voice.

"Find a way of proving if Reed was murdered and by whom, and prove this document was forged."

She sighed, and her shoulders sank. Then she straightened. "What about the so-called debt that Uncle Jack owed to Reed?"

"I'm afraid that seems legitimate, too," Daniels replied, producing a small wrinkled sheet of paper. "As far as you can remember, is that Smithers' signature? The other one is definitely Reed Hadley's."

Laine studied the document outlining a loan to Smithers from Hadley, and nodded dully. "I can't really be sure, but it looks like it." She studied it more. "Wait, I do have something that may help. When I was a child Uncle Jack gave me a little book of poems, and he inscribed the flyleaf. It's with my things at the Harmons'. I'll bring it to you tomorrow morning."

"Fine, fine, anything will help, and we need every scrap of information we can find."

"Doc says he may be able to find out who gave Reed that final dose. I'll tell him he has to get right on that. Do you think we should let the sheriff know what we're up to?"

"Not yet," Daniels shook his head. "The fewer people who know the better, until we have more conclusive proof."

There was a hard knock on the door. The foreman for Mitcham Construction stuck his head inside the office, dusty hat in hand. "Sorry to bother you, Boss, but we've got an emergency down at the new feedmill. You've got to get down there right away."

Travis stood up. "Be right there." He clamped his hat on his head and started for the door. "Anything else right now, Anson?"

"Not at the moment. I'll keep you posted."

Travis turned toward Laine. "I'll see you later, all right? We can go out to Buck and Molly's together. I'm sure she'll be expecting us," he winked and left the office.

Laine felt a flush rise up over her face, and hoped Anson Daniels hadn't caught the subtle exchange between them.

"Well, Miss Coleridge," Daniels stood, "I wish I had more good news for you than this, but I'm afraid I haven't."

Laine rose to leave. "That's quite all right, Mr. Daniels, I think you've been doing a wonderful job on this. If you see Percival before I do, please thank him for me, will you?" She turned toward the door. "And thank you very much for everything."

"Don't thank me yet. We're not through. But, if there's a way to get your inheritance to you, I promise we will do it, and turn it over to you as soon as possible. And I'll pass on your thanks to Percival. I know he will appreciate it."

Laine left the office wondering where all this news would take her. Life with Aunt Sarah certainly hadn't prepared her to meet the kind of complications she was confronted with in Silver Grande.

She pulled her straw hat down against the glare of sun, and smiled. Life in Boston also hadn't prepared her for this hot dry climate, nor for the dust. A cowboy trotted by on a smart chestnut pony. Nor for the people, she thought. Yet, she marvelled now when she thought about how easily she had adapted to it. Perhaps that kind of adaptability was born and bred in a person.

Just like a first love, she thought, walking a bit faster along the boardwalk. Just like an only love. Right now she felt as if she'd been born in love with Travis Mitcham. He lived in every part of her mind, heart, body.

Boston hadn't taken her Arizona roots from her, nor had it taken her love of Travis.

She smiled up at the sun. Even its red hot glow didn't shine as brightly as the light inside her right now.

It was late afternoon by the time Laine finished

her errands at the bank and the emporium. She hurried to the stage depot to catch Buck. Manuel, the Mexican lad who worked for him, informed her that Buck wasn't back from the last run into Flagstaff.

She had the sudden flash of an idea. She wrote Buck a note telling him that she and Travis would be at their house after supper that night, and not to worry about her. Then she asked Manuel for the use of the small carriage and a horse Buck kept for visitors. The young man readied them for her. After a stop at the grocer's, she drove the carriage out of town in the direction of Travis's house.

She hummed as she drove over the dusty road, and fantasized the surprise she would make for Travis. She would do the best she could with a simple supper, candlelight, a nice wine. She smiled to herself at the romantic idea. The glow of their lovemaking still surrounded her.

She'd done the most improper thing a lady could ever do, and yet she had no regrets. She had done it willingly and gladly. Travis had wanted her, she knew that, but it seemed to be more than just desire. She turned her face up to the late afternoon sun. Caught by the tie under her chin, her hat fell back to lay over her long mass of hair. A breeze blew her hair out from her shoulders, and she felt full of the freedom provided by the ride and her sense of purpose.

Travis loved her, he must. She felt that as deeply as she knew the depth of her love for him, and it would be very soon that he would ask her to marry him. She knew it, could feel it intuitively. The fact that he hadn't mentioned it up to now was because of all of the things that had occupied both of their minds. But after last night, this morning, how could he not be ready to ask her?

She wanted to do it herself. She was so full of love for him, she wanted to rush to him, tell him she loved him and knew he loved her, and ask him to marry her as soon as possible. But no, that was simply not done. A lady waited for the gentleman to propose such matters. She felt amused for a moment about how she shed her lady's clothes by making love with Travis, then layered them back on by waiting for him to propose to her.

She drew the horse up in front of the house, jumped down and secured the reins. Grabbing her packages from under the seat, Laine skipped up to the front door and let herself in. She started toward the back of the house and the kitchen, then stopped, thinking she heard a voice. Listening carefully, she recognized Travis's rich baritone voice, and her heart sank. Darn, he was here, and it would ruin her surprise. Well, there was nothing to be done about that now. He would be surprised anyway that she was there, supper in hand.

She rounded the corner to the kitchen and stepped into the room. Travis stood in the center, in a pale blue shirt with the sleeves rolled, exposing tanned muscular arms wrapped around the waist of Kate Hardy.

Chapter Eighteen

Immobile, Laine stood in shock in the doorway, her heart thumping wildly. Travis looked up, obviously surprised at her presence, but did not make any move to drop his arms. Kate Hardy smiled warmly at Laine.

Laine's mind reeled with a thousand questions. She knew she'd been in a love-drenched haze since the night and morning in Travis's bed. Making love had certainly muddled her thinking, made her forget to clarify things. Things such as whether he had another partner. Was it LaBelle Hadley? Or, looking at them now, Kate Hardy?

Had she been fantasizing again about what she believed existed between Travis and herself?

Realizing suddenly that she must be standing there with her mouth open, Laine regained the use of her voice and spoke. "I . . . I'm sorry, I didn't know you were here. No sign . . ."

"Laine! What a pleasant surprise!" Travis dropped his arms at last, took Kate by the hand, and walked toward Laine. "I thought I'd see you in town later."

"Yes, well, I thought I might surprise you . . . and I see I have."

"You certainly have," he grinned with what Laine determined was a pleased look. It bothered her. "Oh, here I am forgetting my manners. Kate, I'd like you to meet my old friend and business partner, Laine Coleridge."

Old friend! Business partner! Laine fumed. He really was incorrigible, standing there holding the hand of a trusting young widow and introducing her as his old friend and business partner. Of all the nerve. Well, she was an old friend, that was true, and she was his business partner, that was also true. But, did he behave with all of his friends and business associates the way he had with her last night? And this morning, for heaven's sake? Chagrin for those previous actions crept into her thoughts.

She calmed herself, and said politely, "How do you do?"

"Well, I'm just fine . . . now," Kate responded with a bright, disarming smile. "And Travis has told me so much about you."

I wish he'd told me as much about you, Laine thought.

"Laine," Travis broke in, "this is my cousin, Kate Hardy. She lives near here, so drops over occasionally. I'm sure you'll be seeing a lot of each other."

Cousin! Now, how could he expect her to believe a thing like that? Laine seriously doubted she would want to spend much time with Kate Hardy. Cousin, indeed!

"Cousin," Laine said flatly.

"Yes," Kate replied. "Travis's mother and my father were brother and sister. There's quite a bit of family resemblance, don't you think?" she added in a friendly tone, leaning her dark shining head close to Travis's for comparison.

I hadn't noticed, Laine thought. "Yes, I think I can see that a little," she said instead.

"And Travis has just agreed to help me out with something," Kate went on happily.

"Oh? In what way?" Laine didn't really want to know, but politeness forced her to ask.

"He's offered to take my son, Tad, under his wing, give him work in construction, guide him a bit. Ever since his father died he's lost interest in everything except getting into difficulties with some of his friends. It's been getting more serious. Travis has generously offered to help Tad regain some direction, maybe even help him think about going into the family business with him someday. For that I am eternally grateful." She leaned up and kissed Travis on the cheek. "You are a good friend, Travis . . . for a relative," she laughed.

Kate picked up her bag from the kitchen table and started toward the back door. "Well, I have to get home now. Laine, it is so very nice to meet you, and I do hope we see each other often. It's difficult out here to make many good women friends, and I am truly in need of one." She opened the door and stepped out onto the back veranda. "Thank you again, Travis. You'll never know how much this means to me."

"I'm glad I could help. Wait, I'll walk out with you to your carriage. Back in a minute, Laine, don't go away," Travis winked at her over his shoulder, then walked out with Kate.

Laine turned her back to the door. Cousin. Kate Hardy was Travis's cousin! Something told her she could believe them. Fervently she hoped she hadn't appeared standoffish to Kate or jealous to Travis. Kate was no rival, might even become a friend, a lovely friend. But, if Kate were not a rival for Travis's affections, why hadn't he even hinted of something more permanent with her?

She certainly couldn't ask him a question like that. Could she? She set her chin higher and sniffed a short breath. Her pride would never let her do that. Perhaps he wasn't interested in marriage with her or . . . marriage at all. Her chin dropped. Perhaps he only wanted her for. . . .

Laine heard Kate's carriage leaving the yard. The back door opened quickly, and Travis stepped in, beaming.

"Well, what do you think of my beautiful cousin Kate?"

Laine turned around slowly, her pulse pounding loudly in her ears. "She is that, beautiful. I didn't know you had family left around here."

"I haven't really. Just Kate. She's had a rough go of it lately. I try to help her out now and then. She's getting along pretty well now, except for my nephew. But, I'll straighten him out," he said firmly, but Laine heard the care in his voice.

"I believe you will," Laine remarked sincerely.

Travis came closer to her. Even from a few feet away she could sense the disturbing warmth of his nearness. "And to what do I owe this lovely surprise

231

visit?" he asked in a low, husky voice.

"Oh, nothing really, I just . . ."

"What's this?" He looked at her packages, then spread them out over the sideboard, peering into each of them. "Food!" He spun around to face her. "You brought supper!"

"It's not much, I just thought I'd . . . but, perhaps I should be getting over to Buck and Molly's. I never did see him today, left him a note saying we'd be out after supper. I've borrowed the depot carriage."

"Well, then, that's exactly what we'll do. We'll go out there after supper. If I'm to be treated to a home cooked meal by a lovely lady, I will not be cheated out of it! I might even help, unless, of course, you've changed your mind." He looked pointedly into her eyes.

"No . . . I haven't changed my mind." She thought for a moment about leaving, but then quickly discarded the idea. What could repaying his hospitality hurt? If she left, he would think she was jealous or didn't really believe him. No, she would stay. They were, after all, friends . . . and business partners. What harm could having supper together do?

"Great! Say, tonight might be a good night for a fire in the outdoor fireplace. We could have supper on the back veranda. What do you think?"

"That sounds very nice," she answered, "I'll get things started in here."

She started taking things out of her packages, and he went out back. A few minutes later she heard him whistling and collecting kindling wood and logs. A shiver ran over her body. How often had her mother cooked meals in this house while her father worked outside?

She looked around at the walls and cupboards. Near the stove a well-worn narrow door covered a small cupboard. She touched the wood, and her hand stayed as if held by a magnet of time and senses. She felt her mother's presence, and involuntarily looked over her shoulder half expecting to see Elizabeth standing there. She shivered again, and shook away the feeling.

A struggle ensued within her. No decent and proper lady would prepare supper for a man unchaperoned in his home at night. But, since we're friends—and business partners, she added hastily— why would we need a chaperone?

No decent and proper young lady would have stayed the night and let the man make love to her either. But, she hadn't just "let" him, she'd wanted him, and she'd made love to him, too. No decent and proper young lady would have allowed such a thing to happen, unless possibly the man and woman were betrothed. Even then, it would raise more than an eyebrow or two if anyone found out about it.

And, Travis wasn't her betrothed. He was her what? Business partner, that's what. That was hardly the way business partners acted. Maybe she wasn't the decent and proper young lady she'd thought she was! But, wait, business partners do have supper together occasionally, don't they? Yes, but they're usually of the same sex. Sex. There was that unspoken word. Decent and proper young

233

ladies never, never speak that word. But, she hadn't spoken it, had she? No! She'd thought about it, though, and she'd certainly participated in it!

Yes, she had, and she'd enjoyed it very much. She supposed no decent and proper young lady would ever admit to that. No, they would never say it, but somehow she knew they would feel it. How could any woman not feel it if she were near Travis Mitcham?

Her preparations for supper were well underway when Travis came inside and began cutting and slicing onions and carrots, humming as he worked. She'd never seen a man cook before, except for the chefs in French restaurants in Boston. She enjoyed watching Travis now, and the sight of him happily engrossed in kitchen duties filled her with a sense of being cared for in a very special way.

"I see you've brought a beefsteak," he said, noting the thick piece of red meat laid out on a wooden cutting board on the table. "Ah, this is my favorite meal. Have you ever had a steak cooked over an open flame? The flavor is all smoky, completely different."

"No, I've never tasted it like that, but it sounds like it might be nice."

"It is. I'll do that tonight. The fire is going really well out back now. Is that all right with you?"

"Of course it's all right, but I wouldn't exactly say that I'm the one cooking supper for you right now," she joked, pointing at his deft slicing.

He peered around her toward the large cookstove. "You made the biscuits and the potatoes, right? Those are potatoes, aren't they?" he asked pointing at a large flat pan containing potato slices, spread out in a fan shape.

"Yes, those are potatoes," she responded indignantly. "Potatoes lyonnaise, to be exact."

"Potatoes lion maze? What's that?" He gave her a small frown.

"Lyonnaise," she pronounced it out for him. "They're French."

"Ooo la la! French potatoes! That's a new one for me, and the outdoor steak'll be a new one for you. Perfect."

He picked up the board containing the steak and went out the back door.

By the time they'd finished supper, the sun had gone down and was casting dark gray shadows along the stretch of desert behind them, backlighting them in a rose and purple glow. Spiny paloverde trees reached toward the sky with black bony fingers against the lowering glow.

Travis leaned against the rustic armchair opposite Laine, patting his stomach with the look of a fully satisfied man. He took the last swallow of wine from his glass.

"That was a wonderful supper, Mademoiselle Coleridge, right down to those lion's potatoes. And I'm sure you noticed I ate a lion's portion of them."

She smiled at him across the low fat candle nestled in its terra-cotta pot.

"And your outdoor broiled steak was as you said it would be, delicious. I'm a bit embarrassed to say I ate enough for a lioness. Must be the air out here.

Sharpens the appetite." She sipped from her wine glass.

The wine, the atmosphere, the presence of Travis made Laine feel warm, relaxed, comfortable. Their being together like this felt right, the most natural thing in the world. She wondered what he was thinking, feeling.

Travis watched the candlelight flicker over Laine's lovely face, lingering to dance a moment or two in the depths of her eyes. He felt comfortable—in the right place at the right time with the right woman. And now was the right time to chance it—chance telling her that David Coleridge, her father, was alive, was his partner, and would be in Silver Grande in a very short time.

She looked relaxed, as if being with him in this house, this former home of her parents, was not unsettling to her. She looked as comfortable as he felt. He drew in a deep breath. He was going to tell her about David now, that was all there was to it.

He cleared his throat. "Laine, I'd like to talk to you about something very important."

Laine's heart skipped. This was it! This must be it! He was going to ask her to marry him, she could feel it! She drew in a deep breath to steady her vibrating nerves, and to be certain her voice would be calm when she responded.

"All right," she said quietly, "but would you like a bit more wine first? I think I would."

Wine. A good idea, Travis thought. "Yes, I would. I'll get it." He made move to get up, but she was up before him.

"No, I'll get it. I want to take these plates inside,

236

too." She picked up a couple of dishes and disappeared into the kitchen.

Travis stared into the dying firelight. How he hoped he was doing the right thing. Neither one of them could go on with their lives if he didn't tell her now. Once he told her the truth, and after she came to accept the fact that her father was his partner, he knew she would understand. Then they could begin to build a life together—all of them. And he wanted that now more than anything.

Inside the kitchen, Laine set the plates down and leaned against a wall. She took several deep breaths to calm her fluttering stomach and slow her crazy heartbeat. Her hands tingled again, always her signal that something exciting was about to happen, and she rubbed them against her skirt. This was the most important night of her life, and she wanted to be calm. She stood away from the wall and went for the wine bottle.

As she picked up the bottle, an envelope caught in the moisture on the bottom came with it. It must have been on the sideboard when she'd set the bottle down, and she hadn't noticed it. She pulled the envelope away and went to set it back on the sideboard, when the address printed in the upper corner caught her eye, and held her paralyzed: David L. Coleridge, San Francisco, California.

She stared long and hard at the name. David L. Coleridge. Her father, it had to be her father. But how . . . ?

She looked at the name of the addressee: Travis R. Mitcham. What . . . ? How could this be . . . ?" How did Travis know her father? And for how long? Why hadn't he told her? How could he have kept this from her?

Against the backsplash of the sideboard, a white paper lay open, one end folded neatly up toward the middle. From where she stood she could see the Coleridge name again printed at the top of the page. Woodenly she reached out and pulled the paper toward her. She lowered the folded end. It was a letter to Travis from David, and it was very informal, as if they'd been corresponding more than just this one time. And then she read the last sentence.

"In all the years we've been partners, Travis, I look forward most to working with you on the railroad construction through Silver Grande. See you soon."

Partners! Travis was a partner with her father! He must be the one Jamison referred to. How had he known? Did everyone know? Everyone but her? How convenient for Travis! He just seemed to go about amassing Coleridge partners!

And the railroad . . . why had he not spoken much about that? He'd said Jamison Hadley was interested in the Smithers property because the railroad might be coming through that parcel. Maybe that was a cover up for him, something to throw her off the track. Maybe it was really Travis who was interested in getting his hands on that property, not Jamison! He wanted it for his own gain, and her father's!

Was it possible . . . was it possible Jamison had been telling the truth all along, and not Travis? Had she been so blinded by her feelings for him she couldn't see the truth?

It seemed Travis was not what she thought, not what she'd dreamed about all these years. He would stop at nothing to get what he wanted, even make love to her if need be to throw her off the track. Probably Anson Daniels, Travis's lawyer after all, and Percival Boynton, too, were in on the ruse. She hadn't even suspected. . . . How could she have been so blind to the game? She crumpled the letter in a tight squeeze.

The wine bottle slipped out of her hand and fell to the floor, shattering in a thousand pieces.

Travis raced through the back door. She stood motionless. "Laine! What happened? Are you all right?"

He searched her face, then dropped his eyes to the shattered bottle on the floor. Raising his gaze to her, he saw that her face was masked, devoid of emotion. And then he saw it, the letter clutched in her hand. Damn! He'd been reading it when Kate arrived, and he'd simply thrown it on the sideboard. He never meant for Laine to see it, at least not until he had the chance to explain things to her. Now it was too late.

"Laine, let me explain everything . . ."

She held up her hand to stop him and spoke wearily, "Please . . . don't bother. I think it's quite obvious what's going on. I've been a fool."

"No. No, that isn't so. Sweetheart, please let me tell you about this, about him. I've wanted to right from the beginning, but you wouldn't let me."

She nodded dully, the letter still clutched in her hand. "You're right. I didn't want to hear about him." She sighed, her throat constricted, and then

239

anger flared inside her and erupted. "But that didn't give you license to lie to me, to cheat me, make love to me, make me think that you loved . . ."

She couldn't finish. One brand of humiliation was enough without adding that she'd thought, had dreamed, they might someday be man and wife.

"Cheat you? I didn't do that, would never do that!" Travis stepped around the broken glass to get to her. He tore the letter from her hand and threw it on the sideboard. "As for lying to you, I didn't do that either, unless it was a lie of omission. Please let me explain it to you now . . ."

"No, I said I didn't want to hear about him, and I still don't, regardless of the fact that he's your . . . partner. Partner . . ." Her voice trailed off into thought. Then a new understanding formed in her mind. "Partner! You're a partner with my . . . with David Coleridge, and in the process it appears you've made me his partner, too! How could you have done such a vile thing? Well, our partnership is dissolved from now on. I . . ."

"That does it." He took her by the shoulders and sat her down firmly at the kitchen table. "I don't care if you want to hear this or not, you're going to. And you're not leaving here until I've had my say, all of my say. And I'm sorry, but I do not accept the dissolving of our partnership, but right now that's not important."

She said nothing, was too weak to move. All she could do was sit staring at her folded hands on the table.

"Your . . ." Travis began again. "David Coleridge and I became partners quite by accident. There was a logging company near the border of the territory and California. I'd put a bid on some timber they had, and so had he. The logging company manager told us each about it, hoping to make double the money in profit.

"Long story short, we began to correspond, found each other easy to negotiate with, and started helping each other out when supplies were scarce for one or the other. That evolved into some building projects both here and there, and eventually in a meeting. We've actually met only twice in the last three years."

She looked up at him once during his explanation, and that was to register surprise that their partnership had started as long as three years before.

Travis continued. "I told him I had the opportunity to buy this house, and asked him if he wanted it himself, or minded if I bought it. He said he couldn't bring himself to come back here, and that he was glad that I wanted it. The bank owned it by that time, so I bought it and simply added his name as co-owner without telling him. It had lain empty for years, and he said he always felt sad about that. It had been a wonderful home . . ."

Here she stopped him again. "Don't talk about that, a home. Just tell me about this partnership. I suppose you've told him about me, about Uncle Jack's place, about the railroad?" Her dark eyes flashed with lightning.

He looked down at the floor, then backed up to lean against the sideboard. "No, I haven't told him about you, that you're here. I haven't been able to bring myself to do that."

When she glared at him, he added hastily, "Whether you believe me or not, I wanted to wait until I could tell you about him first. He doesn't know about the Smithers property dispute, but he does know about the railroad. He's the one who told me about it first. However, I think Hadley had other sources and knew about it before we did. That's the only way I figure why he came back here. Must have heard about it back East."

"And what about your interest in Uncle Jack's property, my inheritance? Do you deny that if the railroad comes through it will make you rich? And did you . . . did you make love to me just because you saw yet another conquest?" Her eyes glazed over with tears, but she fiercely held them back.

He flared, then calmed, and spoke evenly. "My interest in your inheritance was exactly as you know it to be—a desire to help you get what is rightfully yours. It was in my power to do it, and I wanted to help. I said it was a loan, and I meant it. I have no financial interest in the property except for what you plan to do with it, to help you. If the railroad comes through, and I have no doubt that it will, yes, I will be rich. Not because of the Smithers property, but because of my own land beyond that, and what stretches to border the Hadley land.

"And to answer your last question, which surprises me that it even crossed your mind. I made love to you because I desired you, no one else, nothing else but you. Contrary to public opinion, I do not take 'conquests'. And, forgive me for assuming this, but I thought you wanted to make love to me, too." His gaze remained levelled on hers.

She flushed deeply and looked down at her hands. Instinctively she knew he was telling the truth. Yet, she could not forgive him for not informing her who his other partner was.

"I'm sorry I said that. I'm not thinking clearly."

She stood up and walked around the table, keeping it between them. Behind her the sun had disappeared and all was inky blackness beyond the door.

"But, Travis, I cannot bear the thought of you in business with my . . . with that man. He broke my mother's heart when he abandoned her. How could he have done that? Left me . . . He had no heart, did not care about us . . ."

"I don't believe that, Laine. I know he cares about people, and about the land. He's forcefully prevented some money-hungry people from stripping it bare of trees and plants. We've never discussed it, but I believe he must have had a very good reason to have left Silver Grande and you and your mother. If you'd only see him, ask him, I'm sure he could explain it all to you."

"Explain it!" she exploded. "Explain it! How could any father explain that he left a wife who adored him and a little girl who hardly had the chance to know him? He left them penniless, turned a beautiful young woman into a thin, weary woman who compromised all she believed in, all she was used to, first for the love of him, and then for the love of me, so she could keep us together. What kind of man deserts his wife and child, leaving them to God knows what? He probably doesn't even know she's dead or that I'm alive! Unless, of course, you told him. And if you did . . ."

Her tears flowed in steady streams down her face, her breathing labored, her voice hard and constricted. Travis started toward her to comfort her, but she put up her hands to keep him back.

"Tell me this, Travis, how was it your caring and concerned partner never once tried to see the daughter he had in all these years? Tell me that, will you? He deserted us then, and he deserted me for the rest of my life. I will never forgive him for what he did to my mother, and I feel nothing for him now because he has made it abundantly clear that he cared nothing for me. Ever."

She dropped her hands to her sides and sobbed. It suddenly occurred to her that this was the first time she'd ever let out all of her feelings about being abandoned, about losing her mother.

Travis went to her then and took her into his arms, stroking her hair. "Oh, Laine, sweetheart, I don't know why he did what he did. Only he knows that. There must be a real explanation for what makes a man do something like that. Maybe something terrible was happening to him, maybe he couldn't tell your mother, maybe he . . ."

She pushed hard away from him with her hands on his chest and broke from his embrace. "Please, Travis, don't do this. You could have told me before this that you knew him. Knew him . . ." her voice wavered, ". . . you're in business with him! That's enough for me to take right now."

She turned away from him, and Travis dropped his arms. He felt powerless to help Laine, help himself. He couldn't let things stay like this.

"Laine, please, let's not let this come between us. We need to talk more about it. Please believe me when I tell you David Coleridge would not deliberately . . ."

She spun around, and forced the words. "Please Travis, don't make things worse by defending that man to me . . . he doesn't deserve it."

"Then perhaps you'll let me defend myself," a low voice said behind them.

Chapter Nineteen

Travis's head jerked up, and Laine spun around. Outside the screen door a tall man stood in the shadows.

"Please, Lainie—let me tell you about it, let me tell you the truth."

The voice shot into her like a silver-tipped arrow, the sharp point of it piercing her heart and mind. Without truly remembering that voice, she recognized it, then recognized the tall form in the shadows. The man who rescued her the night of the fire in the hotel, the man who sent her safely on the train for Boston and Aunt Sarah's—that man was standing outside the door right now.

Instinctively she knew him. That man was David Coleridge . . . her father.

Laine backed away slowly, stopped by the impact of Travis's body behind her. No, she thought, this can't be happening. This truly must be a dream, a nightmare.

But the screen door opened, and the tall man stepped inside. His big frame seemed to fill that part of the room.

He removed his tan Stetson and held it in front of him with both hands, an action that made him look like a guilty child. A shock of gray-streaked sandy hair fell over his sun-bronzed, lined forehead, and his deeply etched features gave a cragginess to what Laine knew was once a smoothly handsome face. Impeccably dressed, he wore a perfectly cut tan jacket with brown leather trim, sharply creased brown trousers, and heavily tooled oxblood boots.

Laine almost wished he stood in front of her in rags. In her heart she longed to feel something more for him than the hate and anger she'd kept bottled inside for so long, even if only it were to pity him. But all she could feel was numb.

Travis watched David gazing at the woman who was his daughter, pain lingering in the older man's hazel eyes.

"Lainie, I can't believe this. I didn't know . . . ," he struggled, his voice thick and hoarse.

Laine said nothing. Wide and glazed at first, her eyes turned narrow and glassy hard. She spun around quickly and stepped past Travis, and he knew she was going to leave the room.

"Lainie, please don't leave, honey," the big man pleaded, his voice cracking.

She spun back around to face him, eyes blazing, mouth set in a hard angle. "Why shouldn't I?" she spat out. "You did!"

He took a step forward, and she took one back. He stopped still.

A heaviness fell over Laine's chest, and she had to fight to breathe. Her heart pounded so loudly in

247

her ears she thought her head might burst. She turned and ran through the house to the front, then outside to her buggy. She jumped in and reined the horse hard, away from that house . . . her house . . . Elizabeth's house . . . she fought back tears, and . . . David's house.

The last thought spurred on her determination to put as much distance between herself and all that house represented as there had been time between now and when she'd lived there as a baby. She drove the mare hard over the winding road toward town and was more than halfway there before she realized she might be hurting the animal.

She stopped pushing then to allow the mare to rest, and trusted it to know the way. She let the rhythmic jerk of the reins shake her arms, and the steady grinding turn of the buggy wheels vibrate the bumpy road throughout her tense body. Tears blinded her. Let the horse take her wherever it wanted to, she didn't care. There was no one and nothing left for her to trust except this horse, and this moment.

The mare slowed, and the buggy slowed, and Laine's heart and tears slowed. She reached into the pocket of her skirt for a handkerchief. If anyone saw her she didn't want it to show that she'd been crying. The mare plodded to the side of the road and stopped.

"What is it?" she whispered through the dark night toward the animal's pricked ears.

"You know, Laine, it's dangerous for a lady to be out riding alone this time of night."

Jamison Hadley's voice made Laine jump inside her skin.

"What are you doing out here?" she managed to ask him when her frightened pulse calmed.

"I was about to ask you the same thing. I wouldn't think you'd ever want to come back here." He advanced toward her, and she could begin to make him out as her eyes adjusted through the pain of her tears to the darkness.

"What do you mean, 'back here'?"

"You seem upset. Don't you know where you are? You've come to the Smithers Hotel, of course. It holds so many unhappy memories for you, I'd think you'd just want to get as far away from it as you possibly could."

He placed his hand on her arm. She slipped out of his grip quickly, but the lingering pressure of it made her uncomfortable.

"No doubt so you could take it over. Am I right?" she snapped.

"Yes, you are."

"What?" Laine knew he was smiling, but his direct answer surprised her.

"You heard me, you're right. At least I'm honest about it, unlike others of your acquaintance."

Honest. Laine rolled the word around in her mind. Was Jamison being honest? She guessed he was, at least his own kind of honesty. How ironic. The man she'd regarded as her enemy might be the only one telling her the truth.

Jamison started to climb into the buggy. Laine climbed out the other side.

"Now, now, there's no reason to be afraid," Jamison said evenly. "I think you know I only want to help you."

"Out of my inheritance," Laine replied, the suspicious inference beginning to fade from her voice.

"Laine," he sighed, "we've proved to you you didn't inherit anything except debts . . . and ghosts." He crossed and got out of the buggy, standing close to her. "Why don't we let all of that rest in the past and strike a deal of our own? Leave everybody else out of it, lawyers — and partners — included? It will save us both a lot of money."

"What . . . what kind of deal?" Laine gradually realized how tired she'd become. Tonight had almost undone her. Perhaps Jamison was right. They could make their own arrangements, leave everyone else out of it, and she could go back to Boston and Aunt Sarah's way of life, and never have to see Travis — or his partner — again. Her heart ached with what she believed was Travis's betrayal. And the other one . . . she couldn't bring herself to call him her father for that would lend credence in her mind to his existence. If she didn't acknowledge him, she could forget him again just as she had before.

"What kind of deal are you proposing?" she asked Jamison again, regaining some measure of composure.

Jamison tapped his breast pocket. "I have a document here that will solve everything. I've already signed it. Now if you will . . ."

"What kind of document?" Laine's suspicions flared again, but then subsided.

"Why don't we go inside? I've brought a lantern. You can look it over and make your own decision. I'm sure you'll find I can be very generous. Come."

"In . . . inside the hotel?" Laine stepped back.

"Yes, what better place to strike our deal."

Jamison took her arm and steered her toward the front door of the saloon. She held back again, but he urged her on. Then, overwhelmed with the desire to go inside, she stumbled forward. He assisted her, and once inside he lit the lantern and set it on a table. It only vaguely occurred to Laine that he'd been here at least once before and made a clean space amidst the decaying timber. How could he have known she'd come here tonight? Even she hadn't known she would. Her intuition warned her that he'd planned the moment to happen sometime, but she ignored it.

All she could hear was the moan of the wind through broken walls as if it mourned the sad spirits who resided there. Laine felt surrounded by ghosts, could feel their mist brush over her skin, smell the curious mixture of tobacco and beer and old perfume. She shuddered.

Jamison pulled out two chairs and, placing his handkerchief over the seat of one, indicated for her to sit down. He pulled a chair close to her and took out a folded document from his breast pocket.

"As you can see here," he pointed toward a paragraph with the end of a pencil, "I'll wipe out the forty thousand dollars in debts Smithers owed my father, and therefore you owe me, plus give you ten thousand upon your signature on this agreement.

You then surrender all rights to the property. As I'm sure you can see, I'm out fifty thousand dollars, but it's the least I can do to help you through your suffering."

Suffering. Laine read the same sentences over and over in the dim flickering light, not comprehending what she was reading. Jamison's face seemed to float above the light in a yellow wash, his false smile making him look like a gypsy fortune teller. Suffering. Laine supposed one did suffer with the death of dreams, with disillusionment. Right now she couldn't think about them. She had to try to think of how she could just close the door on all of this now.

She'd come back to Silver Grande full of questions. Now she would leave with answers, even if they weren't the answers she'd hoped for.

"That does sound generous," Laine said wearily.

"You're right, again, and if you sign now, I'm prepared to give you the ten thousand tonight." He rubbed his palm over the other breast pocket of his coat.

"Well, I guess this is the right thing to do," Laine ceded. "Where do I sign?" She was vaguely aware of the sound of buggy wheels approaching the building.

Jamison spread the paper out in front of her, smoothing the creases from the line for her signature. He drew the lantern closer, then his hand stopped still. The gritty roll of buggy wheels grew louder, then stopped outside the hotel. He heard Mitcham's voice and someone else's. Without a word of explanation, he grabbed the paper out from under Laine's hand and shoved it in his pocket. Then he beat a hasty retreat through crossed timbers in back of the bar.

"Laine!" Travis called. "Are you in there?" He held a lantern high, inspecting timbers overhead and around him, careful not to disturb any. He entered the saloon and saw her at the table, staring into the lantern light, holding a pencil.

"Laine, thank God," his voice trembled. He rushed to her and dropped down next to her. "What are you doing in here? You've got to leave, it's dangerous."

"Jamison . . ." Laine started.

"Hadley? He brought you here?" Travis's voice shattered the murky darkness. "Where is he? That no good son of a . . . come on, let me get you out of here." He took her arm and gently pulled her to her feet.

"No," she shrugged him off, "Mama's here, I can feel her."

Travis's blood froze. She was scaring him with her detached tone. He feared her sanity may have cracked.

"No," he said gently, "your Mama isn't here anymore, Laine."

"Yes, yes she is, I know it," Laine argued with tears in her eyes.

"Sweetheart, no, it's just a dream. Elizabeth isn't here."

"Yes she is," David Coleridge's choked voice startled them. "I can feel her, too."

253

Laine's senses reeled. That voice, the voice from the shadows. Her shadows. The man who saved her. The man who left her. The man her mother adored. The man Laine had tried to forget all her life. A ghost in a room full of ghosts.

"I can feel Elizabeth here," David whispered again. "I can feel her because she lives in you, Laine. You have her beauty, her warmth . . ."

In the hard yellow flickering light, Travis watched them both, saw David's face contort with pain, saw Laine's eyes glisten with anguish.

"What would you know of my mother's warmth?" Laine hurled at him with a tight, hard voice. She stood up so fast the chair clattered backward. "You drained her of all warmth when you left her, left us." She started toward the door.

Travis placed a gently restraining hand on Laine's shoulder. "Give him the chance, Laine, and give yourself the chance to hear what he has to say. Then decide." His voice was quiet, soothing, yet pleading.

Laine stood shaking under his hand. At last she looked up at Travis with sad, tear-filled eyes, then lowered her head in a gesture of compliance.

"I had to leave, honey, I had to. I had no choice."

"No choice! You had a choice, all right. You chose to desert us, you killed her when you left. She loved you . . . loved you right up to her dying day," she sobbed. "She loved you! You could have stayed . . ."

"I didn't want to leave . . . do you think that was

254

something I wanted to do? I loved you . . . so help me God, I loved you with everything in me. I worshipped your mother. But I had to leave. It was shame drove me away. Don't you understand?!" His face contorted in anguish, and his eyes filled with the tears long held back in self-punishment.

"No . . . you don't understand. I knew nobody would understand. But I had to get out before I hurt her . . . both of you . . . more." He wiped his face with the back of one large hand. "I didn't know . . . how could I know what would happen?"

He searched Travis's face despairingly, then dragged his gaze back to Laine's. "I thought you'd both go back East, back to Sarah's. If you did that I knew you'd be all right, be taken care of. How could I know . . . ?"

David dropped his hands to his sides, his hat hanging limply against his leg, relieved to be given the opportunity to tell the story of the last night he'd seen his wife and daughter.

"I had to get out of here, *had* to," he continued in labored speech. "I've regretted that to this day . . . not the going, just that I didn't take you both with me. I was a failure, and I couldn't stand seeing Elizabeth's lovely face, those trusting eyes looking at me . . . loving me . . . loving a . . . nothing." His body went limp, and he sat down at the table and slumped over his folded hands.

Taking in a weary breath, he continued. "I knew I could make it big again, then I'd send for you. But it took so long . . . I thought by then you'd both forgotten about me anyway, made a new life, a better life. And I figured all the pain I was feeling was nothing short of what I deserved. I deserved to have lost you." He bowed his big head and rested his forehead on upturned thumbs.

Laine watched the big man slumped over at the table, and something inside her gave in, slightly. She wasn't ready to forgive this man for destroying her mother's life, and for deserting her, but she understood his anguish to be real, to be sincere. She took a faltering step forward.

"It was . . . you . . . wasn't it . . . the night of the fire? You saved me, sent me to Aunt Sarah's," she had to hear it from his own lips. When he nodded slightly, she took another step toward the table. "But, how did you know? Were you there all the time?"

He shook his head woodenly, then looked up at her, lantern glow reflected in his eyes. "I'd finally made it, and made it big. There'd never been any woman for me but Elizabeth, never. I dreamed of her, and you, all the time I was away from Silver Grande. I figured by then she'd finally be forced to believe what people had said about me. She always believed in me, never once doubted me. Every business I tried failed, I couldn't keep any work I was able to get, for some reason. I tried gambling to get money back, even though I promised her I wouldn't. I had violated her trust so often, that I couldn't stand to break her heart all over again. So I left.

"But, after I made it, I decided I would swallow my stupid pride, come back for you both and take you out of here, to California, to the home I would make for you both. I prayed all the way that she would take me back, that you would allow me the opportunity to get to know you.

"I came back, discovered you'd been forced to leave the house and were living at the hotel, and I went immediately over there. Oh, I was so excited. I guess I saw myself once again as her hero, riding in to sweep her away to a life of luxury and sunshine.

"When I walked in the place, some filthy bastard had his hands on Elizabeth, and I thought . . . I thought she was playing up to him. I found out later, too late, that he'd taken her wedding ring as a loan in a big card game. Told her he'd win lots of money and split it with her if she put up the ring. She wanted to get enough money to get you both out of there. He won the money, but wouldn't give her the ring back. Decided he wanted her as part of the deal."

His eyes filled again, and Laine felt her heart go heavy as lead. As David was recalling that night, her own memory sharpened after all the years of her purposeful dulling of it.

"He told her if she went with him, he'd give her back the ring and enough money to get the two of you to Boston." He lowered his face into his hands again. "She'd led him to believe she'd go . . . up to a room with him, hoping she could figure a way to get the ring, the money, and both of you out of there. When I walked in, he was . . . he was pawing her.

"I saw red, I guess, and I snatched his hands off

257

her and hit him. I knocked him down and jumped on him, pounding him till my hands were raw. I'd have killed him with my bare hands, I know it. He drew a gun, we struggled, the gun went off, and one of the shots . . . hit Elizabeth." He stopped, swallowing hard.

"I was blind. I ran to her, picked her up in my arms. She smiled at me, said she knew . . . knew I'd come back for you both, and . . . she told me she loved me, had always loved me. But, she was too far gone . . ." A sob burst out of him, and the tears flowed freely down his face. He stared into a space near the crumbled bar.

"She . . . she told me you were at the back door waiting for her. She told me to get you, make sure you got away, send you to Boston. By that time the whole place had erupted into a brawl, and some oil lamps got knocked over, I guess, I don't know, but suddenly the place was an inferno.

"She kept saying your name over and over, and then something else. I couldn't hear her at first, and I put my ear down close to her lips. She . . . she said she wanted her ring. I laid her back down and put a table near her to protect her, and then I found that son of a . . . I don't know how, but I did. I couldn't see . . . the smoke, and I was blinded with rage and remorse . . . and my own tears, I guess. But I found him, right over there." He pointed to a dull spot on the floor near the bar. "He just lay there moaning he was hurt, and I hit him again, and again. That time I knew he was dead. I'd killed him, and I felt nothing. I went through his pockets and found her ring.

"I ran back to her . . . she was bleeding bad. I lifted her head and took her left hand . . . I . . . I told her we were married all over again, forever, and I . . . I slipped the ring on her finger, and kissed her hand, and told her I loved her, had never stopped loving her. She smiled at me . . . she actually smiled at me, after all that had happened to us . . . was happening around us . . . she smiled at me as she always had."

Overcome with the depth of raw emotion, the big man buried his face in his hands. His shoulders wracked with shudders from deep inside him. For a moment Laine felt an overwhelming urge to drop down on her knees next to him and throw her arms around him, but she couldn't bring herself to move.

As he fought back his own surge of emotion, Travis stood close to her, but did not touch her.

In the next moment David contained himself and with a deep breath resumed the painful retelling. "I held onto Elizabeth, tried to get her out, but she stopped me, said it was too late for her, that I had to get you. And she died . . . right there in my arms. I wanted to die right there with her, I couldn't let her go, couldn't leave her. The fire was raging all around us, and I wanted to go up in smoke right there with her.

"But there was you to think of, waiting all alone, probably scared, counting on me. I couldn't let you down again. I'd ruined her life, but you . . . you had meant so much to her, to both of us, and you were her dream. I couldn't let it die. I had to save you from it all, no matter if I had to live out the rest of my life in my own hell, tormented by everything I'd done wrong. But I couldn't let her dream . . . you . . . die.

"I let her down easily, covered her beautiful face with my handkerchief, then ran out to the back to find you. You wouldn't come to me at first, but then there was an explosion . . ."

"I remember," Laine whispered hoarsely. "I woke up on a train, scared to death."

"I know. I'm sorry. For one insane moment I thought about taking you back with me to California, but I knew I was no good for you. I bought your ticket and paid the conductor extra to insure your safety to Boston. I thought I was doing the right thing. Your mother dreamed you would have a good life, a better life. She thought it would happen for you in Boston. I knew she was right, and I couldn't let you both down again. So I sent you to Sarah's.

"I wrote Sarah, asked how you were, wanted so desperately to see you. Sarah wrote back once, said it was my fault your mother was gone, said you never talked about it, you'd forgotten about me, and that the best thing I could do for you was stay out of your life . . . for good.

"I couldn't stand the thought of that. Seeing you again made me crazy to be with you all the more. You were part of Elizabeth, part of me, part of our love. Oh, honey, we loved each other, and we adored you. I thought I did the right thing. I loved you so much, I wanted only the best for you, and I knew Sarah would provide that.

"I never thought my staying away from you would . . . would actually hurt you this much. I never knew . . . I never meant that, never meant to hurt either of you. I only wanted to give you everything. When I hadn't, and then Sarah blamed me for Elizabeth's death, I knew she was right. And I thought they'd hunt me down for killing that bastard in the saloon. I couldn't subject you to that either. The best thing for you was to put the nightmare behind you and to forget I ever existed. And I believed you had.

"I thought about you growing up, your birthday, going to school. I knew you'd be beautiful, just like Elizabeth. And I hoped some no-account cowboy like me wouldn't come along and ruin your life like I ruined hers."

He dropped his face back into his hands. "I'm so ashamed, Lainie . . . I wanted only to make you both happy, be the hero to both of you. I don't expect your forgiveness . . ." His voice trailed away, and he sucked in a ragged breath, keeping his face hidden from her.

Laine's throat ached from swallowing sobs as her father spoke. This big man had been a beaten man, a man whose only weakness was in wanting too much for his wife and daughter, and being unable to accept less than perfect delivery on his promise. He'd fought his way back, but it had been too late.

She raised her eyes toward Travis. He was silent, a soft look of compassion dwelling on his face. Her gaze pleaded with him for an answer to the unasked question of what she should do, but he could only look first at David, then back to her with an aching sadness in his eyes for both of them.

She raised her gaze overhead and prayed silently. Oh, Mama, would you forgive him? Instinctively she knew Elizabeth would have done just that. She wasn't certain she could completely forgive him herself, but she knew she had to try, for her mother's sake, and for her own. And even for David's.

With leaden feet, Laine walked toward the slumped form of David Coleridge, a man she didn't know, but a man who'd opened his heart to her and laid bare all his wounds, taking the chance of being wounded more. She knew he'd spoken the truth. It took a strong man to open himself to criticism by his daughter and yet be sensitive to her burning need to know the truth. He seemed to trust her enough to be honest. She reached out and placed a faltering hand on his shoulder.

Slowly the big shaggy head raised, and the misty hazel eyes lifted to hers. The love Laine saw burning from them was as much as she'd seen in her mother's eyes when she left her alone in the room that fateful night. In her heart Laine knew her father loved her, had always loved her. And much as her mind wanted to deny it, she knew he had acted in the only way he knew how, out of his love for her and her mother.

Tears streamed steadily down her face and fell on his sleeve.

He pushed away from the table and rose slowly. Pulling his big frame to its fullest height and towering above her, he looked at his daughter with new eyes, clear eyes, drinking in the very sight of her, quenching his dry and barren soul.

"God, you look so very much like her. Her life is in your eyes, her beautiful light lives in you."

Then suddenly he engulfed her small frame in a fierce embrace, sobbing quietly into her hair. His arms went around her and locked in a steel circle across her back. He hung onto her with a strength that would never be broken again.

"Daddy," she whispered against his chest.

Travis touched the corner of his eye with a finger, then turned and left the two alone . . . together at last.

Chapter Twenty

Laine alighted from the buckboard and followed Buck inside the stage depot.

"Promises to be a hot one today," Buck said, watching her and thinking how cool she looked in her rose-colored frock. He removed his hat and wiped his brow with his forearm at the same time.

"I love it," Laine replied.

"Thought you Easterners hated the heat." Buck dropped down behind his desk and checked the day's passenger lists.

"They do. I'm from Silver Grande," she replied with pride in her voice.

Buck grinned up at her. "And what are you up to today?"

"A few things. Have to see Mr. Daniels, for one, and I'm having lunch with my father at the hotel."

Buck set his pencil down, and tipped his chair back.

"Ah, yes, it's good to see David Coleridge back here. Always liked him. How've you two been gettin' on? Gettin' reacquainted?"

"Well, there's a lot to learn, a lot to catch up on, and it will take more than this past week to do that, but I think we're making a lot of progress."

"Wal, honey, I hope you don't blame yer father fer ever'thin' that happened. Some things just wasn't his fault."

"I don't, now that I've learned more. I just wish things could have been different . . ." Her voice trailed off into the distance.

"I know, but all we have is to keep a'goin' no matter what, and sometimes that ain't easy."

Laine nodded in full understanding, then turned to leave. "Thanks for the ride in this morning, Buck. I'll stop by before your last run."

She strolled along the boardwalks, taking a turn around the town, looking into shops, talking with people as if she were seeing Silver Grande for the first time. Aside from the still pending business over the hotel property, she was feeling rather good inside.

Seeing her father again, talking with him for hours over the last week, asking countless questions of him, and answering his many questions, had left her emotionally drained.

Travis had spent time with them as well, and Laine was warmed to see the genuine regard for each other the two men displayed. During the week, the three of them became comfortable when together, and when they joined Buck and Molly for supper one evening, the talk and laughter came easily.

As Laine strolled the boardwalks, she thought

back to the night her father had appeared at Travis's home. She thought about the outdoor supper she and Travis had shared, right down to the wine. She could still see the rosy glow of the waning daylight hours, and how the candlelight played over his face and caught the dark shadows in his hair.

Then there was that letter from David, and that awful confrontation. Travis's words still bounced around inside her head, "Sweetheart, please let me tell you about this . . ."

Sweetheart? Had he really called her sweetheart, or was her mind playing tricks on her now? She stopped at an intersection of two streets. The voice inside her head was insistent. Did I hear that right? Did he call me sweetheart? If he did, does that mean . . . ? Oh, I can't be sure. And I certainly can't walk up to him and say, "Travis, did you call me sweetheart the other night? And did you mean it?"

She started walking again, and came upon Ella Cooper's dress shop. She decided to go in and browse a little. She passed Percival Boynton coming out.

"Percival?" She knew she sounded surprised.

"Good day, Miss Coleridge," he tipped his hat nervously.

"What brings you to a dress shop?" she smiled brightly.

"I . . . uh . . . nothing, really. It's uh . . . my cousin's birthday, and . . . uh . . ."

While Percival stammered, Laine thought about

266

Kate Hardy, Travis's cousin. People certainly seem to be full of close cousins in Silver Grande, she thought.

"Of course," she answered, trying to put him at ease. "It's nice to see you."

"Yes, it is," Percival whispered hoarsely. "I mean, it's nice to see you, Miss Coleridge. Uh, good day again, Miss Coleridge." He scurried away.

Laine shook her head and went into the shop.

Inside, Ella Cooper was dusting some shelves and replacing the contents in neat order.

"Good morning, Mrs. Cooper," Laine greeted her brightly. "How are you today?"

"Good morning, Miss Coleridge. I'm fine." Her response sounded guarded to Laine, the reason unclear. "May I help you with something?"

"I'm just looking right now." Laine started around a rack of long dresses.

The chintz curtain covering the small door to the workroom opened slowly, and a petite young girl emerged, a voluminous black and gold dress flung over her shoulder, a needle and thread clenched between her teeth.

"Hello," Laine greeted her. "I don't believe we've met. I'm Laine Coleridge."

Ella rushed over to the girl. "This is my daughter, Ada."

"Ada, how very nice to meet you." She leaned down and took a closer look at the dress Ada was working on. "Did you make this?"

Ada wrinkled her pert nose and took the needle out of her mouth. "Good heavens, no." She had a

267

husky voice that didn't seem to fit her. "This is one of LaBelle Hadley's castoffs. She gives me a dress once in awhile. Pretends she's doing me a big favor by giving me one of her 'best frocks' as she likes to say. Percy says I should just refuse it and tell her I don't need charity."

"Ada!"

"Sorry, Mother." She turned to Laine. "Mother doesn't like it much when I say things straight out as they are."

"Percy . . . says that, does he?" Laine said, thinking the girl's direct response refreshing.

"Yes, he does," Ada looked down, blushing.

Laine watched the young girl, a smile playing at the corners of her mouth. Percival must be courting Ada, and he's so shy he doesn't want anyone to know.

"I think Percival could be right," Laine said. "I wish I could have said that when I was a child and received my own share of LaBelle's castoffs."

Ada set down the needle and unfolded the dress, holding it up to her shoulders and letting the skirt fall to the floor. She wrinkled her nose again and watched for Laine's response.

Laine cocked her head from side to side, and cast a critical eye over the gaudy gold dress with the large red, black and gold triple overlaid skirts. She flicked her fingers over the huge ruffled roses on the shoulders.

"You're right, Ada, it's dreadful. Just like always," Laine mused aloud. "Now, what are you going to do to fix this thing?"

Ada laughed with an enthusiastic air of complicity. "First . . . those awful flowers!" She pointed with disdain at the shoulders of the dress.

"You're right about that!" Laine laughed. "Get some scissors and let's get to work!" She set down her bag and took off her hat.

They pulled the garment over a dress form and went to work. In less than an hour Ada's deft hands had fashioned the effect that both women's creative minds devised. They removed the triple skirts overlaying the full gold one, discarded the red one, and tacked the filmy black one over it so that the gold shimmered through in the light. When they removed the oversized flowers from the shoulders, they discovered that the top could be brought down to form a modest décolletage.

A gold satin sash was made by unrolling one of the huge roses. Pulling it tightly about the slim waist, Ada swiftly tied it into a rather bouffant bow at the back, letting the ends stream down the full skirt. Then the two stepped back, admiring their handiwork.

"Well, Mrs. Cooper, what do you think?" Laine asked, walking around the form, fluffing the skirt.

"Oh," Ella breathed, both hands on her face, "it's beautiful. Miss Coleridge, you've done a magnificent job on that gaudy old thing."

"It wasn't all me," Laine said, throwing an arm around Ada's small shoulders, and noting that Ella had dropped her earlier guarded response. "Your daughter did just as much, if not more." She smiled warmly at the young girl. "You," she smiled, cup-

269

ping Ada's small chin in her hand, "are a creative genius!" Ada blushed under Laine's lavish praise. "Tell me, Ada, do you do a lot of this for the women in Silver Grande?"

"Oh, no," Ada answered, bustling around picking up threads and bits of fabric. "Nobody knows I do things like this. Most of them look down their noses at me anyway, so I wouldn't do it even if they asked me," she sniffed.

Laine stood for a thoughtful minute, appraising the fine work so quickly performed on the dress in front of her. She looked back at Ada. She had a flash of being outside herself looking into the face of her own past.

"I want to tell you both something," she said, turning to include Ella in the conversation. "What I plan to do, hope to do, is to open a shop of fine women's clothing, devised from my own designs. I want to make it a large shop, part of which could include things brought in from large cities!" She began to walk back and forth around the shop, not looking at them, thinking and planning out loud with ideas forming more rapidly than she could speak them.

"And there could be room for another person, a designer of clothing for the woman who has limited funds to spend, but who wants attractive and fashionable things. That has become the trend back East, and it will surely arrive here eventually."

She spun around. "And that's where you come in, Ada. You might even have your own shop inside the large one where you refashion garments, alter them, as well as design some of your own if you wish. And Mrs. Cooper . . . Ella, if you would want to do this, you could manage the shops, handle the buying and inventory of the ready-made things we bring in."

The two women watched with widening smiles as Laine moved around, excitedly making plans and spouting ideas. Her enthusiasm was infectious, and soon they were coming up with ideas of their own, and Laine would agree vigorously, saying, "Yes! Yes!" over and over.

When at last she stopped talking, Laine stood breathless, face flushed from the exhilaration of the birth of a good idea. Ella and Ada stood watching her, smiling so broadly Laine thought their faces might break. She returned their smiles, then impulsively hugged both of them.

"I think the three of us may be seeing a lot more of each other in the future. What would you think about that?"

"We would both be so very grateful for that, Miss Coleridge," Ella said quietly.

"It is I who will be grateful to both of you. And please call me Laine. You'll hear from me soon, but for now let's just keep this our secret, all right?"

The two women agreed. When Laine started to leave the shop, Ella walked with her to the door.

"Laine, there is something I'd like to tell you, if I may, and if you have the time now." She spoke quietly, watching over her shoulder to be certain Ada was busy with something and wouldn't hear her.

"Of course, Ella. What is it?"

271

"I . . . will have a little money to put into the business with you, and of course we can use or sell what's in this shop. But, I just want you to know that we can contribute, you won't have to support us. I . . . I will be coming into some money . . . very soon."

Laine registered understanding. She placed a hand on Ella's arm. "Reed Hadley?"

Ella's eyes darkened, then misted. "You know?" When Laine nodded, she went on. "But I haven't told Ada yet."

"Don't worry. I won't say anything to her, or to anyone. Are you certain . . . you will receive the money?"

"Oh, yes. Reed told me he'd provide for us in his will."

"I understand, it's just that Jamison . . ."

Ella sighed. "I know. He broke his father's heart. When he returned to Silver Grande, Reed could see how corrupt he'd become."

"I'm afraid it's worse than that, Ella."

Ella frowned. "How so?"

"I'm not really at liberty to say yet, but rest assured if you are due something from Reed Hadley's estate, I will see that you get what you are entitled to."

Ella's eyes glistened. "Thank you, Laine. There's something more I want to tell you." She took in a deep breath. "I knew your mother."

Laine's eyes widened in curiosity.

Ella pressed on. "I worked in the saloon when Elizabeth was there." She looked down at her

272

hands. "I'm not proud of that, you understand, and neither was your mother. We had no other choices that we were willing to take. But, I just want you to know that your mother was a wonderful woman, and she loved you so very much. She always talked about you and what a fine lady you were going to be when you grew up."

Laine smiled, but her heart ached just a little. If only her mother could be with her now.

"And I hope you know that your mother never . . . she never went with any of those . . . men. Never. No matter what people said. She wouldn't. Not that all those men didn't want to, and some of 'em even bragged they did. But it was all talk because they couldn't take it when she rejected them. But she never would go with them. She loved David . . . your father. She believed he'd come back."

"Were you there, the night of the fire?" Laine asked in hushed tones.

Ella sighed. "Yes, I was. Reed was there, too. We had an argument. He wanted to tell his family that Ada was his child and wanted to take her there to live with them, and I refused him. I couldn't let her go to that house. If Reed had wanted us to live with him alone, I'd have agreed to that. God knows that would have been wrong, too, but I couldn't let him take her away from me. Just like your mama wouldn't let go of you, I wouldn't let go of Ada. We were all we had, just each other." Her eyes filled with tears.

"I know. Mama and I, well, we were everything to each other. And she kept her promise to me. She got me out of there."

"Oh, yes, but your father . . . When he came into the place that night it was as if a blazing sunrise had suddenly shown on Elizabeth. He was the sun for her always. I saw her face. She looked, oh, somehow free, more alive than I'd ever seen her. Who knew that in a few short minutes . . . ?"

Laine's shoulders sagged slightly, and the older woman stepped forward and embraced her, rubbing her back as a mother would a hurt child. Then she stepped back.

"It was Reed who shot the man who attacked your mother. He knew David thought he was the one, hitting him like that. But he was already dying from Reed's gunshot. Jack Smithers knew it, too. And Jamison, because he was there."

Laine dropped her hands. "My father still thinks he killed that man. We should tell him . . ."

"Maybe . . . David had to feel he'd done something to earn your mother's forgiveness for leaving her. Maybe thinking he'd killed that man has helped him. Anyway . . ."

"Wait," Laine held up her hand, "Did you say Jamison Hadley was there that night, too?"

"Yes, although the reasons why aren't clear to me. He always used to get into a lot of trouble, and Reed sent him away to a boarding school that employed the strictest discipline as part of the teaching. Mr. McCauley knew about it. I remember Reed was surprised when his son appeared. And Jamison was gone soon after that night. Reed never spoke to me about him after that."

Laine said nothing. Ella watched her for some response, and seeing none, continued.

"Anyway, after that night, Reed was a changed man. He wanted me out of that place even after Jackson tried to get money enough to rebuild. Poor Jackson. He was never the same after the fire, a sad and broken man. Reed tried to help him some, especially since Jackson never told the sheriff who really killed that man. But Jackson wouldn't hear of it. So Reed made sure through a lawyer that funds were available to help him out, give him something to live on, but he wanted it done anonymously. Jackson never knew that his benefactor was Reed Hadley."

Laine jerked upright. "You mean, Uncle Jack never borrowed any money from Reed Hadley?"

"Oh, no. He was too proud to do that, too honorable. Given what was between them, don't you see? He thought it would put them both in an compromising position. Even after his brother got into a lot of trouble, and Jackson paid his debts with everything he had, he wouldn't borrow a cent no matter how often Reed offered it. But, he hung onto that old hotel, God knows why."

"I think I know why. He did it for me. The lawyer you mentioned — by any chance was that John McCauley?"

"Why, yes, I believe it was."

"Of course. Then he turned it around to make it look like a loan, a debt . . . And now Jamison and McCauley are trying to cheat all of us out of what's rightfully ours, and they are doing it with what I believe to be forged documents."

"Oh no!" Ella blanched. "Can they do that?"

"They can if we can't prove otherwise."

"Maybe we can . . ." Ella's voice trailed away. "I truly believe Reed wanted to make amends for all of the trouble he and his family caused people in the past. I loved him, in a way. And from what I saw, I may have been the only one. We might have . . . I'm sorry he died so soon."

"Yes, it was a rather untimely death."

Ella frowned. "You don't think . . ."

"I'm not sure what to think, Ella. So much has happened . . ." She opened the door to leave the shop. "I really have to go now. I'm due in my attorney's office soon. But, rest assured I'll keep you posted. And thank you, Ella, thank you for your honesty and faith."

"Laine, there's one more thing I have to tell you."

"Yes?"

"The gloves I gave you? After the fire I went back to clean out my room, and I went into your room, too. Jackson was too distraught to even look in there. He loved your mother and you, you know. Most everything was charred or ruined except for a locket . . . and those gloves."

"Those gloves . . . my mother's. That's why you told me the initials weren't yours. Of course. I never put that together . . . a locket? Did you say there was a locket?"

"Yes. I'll give it to you as soon as I see you again. I have it locked away for safekeeping. I believe Elizabeth said David gave it to her. There are

276

pictures of them in it. I thought someday . . . someday you might come back, or I'd find you somehow to make sure you got it. I knew she'd want it that way."

"Oh, Ella!" Laine stepped back inside and hugged the woman closely. "You'll never know what all of this means to me. But I'll pay you back by getting what is rightfully yours."

"I'll help you in any way I can. Just don't let those thieves take what doesn't belong to them."

"Count on it!" Laine said, and left the shop feeling lighter and happier than she'd felt in weeks.

Chapter Twenty-one

With a spring in her step, Laine rounded the corner toward the Mitcham Construction office. She spotted Travis coming up the boardwalk, Percival Boynton at his side. As always, the sight of Travis's long muscular body striding toward her in worn denim pants and open-necked shirt made her breath catch in her throat. And this morning it moved her to remember him without his clothes. She felt the heat of flush rise up her throat and cover her face.

"Good morning," she called out as they drew near. "I was just coming to see you. I have some very interesting and exciting news."

"And we have news for you," Travis said, pointing to a thick envelope Percival held in his hand.

"Percival, hello," Laine smiled at him. Boynton nodded back, blushing slightly. "What news?"

"Percival has found a new twist to the story. Seems Reed Hadley acquired your father's property and money through devious means of his own. The deed and supporting statements are in here." He tapped the thick envelope. "Apparently Reed was going to tell you about it, and turn these papers over to you. Strikes me Jamison had a strong motive for doing in his own father. Although I can't be completely sure."

Laine frowned. "What should we do next?"

"I'd say we find David and let him and Anson know all about it. Then I think we should stage an impromptu meeting in McCauley's office. Percival, you up to getting Hadley there?"

Percival nodded enthusiastically. "And I have a couple of ideas of my own," he said more firmly than the others had ever heard him speak. "One hour long enough?"

"One hour. We'll be there," Travis said, clapping him on the shoulder as Percival took off on a run. "Now, Laine," he said, turning a smile on her, "what's your news?"

"Ella Cooper told me that Uncle Jack never borrowed any money from Reed Hadley. Reed made some funds available to him anonymously through John McCauley. I guess he was trying to pay him back a little for something he'd done to Uncle Jack in the past. And now with Percival's information, we know what that is."

Travis frowned. "That makes it all the more possible that Jamison had something to do with his father's death. He must have known what Reed was planning, and he didn't want to see all that money and future wealth slip out of his hands."

"And Ella was also due to inherit from Reed's estate. No doubt Jamison knows about that, too, and will try to bilk her out of what Reed had designated for her."

"Ella? Why?"

"Ada is one reason. She's Reed's daughter."

Travis whistled low. "Would she be willing to testify to those things if need be?"

"Yes, I think so. After all, we're planning on going into business together," Laine smiled.

"You are building an empire, aren't you?" Travis chided her.

"Possibly," she turned her head smiling, "just possibly."

"Well, then let's get started with it, what do you say?" He held out his arm to her, and she linked hers through it, and together they walked to Anson's office.

"And that's what we have so far," Travis said to David as the three sat in Anson Daniels' office.

"And McCauley's as big a crook as the rest of them," David said, his eyes narrowing. "That swindling little son of a . . . well, I have ways of dragging a confession out of him."

"No, Dad," Laine cut in, "I think we have to take care of this calmly and coolly. Give them enough rope, and they'll hang each other."

"And we've got to have that circuit court judge here," Anson added.

"That may take too long," David said. "I could just go over there and beat the truth out of him."

"No," Laine said firmly, "then you'd be in jail,

and the biggest rat of all would get away. No, we have to do this inside the law, and so subtly they'll never know what hit them till it's all over."

"Give it up, David," Travis grinned. "You're up against a formidable opponent here."

"Yes, well, apparently my daughter has a stubborn streak in her—where she gets that from, I have no idea." His eyes crinkled at the corners when he smiled.

"Hah! You don't know the half of it!"

"I guess not," David said quietly. Travis started to apologize for the remark, but David stopped him. "I guess you're right, honey. I'll do it your way. What happens next?"

Travis stood up quickly and picked up his hat. "Shall we take a stroll, partners? Say, over to the office of one John T. McCauley, attorney at breaking the law?"

"Right," Laine said, standing and grabbing her bag.

"Sounds like the right move to me, partners!" David was up and out the door before Travis could get his hat on his head.

"I'm right behind you," Anson said, stuffing a briefcase with the pile of papers on his desk.

Father and daughter Coleridge and Travis strode arm in arm down the boardwalk, Anson bringing up the rear. When they opened the door to McCauley's office, the tinny bell rang out once again, and Laine smiled, visualizing trumpets heralding the arrival of an avenging contingency to the court of a corrupt king.

Boynton stood up quickly as they entered, trying hard to suppress a persistent smile. "I'll announce you," he said in a purposely formal voice. "The other member of the party has already arrived. Early, I might add."

He winked, then went to the big door and rapped lightly. A muffled, hard voice responded from the other side. Boynton opened the door wide, one arm extended toward the waiting room.

"Miss Laine Coleridge . . . and company!" he announced loudly, and the four of them marched in a single line into McCauley's office.

"What!" McCauley stood up quickly, banging his knee on the desk. Frowning in pain, he boomed at Percival, "Boynton, I told you we were not to be disturbed!"

"Too late . . . sir," Boynton quipped as he pulled the door not quite closed and went to his desk.

Jamison stood at one end of the room, his usual unruffled demeanor clearly cracking.

"Isn't this nice?" Laine said sweetly. "We're all here. I know we can take care of everything quickly and cleanly now, can't we? I'm here to sign the necessary papers turning the hotel property over to me, solely. It is rightfully mine, and unencumbered, and I now have the proof I need."

Her coolness unnerved the perspiring McCauley. Squinting his eyes, he begged Jamison to speak, to help him out of the situation, but Hadley stood silently, the muscles in his lower jaw twitching.

McCauley dropped down in his chair and moved to reach for a pen at the edge of his desk, banging his elbow on the corner of it. Pain and anger played across his puffy cheeks, and his blood pressure pulsed in his neck as he checked himself from spewing profanity.

"Files . . . I have evidence in my files that will dispute . . ." he sputtered.

"Evidence, Mr. McCauley? Evidence of what?" Laine leaned forward. "Of debts owed to Jamison Hadley? If indeed you do have such evidence, may we see it? I would venture to guess that it is contrived, forged . . . in any case, invalid."

McCauley rubbed his elbow. Beads of perspiration stood out along his upper lip. Did she really have anything new to challenge him with, or was she merely trying to outwit him? His powers of perception were failing him now, and Jamison Hadley was contributing no help.

"You have no way of proving anything," McCauley growled, searching her face. Laine knew he hoped he would find in it a lack of any real knowledge, or the trace of a crack in her presentation. She also knew he would find neither.

McCauley's eyes scraped over the three men behind her. The spark of recognition glimmered in his eyes when they fell on David Coleridge, but Laine saw him work at concealing his unsettling feeling about him.

"What do you think you're all doing in here?!" McCauley stood up so quickly his chair plummeted back against the wall. "Boynton!" he boomed. "Get these people out of here! This is a private conversation!"

"Not as private as you'd like it to be, I'll wager," David Coleridge's eyes narrowed, and his large frame moved beside Laine.

McCauley's face drained of all color as rapidly as it had reddened earlier. "Coleridge . . ." he exhaled, and his eyes bulged as he glared at Hadley.

Blank terror flattened Jamison's features, but he quickly regained his composure.

"Right you are . . . for the first time in a long time," David said evenly.

McCauley sucked in a sharp breath, and avoiding David's eyes, he began, "Miss Coleridge, if there is something you do not understand, something I can help you with . . ."

"Yes, I'm sure you'd like to help me, Mr. McCauley. Help me and my family and friends out of what you and the Hadleys managed to swindle from them a long time ago."

"Why, whatever do you mean?" McCauley stepped back, visibly shaken by her statement.

Jamison squirmed under her accusations, then pulled back into his smooth demeanor. "Laine, I know you will understand my position. I was merely trying to help my family regain what my father had so carelessly lost in his weakness. Isn't that just what you're trying to do now, regain something your weak father lost when he deserted you and your mother?" He shot a triumphant glance at

David.

Wrenching free of Travis's grip on his arm, David lunged toward Jamison. "You conniving little bastard . . ." Travis reached out for him again and restrained him.

"Look," McCauley said, wiping moisture from his moustache, "there are entirely too many people in here. This business should be conducted among only the two parties involved, Miss Coleridge and Mr. Hadley. It's no one else's business but theirs. The rest of you will please leave."

No one made a move to leave. "They're all involved," Laine said calmly. "We're partners, and Mr. Daniels is our attorney. They all have a right to be here. And further, we represent the interests of Mrs. Ella Cooper, and her daughter Ada."

McCauley and Jamison exchanged glances, and Jamison shook his head disdainfully.

Daniels withdrew a document from his briefcase and presented it to McCauley. "It is my clients' contention," he began in a crisp, authoritative tone, "that you and Mr. Hadley conspired to forge the signatures of Jackson Smithers and Reed Hadley on deeds and loans for the gain of Mr. Hadley and yourself. My clients further contend that Mr. Hadley murdered his father when he learned that the elder Hadley planned to tell Miss Coleridge the truth about everything."

Jamison blanched, and McCauley shot him a desperate glance. "If that were true," Jamison said tightly, "you would have to prove it."

"We have witnesses," Daniels continued, his strong announcement belying the flimsy evidence to support his statement, "who will swear that you gave an overdose of nitroglycerine to your father the day he died."

"What witnesses?" Jamison boomed, beads of sweat popping out on his forehead. "There was no one in the house that day but me . . ." He clamped his mouth shut, realizing he'd said too much.

McCauley glared at him, then looked over the document Daniels presented him. His hands shook as he lifted each page. He was stalling for time to think, and he knew the others knew it.

"This doesn't mean a thing, Daniels. The papers we have in our files which bear those signatures concerning the properties will stand up in any court in this territory." McCauley pursed his lips.

"Let me see those papers," Daniels demanded firmly.

"Daniels," McCauley placated, "you are beaten. Why don't you just convince your clients to take a cash settlement . . . and then all of you get out of Silver Grande, out of the territory? No more questions asked." He smiled and shrugged his shoulders, palms open.

"The papers," Daniels demanded again.

"All right." McCauley was aggravated. "Boynton! Bring the Coleridge files!"

"Right here," Boynton said calmly, pushing the door open wide and producing several brown folders. He had withdrawn the files from the cabinet and had been holding them outside the door during the argument, waiting to make a dramatic entrance.

McCauley sifted through the files confidently. Appearing not to find what he was looking for, he went through them again more slowly, spreading everything out before him on the desk. "Where . . .? Boynton!"

"Yes, sir?" Percival answered quickly, looking over the rims of his spectacles.

"Is this every file we have on the Coleridge and Smithers properties?"

"Yes, sir, it is. You know I keep precise records."

"Yes, I know, I know. But there . . . there seem to be some things missing." McCauley's neck showed expanding veins like blue cords.

"Oh, I really don't believe so, sir. How could that be?" Percival feigned concern, peering across the desk into the open file folder in front of McCauley.

"Because you are a bumbling idiot, that's how!" McCauley shouted at him.

"Really, sir," Percival came back quietly, removing his spectacles, "there is no need to raise your voice. Perhaps you've misplaced what you're looking for. Or, perhaps it was stolen."

Laine stole a glance at Percival's face. It was more relaxed than she'd ever seen it. Percival had the entire situation in control, and he knew it. And she knew it!

"Stolen?! That's ridiculous!" McCauley's frustrated voice resounded around the room.

Jamison moved in behind the desk and desperately riffled through all of the papers. "You fool, McCauley!" He slammed his fist down on top of the papers.

"It's your negligence!" McCauley pointed an accusing finger at Boynton, his face now a purplish red. "You're incompetent . . . and you're fired!"

"I'm so sorry, sir," Boynton said calmly, smiling with self-satisfaction, "but if you'll look at that letter . . . yes, that letter right there on top . . ." he pointed to a sealed envelope sitting squarely atop the jumbled pile on the desk. ". . . you'll find my resignation, dated today, one hour ago. I no longer work for this firm."

He turned and left the room, smiling broadly, and with a spring of freedom in his step. McCauley's perspiring face dropped.

"McCauley," Travis said evenly, "admit it. You've been caught red-handed dipping into a pot you shouldn't have even been near."

"That isn't true," McCauley blustered. "I didn't . . ."

"Of course you did, Mr. McCauley," Laine said with sympathy. "But we can certainly see why. I'm sure Jamison Hadley pushed you into it, threatened you or something. Isn't that right?" she added, leading the visibly squirming lawyer.

"Well, he did say he would give me a percentage . . . that is, well, his father made me do some things . . ."

"Shut up, McCauley," Jamison shouted, "before

288

you say too much. I'll testify in court that you engineered everything, and they'll hang you for it."

"Me?! It was you . . . you and your father!" McCauley backed away from Jamison, trying to move around the desk toward the door. David Coleridge blocked his exit. "Sure, sure I witnessed some of those signatures. I knew he'd forged his father's name. He forced me to sign Smithers' name. And he set the hotel on fire to cover the fact that his father killed someone in there that night. But when he murdered his own father, I wanted out!"

"Shut up, McCauley. I'm warning you!" Jamison spat through clenched teeth.

"No!" David boomed. "Wait a minute, wait a minute. Who did Reed kill in the saloon that night? Did he shoot Elizabeth?"

Laine's eyes snapped to her father's face. She saw a raging fire in the glare he pinned on Jamison Hadley.

"No, not Elizabeth," McCauley came back, wiping his perspiring face. "He was in love with Elizabeth once, only she wouldn't have him. He was sweet on someone else by that time. Some other man was grabbing your wife, and Reed started shooting. The other one started shooting, and I guess Elizabeth got caught in it. Reed saw you beating him to a pulp. He knew you thought you'd killed him, but Jamison didn't know that, and he started the fire to cover what he thought was his father's crime. Then he got out of town."

David stepped back and leaned against the door,

visibly moved by McCauley's story.

"Reed was going to change everything after that," McCauley went on, "but Jamison wouldn't let him. He knew the railroads were coming in, and the Smithers property would be worth a lot then. Reed wanted to turn it over to Miss Coleridge and pay her back for what he did to her father. No one knew Coleridge was still alive. They all thought he was dead."

"What do you mean what Hadley did to me?" David demanded, stepping forward again.

"As I said, he wanted your wife. When she refused his advances, he did everything he could to ruin you. Poisoned every employer you had and every business you started. Thought by getting rid of you, he'd have a clear way with Elizabeth. But still she wouldn't . . ."

"How did Ella Cooper get involved?" Travis asked.

McCauley dropped into his chair. "She seduced Hadley to get him away from Elizabeth because she'd been good to her. Then Reed and Ella seemed to actually like each other. Something happened to him after that. Started getting philanthropic, I guess. He came to me with a lot of new ideas. That's when I let Jamison know everything."

McCauley took in a shaky breath. "I wanted out a long time ago, but when Jamison came back he wouldn't let me. Said he'd make public what I'd done, ruin me. But when it came to murder . . . well, I wanted nothing to do with that. I couldn't . . ."

McCauley was wailing now, his eyes bulging, and he mopped perspiration from his brow again with a white handkerchief.

"That's right, you couldn't, you weak old . . . you're just like my father." Jamison flew over the desk and grabbed McCauley by the throat.

Travis lunged after him, grabbing him around the neck in the crook of his arm, then spinning him around and pushing his face down onto the desk, bending his arm up toward his shoulder blade.

"He did it!" McCauley shouted. "The day of the funeral . . . his father wasn't even cold in the ground . . . he was plotting how to get all the money."

"And then he tried to bribe me," Laine said quietly.

Travis looked at her questioningly.

"That night when you and Dad found me in the hotel. He'd been there and ran out when he heard you coming."

"You can't prove a thing," Jamison hissed, "not any of you."

"But we can," Ella Cooper entered the office, Ada behind her with Percival's arm around her shoulders.

"What's she doing here?" Jamison muttered, his face a dark red, his lips twitching.

"I . . . we wanted to come," Ella said. "My daughter," she swallowed, looking toward Ada and Percival. They smiled their support, but Ella couldn't speak.

Ada stepped forward holding Percival's hand. "Reed Hadley was my father," she said directly.

"That's preposterous!" Jamison sputtered. "They're just trying to get their hands on my father's money."

Ada turned on him. "Much as I hate to think of you and LaBelle as my half brother and sister, I always suspected Reed was my father. And now we have the proof, thanks to Percy." She smiled at the shy young man who looked at her with love.

Percival handed Ella two bound volumes.

"It is the truth," Ella let out a relieved sigh. "A couple of days before he died, he came to me. Said he wanted to publicly acknowledge Ada was his daughter. He left me with this journal and this account book. Said he didn't trust Jamison, and if anything happened to him, to give these to Miss Coleridge and Mr. Mitcham. Percival was visiting Ada that day, and Reed asked him to set some kind of seal or witness that these were his books, and, if you'll look in the back of the journal, his last will. Percival went to his office to get the necessary things, and ran back to witness and seal everything."

Percival stepped back and pushed the office door wide open. Then he motioned into the waiting room. A tall, portly man and a muscular younger one entered McCauley's office.

"Did you hear enough, Sheriff?" Percival asked

firmly.

"Plenty," the big man growled. "Hadley, you're under arrest. You, too, John T." He snapped handcuffs on Jamison's hands still held behind his back by Travis. The deputy snapped cuffs on McCauley, and they were led out of the office.

Laine dropped down into a chair, heart pounding, hands shaking. David went to her side and placed a protective hand on her shoulder.

"I'm glad that's over," she breathed hard. "I wasn't sure they'd confess, they were so slippery. It scared me for a moment."

"You? Scared?" Travis laughed. "I didn't believe I'd ever hear you say that."

Laine shot him a half smile.

"You did wonderfully, honey," David said with love evident in his voice.

"I'll say," Daniels agreed.

Boynton came back into the room. "Gentlemen . . . and ladies . . . may I present the honorable Joseph R. Buskirk, Circuit Court Judge of the Arizona territory." A short white-haired man in wire-rimmed spectacles entered the room. Boynton handed a thick brown envelope to him.

"These are all the necessary papers you'll need, your honor, and these are all the necessary people." He brushed his hands together in satisfaction. "All's well that ends well," he grinned, and left the office, closing the door behind him.

"Boynton, you're brilliant!" Travis called after him.

Chapter Twenty-two

Laine stood in the Harmons' kitchen looking out of the back door toward the far snow-capped mountain peaks. The last few days had been emotionally draining, but she felt excited and happy.

Everything seemed secure now. The hotel property was in her name. She'd begun plans with Ella and Ada for the renovation, and Travis and her father had begun architectural drawings and lists of supplies. They'd all had dinner together one evening at the Black Canyon Hotel to celebrate.

But now a kind of letdown had set in. She'd been riding high on the final results of disposition of the property and funds to everyone involved, reunion with her father, and partnership with Travis. Her life was moving along just as she'd dreamed it. Then what was wrong?

She knew what it was. It seemed her relationship with Travis had come to a standstill. The times they'd spent together lately had all been related to the business. The days had been hectic, that was true, and they'd all been very busy. But would

Travis always be busy, too busy . . . ?

"You all right, honey?" Molly placed a loving arm around Laine's shoulders.

Laine turned around and hugged the older woman. "Yes, Molly, I'm fine . . . or I will be fine. I'm just . . . I don't know . . ." She turned around again and stared blankly across the vast country.

"You been through a lot lately, honey. You just don't feel settled yet," Molly said with the knowledge of years of becoming settled. "Takes awhile . . . don't be in a hurry. And don't skip any steps." She patted Laine on the shoulder, then busied herself preparing supper. "Should I set another place fer yer . . . David?"

Laine turned around, smiling. "Yes, Molly, my . . . father will be staying for supper tonight." She went to a cupboard to take down some plates. "My father . . . oh, Molly, that word seems so strange to me, yet so wonderful, so right." She stood by the table, fingertips resting on the edge, and spoke dreamily. "He told me all about how he and Mama met and fell in love. I didn't know love like that truly existed anywhere, let alone in my own life. I fantasized about it, but I'm not sure I really believed it could happen to anyone."

"And yer thinkin' why can't that happen to you, ain't you, honey?"

"How do you always know what people are thinking, Molly?" Laine smiled at the ruddy-faced woman she'd grown to love like a second mother. "I used to dream that a handsome, wonderful, dashing man would find me, tell me I was the woman he couldn't live without, that he loved me for the person I am and want to be. And I knew I'd love him so much I could never even look at another man." She stared dreamily down into the flowered tablecloth, then lifted her head sharply. "Not take care of me, though, you know?" she added hastily. "I can do that myself. I can do most anything myself . . ."

"Mebbe you kin, honey, mebbe you kin. But it shore does take the right man to make all that you do fit, somehow, fit in all the right places with you n'him . . . oh, I dunno what I'm sayin' . . ." Her voice trailed off, and she went about slicing a big loaf of fresh bread and placing it on a platter.

"Yes, you do know what you're saying, Molly. You and Buck, you fit each other." Laine said it with love and a trace of awe in her voice. "That will probably never happen to me."

"Aw, now shore it will, honey," Molly reassured her.

"Molly, I've met a lot of men. Boston is full of men who think all women fit them." She shook her head in recollection of several of the young men she'd known. "But, I was different. None of them fit me. They tried, though!" she laughed. "But, maybe it won't really matter now. I have my father, and . . . a partnership with Travis, and a new life and a lot of work ahead of me. I'll have no time for such things."

Molly set some flatware on the table, lost in thought. She had something on her mind she wanted to say, but she wanted to be certain it was said right. Finally, she broached the subject.

"Even with a lot of work to do, people have to make time fer such things, Laine. We wuzn't meant to go through life alone. There's probably somebody right now who wants to be with you." She placed the knives at each plate with deliberate movement.

Before Laine could answer, Buck was on the back porch smacking his hat against his pantleg. " 'Nother hot one," he announced as he opened the door and entered the kitchen. He tossed his hat up on the rack near the door with practiced accuracy.

"How come yer home so early?" Molly wanted to know.

"Wal, thanks fer the welcome," Buck grinned. He walked past her to the sink and patted her behind as he went. "My driver's back, and he's takin' the late run t'day, so I thought I'd come home early. 'Course if'n ya don't want me here . . ." He lowered his head in feigned rejection.

Molly assured him with laughing eyes and a kiss on his wrinkled cheek that she did want him, and he plunked himself down at the table.

"Oh, Travis is on his way out, too," he remarked offhandedly, stealing a sidelong glance at Laine.

Molly went to the cupboard for another plate. "Wal, I best set another place. Got anymore surprises for me, Buck?"

"Nope. Didn't think you'd mind havin' Travis. Said he wanted to stop after he'd been out to the Hadleys'. Said he had to see LaBelle about somethin'. Said it would only take him a few minutes

. . . wouldn't be there long . . . uh, couldn't be nothin' important if he wuz gonna leave so soon . . ."

Molly sent a glare to Buck with the unspoken instruction to shut his mouth. Buck did not know why Travis was going to the Hadleys', but it never occurred to him that he had to keep it a secret. He wasn't very good at keeping secrets anyway.

LaBelle. So that was it, Laine thought. Perhaps he was more interested in her than he'd led her to believe. Perhaps their relationship hadn't been totally the trumped up idea of LaBelle's.

"Hello!" Travis's voice came from the porch and shattered her thoughts.

He opened the screen door wide and stepped into the kitchen, taking off his hat. Laine's heart jumped wildly in her chest. She could almost smell the sun and wind on him, and could sense the rippling in his back and shoulder muscles as he lifted his arm to drop his hat on the rack. He turned back toward her. Their eyes met, but she averted hers and moved to help Molly with some vegetables she was preparing. Molly put down her knife and turned around, wiping her hands on her apron. She stepped quickly toward Travis, arms outstretched.

"Travis, it's so good to see you." She hugged him closely, and he held her for an extra minute.

"Good to be here, Molly," he said warmly, kissing her cheek. "Hello, Laine."

She turned around for a brief moment and gave him a half smile, then went back to her work. David's heavy step sounded from the porch, and he entered to a chorus of greeting. He went over to Laine and put his arms around her waist when she looked up at him.

"And how is my little girl today?" he asked, kissing the top of her hair.

"Now, Dad," she admonished him with good nature, "you've got to stop thinking of me as a little girl. I'm a grown woman."

"Stop! Don't say that!" he laughed, holding up his hands to prevent more words. "Makes me feel so old!" He hugged her again. "I guess it's just that I've missed so much of your life, I want to keep you a little girl for awhile longer. Indulge me some, daughter!" he commanded with amusement.

Laine stood on tiptoes and kissed her father warmly. "All right . . . Daddy. Just so long as you treat me like a partner when we're out in public."

"Done!" he said and shook her hand as if they'd just sealed a major business deal.

Molly set supper on the table, and they all sat around it laughing and talking about everything and nothing. An air of lightheartedness permeated the conversations. Laine felt good inside, warmed by the atmosphere, satisfied with the feeling of family that filled her. Yet, there was still one empty, hungry cavity deep inside her that yearned to be filled.

"So," Buck said, "Jamison Hadley's lyin' tail's gone from these parts now, isn't it?"

"Sure is. And," Travis said, enthusiasm in his voice, "Anson Daniels has asked Percival Boynton to come into his firm. Soon as he's licensed, they'll be partners."

Laine smiled with satisfaction. "That's wonderful. Percival will do a fine job. I'm so happy for him."

"And that leaves LaBelle," Travis opened the subject. All eyes were on him, except for Laine's. Travis felt unsettled, uneasy. It had not been a pleasant final confrontation with LaBelle, but he'd done it.

"She had big plans. You know how spoiled she is, how full of herself she is," Travis paused, watching Laine, but still her eyes remained downcast. He longed to cup her chin and pull her face up so that he could look right into those disturbing violet eyes and force her to look at him.

"After all this time, and all I've said, she still thought marriage between us was the right thing to do, with the merging of our properties and so forth. Stubborn woman.

"She's decided that a big wedding is just what she needs to cheer her up since her father died." No one at the table moved. Why did he get the feeling his words were coming out all wrong?

Laine's ears reddened and burned at the tops. Carefully, and without looking up, she pushed her chair away from the table. "Excuse me." She stood up with her plate and turned toward the sink. "I just remembered I haven't exercised Lady yet today. She expects that," she moved toward the back door, "gets restless, full of energy. Should do it before dark." Then she was out the door and on a run toward the barn.

Molly watched Laine go, and then shot an exasperated look at Travis, who sat motionless. Under the table Molly kicked Buck in the shin. He let out a groan, then purposely clamped his mouth tightly shut showing Molly that he was not about to say anything to his young friend.

Travis's shoulders slumped. "I have to tell her . . ." He looked around at all of them. "It's time now . . ."

"Travis," David said firmly, "it would have been more seemly if you had tried to speak to Laine alone about your marriage to LaBelle. I can't believe you're not aware she's in love with you. If you break my little girl's heart . . ."

"Marry LaBelle!" Travis jumped to his feet, pushing his chair back. "Marry LaBelle? Are you crazy? I would no more . . . I never intended to marry her! That was her little scheme to trap me. Good Lord, that could never happen!"

"Wal, then, why'd you go over there if you wuzn't settin' up plans with her? What were you talking about?" Molly was agitated now.

"Well, to square things with her, of course. To set things straight with her once and for all, of course! She's decided to move to Flagstaff to her mother's people. She met some fella there she says has more money than I have who wants to marry her." Travis started to pace the room. "Why would anybody think . . . ? Does Laine think LaBelle's whole fabrication is true?" He looked around incredulously at all of them.

"Wal, it's obvious she does, you idiot!" Buck could not contain himself any longer. "How wuz she to know different? You shore didn't tell her!"

"I did too tell her, once. I just assumed that

301

would be enough. I didn't think she would ever keep imagining such a thing . . ." Travis ran a hand through the front of his hair, letting the dark strands sift through his fingers slowly. He turned around completely. "Of course, as always, her imagination ran away with her. Why does she always do that?! That woman exasperates me! Always has, always will."

Full of frustration, Travis could not stand still and kept pacing and turning back and forth.

"Are you going to just stand there spinning around like a top out of control?" David asked with a grin. "Are you going to let my little girl go on thinking that you are going to marry someone else . . . when what you really want to do is marry her? Of course, I could be wrong . . ." He made a broad attempt to scrape remaining food particles from his plate.

"Oh, of course you're not wrong!" Travis declared loudly. Then he stopped short, and looked up as if the idea had only just that moment crossed his mind. "Of course you're not wrong," he repeated evenly. A wide smile lit up his face. "I do want to marry her. What do you think of that?" He ran his hand through his hair again. "Travis Mitcham wants to marry Laine Coleridge . . . always wanted to marry Laine Coleridge. But, what if she doesn't want to marry me, now? She's made it clear she doesn't trust me completely yet. She's got all those ideas about what she wants to do, the business. And we could continue to do them together. I would do anything she wanted. Anything . . ."

"Wal, don't tell us, you lovesick fool!" Buck boomed and jumped to his feet. He grabbed Travis by the shoulders and pointed him toward the door in the direction of the barn. "Git outta here and tell her afore she gits away!"

Travis started on a run. "I'm going, I'm going!" he shouted over his shoulder to a chorus of laughter from the kitchen.

Chapter Twenty-three

Laine patted Lady's neck, and the mare responded with an excited nuzzle in anticipation of a brisk run. Her eyes stung, while her stomach churned over and over, and Travis's voice echoed in her head, ". . . a wedding . . . soon." She'd been dreading hearing those words, but now that they were out, she should be relieved of the tension and get on with her life.

Come on, Laine, she urged herself, you're a big girl now. There's no more fantasy world for you. Let go of those little girl dreams about Travis. Your lives don't fit together. Fit. That's what Molly said. You have to find someone who fits all the parts of yourself. Once you know yourself well. You know yourself well now, don't you? She shook her head and shook the tears back with it.

Reaching up, she grabbed for the bridle on a wood peg, but the reins tangled themselves, and she could not wrest it from its snarled hold. Her inability to untangle the reins only frustrated her more, and the tears welled up once again and threatened to burst forth.

"Damn!" she muttered. She pulled hard, and the

reins knotted tighter, making her angrier. She threw them against the wall.

"I can help you with that, if you'll let me," Travis's rich voice came from behind her.

She whirled around. He stood there, hands to his sides, confusion apparent on his face. Laine worked to check her frustration; she would not let Travis see her in such a state.

"Thank you," she whispered, wishing she could summon a stronger voice, "but as soon as I find something to stand on, I'll be able to free the bridle myself." She busied herself looking around for a stool or some other sturdy object to stand on.

"Laine," Travis began, "I . . . there's something I have . . . want to talk to you about."

"Of course, Travis," she answered too quickly, her voice wavering, "I'll stop over to your office sometime next week. We have a lot of . . . loose ends to take care of, I know." She kept moving, searching for a stool or a box, or something, anything.

Travis followed her with small steps as she looked around frantically. "No, I mean, we have to talk about it . . . now." He seemed not to know what to do with his hands, or where to stand.

Laine felt mounting emotion that she knew would explode and shatter if she didn't get away from him right away.

"No! I mean, I'm sure it can wait, Travis. Really, I have to exercise Lady right now. You can see she's ready." She ran around even more frantically, looking more for an escape now than for something to stand on.

"But, Laine, please . . ."

She didn't answer him. Tears were pushing insistently at the backs of her eyes. Then she spotted the ladder leading to the haymow. Running toward it, she took a step up, and, with her back to him, said, "Yes, next week, Travis. I'll be sure to stop in. We have so much to talk about . . ." She started up the ladder, and the tears started down her cheeks. "The business, and . . . everything. Next week."

She ran up the ladder, stumbling blindly.

Reaching the top, she kept moving until she came to a corner with hay piled high in the back and low in the front from where it had been pitched to the floor below. She sank down in it, dropped her head back, closed her eyes, and laid her forearm over them, gasping for air. The heat and her nervousness overtook her ability to relax and breathe evenly. All she needed was time alone to compose herself.

She lay there for what seemed like hours until at last her breathing became more even, and she'd stemmed the flow of tears. The smell of hay evoked the memory of the last time she was in the haymow, the time when she and Travis exploded in each other's arms, and sharpened the hunger in both of them with the heat of their passion.

She clamped her eyes shut, but the vision shot into focus of them in Travis's house, his bed, each other's arms, their bodies melding together completely, fitting together.

Fit.

There it was again. But that was past, gone forever. I am so fortunate, she thought, and I must remember that. There is so much more for me in the future. My life is much better than any of my fantasies ever were.

She took a deep breath. More memories came flooding back, and with them the scent of Travis, his body, his clothes. She clamped her eyes tighter. The scent was so real!

Would she ever get over him? The truth hung in front of her mind like a banner. She loved him, and there was nothing she could do about it now. Time, perhaps in time she would be able to, but not now.

Maybe in time she would go back to Boston. Arizona had compelled her to come, and now the starkness of that same Arizona was closing her out of what she wanted most. No, it wasn't! How could she think that? It still compelled her to stay, more than ever. She would never go back to Boston to live. Here was where she belonged. Arizona fit her, and she was learning to fit Arizona.

All right, all right, she would give in to it and stay here, do whatever came her way. After all, she had her father. She would simply learn to stay out of Travis's way as often as possible.

She felt better, she thought, calmer. She would go take Lady for a run. It would clear her head, get her on the right track. She took another deep breath. The scent of Travis filled her senses, and her hands began to tingle.

Damn! She cursed the air. How long would it take before the very essence of him did not affect her so completely?

She opened her eyes, feeling all at once uneasy

with no real explanation. Her hands tingled more sharply. Nothing exciting was going to happen now, that was for sure, so why were they doing that? She rolled her head to the side.

"Hello." Travis sat in the hay a few feet from her, one stalk of it dangling loosely from his front teeth.

She jumped, his presence so startled her. His shirt was open far down his chest, and she could see dark hair curling near the vee. She swallowed hard, trying to force her pounding pulse down below her throat, and tried to push herself up.

Travis took the piece of hay from his mouth and tossed it aside, then slowly and deliberately leaned over on all fours. With one hand on her shoulder he pressed her back down into the hay. She struggled again to get up, but he held her fast.

"Travis! What are you doing? Let me up!" Her frustration began to mount.

"No," he said with cool strength. "I told you I have something to tell you, and you are going to listen to me. If I have to pin you here all night, I will. I'm going to say it, and say it now, and you're going to hear it, and you're going to hear it now. Not next week, now!"

"I don't feel like listening now, or talking now. So let go and let me up. I told you next week, and I meant that!" She pushed her elbows hard into the hay trying to get up.

Travis pushed her back down. "And I told you now, and I meant that! I am going to tell you about LaBelle, and . . ."

"LaBelle!" she spat the name out. "Thank you,

but I had enough of LaBelle when I was a child, and I've had enough of her since I came back. There's nothing you can tell me about her that I want to hear." She narrowed her eyes and set her jaw hard. "Now, let me up or I'll scream."

"Go ahead, scream," Travis said evenly. "No one's going to help you. They all made me come after you. I'm going to have my say, and it will be the truth." She turned her head away from him. "You can pretend you're not listening, Laine, but I know you are."

He looked longingly down at her. She was so beautiful, so spirited. He would make her learn to trust him, to believe in him. He desperately wished to be her hero once more, in her fantasies and in her reality.

"I went out to the Hadleys' today . . . stop struggling! I went out to the Hadleys' to talk with La-Belle. All her talk about engagement and wedding had to be stopped. I knew it hurt you, and it was making me damn mad."

Laine clamped her folded arms over her chest and stuck out her lower lip, affecting an air of imperviousness to his speech. Travis smiled with amusement at her. She was one willful woman, but in the best possible way — strong in her own sense of purpose. He shook his head for a moment. He didn't want to tame her. On the contrary, he wanted to be beside her, sharing in that strength, giving her some of his own.

"Will you please get on with it," Laine snapped, "so that I can get on with my life . . . er, my ride?"

"Of course," Travis smiled, his heart lifting. Now he knew more than ever that she cared for him. A glimmer of fun sparked in his heart. How long could he string this out? How long could he tease her before she took the bait and gave it back to him, and in the process tell him out loud how she felt at last? This would probably be rather cruel, but . . .

"The housekeeper answered the door, so I asked to see LaBelle. The housekeeper said she wasn't there. I asked when she'd be back, and the housekeeper said she didn't know. I asked if she went shopping, or maybe out for a carriage ride, or . . ."

"Travis, for God's sake! Stop giving me the agenda for a day in the life of LaBelle Hadley and get to the point!"

This time Laine's anger afforded her the strength she needed to get herself up and out of the hay.

She stood up straight in front of him, pieces of hay stuck to her clothing and entangled in her golden curls. Her eyes snapped with violet fire.

She's so beautiful, Travis thought again. He almost gave in, but decided to keep it going just a bit longer. He sighed long and loud.

"All right, all right, hold your horses. You're getting mighty impatient, ma'am."

"And stop playing cowboy with me!" She stamped her foot, but the almost inaudible thud in the hay offered no emphatic underscore to her statement.

"Try to remain calm, Laine," he baited her. "I'm sure it's not good for a delicate lady like you to get

310

all riled up." He looked down at his hands, a crooked smile etched at the corners of his mouth.

Laine was growing more and more furious with him. She clenched her hands which seemed to be tingling so strongly she thought something might be physically wrong.

"Travis," she spoke in a hoarse whisper, "I will give you one more minute to say what it is you have to say, and then I am leaving — regardless of whether you think you've had your say or not. I've taken about all of this I'm going to."

"All right. It's just that you keep interrupting me . . ."

"Travis!"

He put up both hands to repel her anger. "I know, I know, get on with it. Anyway, LaBelle came in just as I was talking with the housekeeper."

Laine glared at him again. "I'm getting on with it, don't worry. LaBelle went into her act about my being there to discuss plans for the wedding . . ." At that moment he decided to minimize the complete confrontation with LaBelle. It was unpleasant and would serve nothing to repeat it. He decided to alter things just a bit.

" . . . and in the next minute she was saying that she was moving to Flagstaff. She's met some rich dude and roped him into marrying her right away. She's leaving Silver Grande for good!"

Laine stood still, staring at him, waiting for him to go on. But he did not continue.

"That's it? That's all? No wedding plans for you?" she managed to ask.

311

"Guess not. At least not with LaBelle Hadley." He looked down, working hard to affect a sadness he did not feel. Considering his mounting euphoria, this was a difficult feat.

"Well, it doesn't sound as if you had anything to do with stopping those plans yourself. In fact, you're probably disappointed at being rejected. What are you going to do now?"

Travis kept his eyes downcast in mock dejection. "Oh, I don't know. You don't really need me in your business. And I have a very capable crew who could probably run my business much better than I do. I suppose, I could always go to Flagstaff . . ."

"Oh, don't be ridiculous!" Laine whirled around with her back to him.

"I know. I suppose it would be fantasy for me to think I could make a good life in Flagstaff, start all over again. But I guess I could make do anywhere . . ." He deliberately made his voice sound weak, playing upon her sympathies.

"Fantasy?!" She spun around to face him again. "Have you lost your senses? The fantasy is here . . . now!" She dropped to her knees in front of him, an earnest expression over her face. "This is where you belong, Travis, and you know it. Right here, with the land you grew up on, the people you care about, and who . . . care about you. Buck and Molly—what would they ever do without you? And David . . . my father, your partner, he needs you, wants you to be a part of his life. You can't leave here, Travis, you belong here!"

She was breathless, her eyes alive with spirit and

312

fire. Travis marvelled at her beauty and spark.

"And what about you, Laine?"

She leaned back on her heels, her face flushed. "Me?"

He smiled broadly at her, flashing white even teeth that lit his face. He leaned forward and grasped her hands, and the warmth of his fingers caused the tingling to explode in tiny jets.

"Who are you trying to convince? Me? Or you? What do you want?"

The way he looked deeply into her eyes, Laine knew she'd just been tricked into that little sales pitch to keep him in Silver Grande. She pulled her hands out of his, positive he could feel heated frenzy racing through hers. She would take a new direction.

"Well, I could go back to Boston . . ." she said quietly, dropping her eyes and entwining her fingers.

Travis wasn't exactly certain of this, but he thought she may have been onto his little game all along and had now reversed it. Was she playing the same game, or was she in earnest about going back East?

"Boston? Now what are you saying?"

"Well, Aunt Sarah always thought . . . that is, she wanted me to take over her house for her, entertain . . . do charity work."

He peered deeply into her eyes. "Do you really think Boston is where you belong?"

"Quite possibly," came the soft answer.

Travis couldn't take the chance anymore of wondering if she was playing his game. He would have to play it straight from now on. He stood up quickly.

"Why? So you can be a prim and proper lady living in a big mansion? Fulfill all your childhood dreams? Live in a fantasy world again and shut out reality so you don't have to feel anything? Don't have to feel hurt, or even feel happy? Don't have to take any risks?!"

He paced up and down the full length of the loft. "Well, you can't leave, I'm not going to let you leave. Did you forget that we are partners, we made an agreement? And then there's David to consider . . ."

"Oh, Travis, we both know that partnership isn't binding. You can get out of that. So can I."

"Hah! That's what you think! It's binding all right. Try and break it. I'll take you to court!"

"Travis . . . why are you saying these things to me?" She sounded genuinely hurt by his outburst.

He stopped and took long strides back to her and dropped down on his knees in front of her. "Because, Laine, you're a woman, a living, breathing, loving woman in the here and now, full of the fire of life. You belong here as much as I do. You're part of this place, and it's part of you. Your father's here, Buck and Molly think of you as family, now, too. These are people who love you."

She gazed back at him as he spoke. He meant what he was saying. She knew that in her heart. What else did she see in those eyes? Love?

"Maybe that's all fantasy, just like everything else.

314

Even you were my fantasy, Travis. Did you know that?"

He leaned forward and gently put his hands on her face. "Laine, nothing is fantasy anymore. It's real, and you can have it, hold it, feel it in your heart. And, I don't want to be a part of your fantasies anymore, Laine. I want to be a part of your . . . reality, if you'll let me." His gaze penetrated deeply into hers.

God, if he doesn't say it soon, Laine thought, I'm going to flatten him in this hay and make love to him until it's the only thing he can say!

"What are you saying, Travis?" she said instead, leading him she hoped beyond this game to the win, the prize being the words she'd been longing to hear from him. She'd always needed him to say the words, as much as she needed to say them to him.

"I'm saying, sweetheart, there has never been anyone else in my heart. There's never been anyone but you. I guess I always knew something kept me from being involved with anyone, even in college. I know now that it's always been you. And if there is to be a wedding, it will be yours and mine, if you'll have me. All you have to do is say yes to the next question. Look, I'm even on my knees!"

He took both of her hands in his, his heart in his eyes when he gazed at her. "Will you marry me, Laine?"

Laine looked at him with happy surprise. Travis enjoyed the pure freshness of her. Then she narrowed her eyes and turned her head, giving him a sidelong glance that would wither a lesser man, and

315

he suddenly felt his confidence waning.

"Travis, you . . ." she whispered. Then she pushed him back into the hay. "You're the meanest man I ever met!"

"What?!" He leaned up on his elbows. "I can't believe this. I've just asked you to marry me, and that's mean? What goes on in that imagination of yours?!"

She leaned over him, her face a few inches from his. "If this is your idea of fun, or a joke to make sure I don't go back East and renege on the loan you gave me . . ."

"It's a way of keeping you from going back east, yes, but it's no joke!" He was breathing hard.

She started to get up, but he grabbed her arms and held her down. "Where do you think you're going?"

"I'm going for my ride now." She struggled to get up.

"That's what you think!" He rolled her over on her back so quickly she had no time for defense. He flattened her back into the hay, and pinned her down with the full length of his body. She squirmed, but his weight and strength held her fast. He took her face in both hands and forced her to look at him.

"You are the most impossible, strong-willed, most beautiful woman I've ever known. But I love you, have always loved you, will always love you. And you love me, too, I know it. Say it!"

"You are the most impossible . . ." she began.

"Not that!"

316

"What?"

"You know what!" He shook her head gently, then dropped his lips down next to her ear and whispered, "Say it, Laine. I need you to say the words."

"Aha!" She ran her hands into the back of his hair and pulled his head up.

"Aha?" He looked down at her quizzically.

She started to laugh lightly, and then a warm, full laugh bubbled out of her.

"What is this?"

"This, my darling, is me saying I love you, in fantasy and reality. I love you, have loved you all my life."

His face registered elated shock. "Then . . . are you saying you'll marry me?"

"Of course! I thought an eternity would pass before you would say those words to me! I thought you were never going to ask me to marry you! I had to do something . . ."

"You mean this has all been a trick?" He pushed up from her, a wide smile on his face.

She laughed lightly. "I'll never admit to it."

He threw his arms around her and rolled over and over with her in the hay until she was atop him, hair tumbling around her face and his, hay and leaves tangled among the curls.

"Oh, it will be fantasy come true to be your wife," she said breathlessly. "We'll work side by side in business. We'll live in my father's house, our house, I mean, and we'll plant roses by the veranda . . ."

"Roses! Out here?" Travis lifted her hair up and pushed it back from her face. "Oh, sweetheart, you are still a dreamer. Roses won't grow here, they're too delicate. Just like you . . . wait, I take that back!" He gazed into the fire in her eyes. "But you . . . yes, I do believe you probably could make even the cactus bloom when it didn't want to."

Laine smiled softly, lowering her lips to his, and fitting the length of her body against his until she felt his firm response.

"And I promise you I'll make the roses bloom for you, too . . . you'll see."

DANA RANSOM'S RED-HOT HEARTFIRES!

ALEXANDRA'S ECSTASY   (2773, $3.75)

Alexandra had known Tucker for all her seventeen years, but all at once she realized her childhood friend was the man capable of tempting her to leave innocence behind!

LIAR'S PROMISE   (2881, $4.25)

Kathryn Mallory's sincere questions about her father's ship to the disreputable Captain Brady Rogan were met with mocking indifference. Then he noticed her trim waist, angelic face and Kathryn won the wrong kind of attention!

LOVE'S GLORIOUS GAMBLE   (2497, $3.75)

Nothing could match the true thrill that coursed through Gloria Daniels when she first spotted the gambler, Sterling Caulder. Experiencing his embrace, feeling his lips against hers would be a risk, but she was willing to chance it all!

WILD, SAVAGE LOVE   (3055, $4.25)

Evangeline, set free from Indians, discovered liberty had its price to pay when her uncle sold her into marriage to Royce Tanner. Dreaming of her return to the people she loved, she vowed never to submit to her husband's caress.

WILD WYOMING LOVE   (3427, $4.25)

Lucille Blessing had no time for the new marshal Sam Zachary. His mocking and arrogant manner grated her nerves, yet she longed to ease the tension she knew he held inside. She knew that if he wanted her, she could never say no!